VIPERS ARE FORBIDDEN

GODS AMONG MEN SERIES

ALTA HENSLEY

To all the powerful women out there who have had to fight to get where they are.

NEWSLETTER

ALTA HENSLEY'S HOT, DARK & DIRTY NEWS

Do you want to hear about all my upcoming releases? Get free books? Get gifts and swag from all my author friends as well as from me? If so, then sign up for my newsletter!

Alta's Newsletter

WARNING

Enter this tale at your own risk. It's dark. It's dirty. It's the love story of a viper and those who try to destroy her.

It's impossible to enter a pit full of snakes and not get bit.

Until you meet me, that is.

My venom is far more toxic than the four men who have declared me their enemy.

They seek vengeance and launch a twisted game of give and take.

I'll play in their dark world, because it's where I thrive.

I'll dance with their debauchery, for I surely know the steps.

But then I discover just how wrong I am. Their four, not only matches, but beats, my one.

With each wicked move they make, they become my obsession.

I crave them until they consume all thought.

The temptation to give them everything they desire becomes too much.

I'm entering their world, and there is no light to guide my way. My blindness full of lust will be my defeat.

Yes... I am the viper and am forbidden.

But they are the end of my beginning.

CHAPTER ONE

Athena

I've never asked to be liked. In fact, I'd rather you didn't.

Cold. Heartless. Bitch. I've heard them all, and don't consider one to be an insult. On the contrary, if you were to call me sweet, nice, or endearing, I'd be livid because it would mean one thing.

You'd be underestimating me.

I quite enjoy being the villainess in the story.

"Look, I know you prefer to deal with my father, and you expected to be working with my brother, Apollo, but you aren't. You're dealing with me." I pause for a moment to draw a deep breath and not throw the phone across the room. I'm over tip toeing around this asshole's thinly veiled misogyny. "Let me explain how we are different. If you cannot hold up your end of this contract, my father would have burned your stadium to the ground. My brother, well he's a little more hot headed. Apollo has yet to mellow with age, like my father. He would burn your stadium to the ground with several workers still inside."

"Look, little girl," the current owner of The Titans says. "Before I sell one of the top NHL hockey teams to your family company, I need some reassurance that you actually know something about the sport. The people of Seattle need—"

"The only thing you need from me is money. My job is not to reassure you. And before you call me *little girl* again, I'd think twice." I close my eyes and take a calming breath. "Like my father and my brother, I'd burn down the stadium, too. But then I wouldn't stop there. I'd also burn down your house. And I'd have to report to your insurance company that my *female* intuition told me it was arson, and they should investigate. I'd let them know exactly where to find the evidence. What evidence, you ask? I'll fabricate, then plant plenty of evidence showing you burning down your own house, and I will have you arrested for arson and insurance fraud. Like a bitch with a bone, I wouldn't even dream of stopping there. Not until your other businesses were all ashes, your reputation in tatters, your family destitute, and you are sitting behind bars, so I know exactly where to find you in case I wanted to fuck you harder."

I don't know when I rise, with my hands on

either side of the phone, as I bend over the desk to talk into the speaker. With another deep breath, I take my seat, leaning back into the plush leather chair as my nerves settle.

The other side of the line is almost silent. The only thing coming from the phone is his shallow breaths. I honestly hope he pisses himself, and he should.

My bite is deadly, and he had better fucking learn that.

"Don't ever call me *little girl* again. Do I make myself clear?" My voice is much calmer and more pleasant now. I even put on a smile so he can hear it over the phone.

"This is not the way business is done." His voice is shaking.

Good.

"No, this is not the way business *was* done, but it is how it *will be* from now on. I suggest you make your peace with that and—"

"I swear I will—"

"You will what?" Venom drips from my words. "Tell my daddy? What are you going to say? That his daughter is being mean to you? That you tried to fuck him and Medusa Enterprises over, and I wouldn't roll over and take it? How do you think that is going to play out?"

"I—"

"I'm done letting you waste my time. Here is what is going to happen. You are going to deliver the signed documents on time. And just so you don't piss me off, you are going to take ten percent off the top of your cost, or I will burn everything you have ever loved... with a smile on my face as I do."

With a quick tap on my phone, I disconnect the call. He'll come through. If he doesn't, I mean every single word. I'll ignite an inferno.

Staring at the Medusa Enterprises family logo on the massive sign outside my office through the large glass windows, I settle my temper. The one thing I pride myself on is not losing my cool. I'm far more lethal if I am always calm and collected.

Godwins don't show rage.

We may feel it. We never show it.

A knock sounds on my door, and Toria Lancaster peeks her head through the partially open door. "You asked to see me?"

I motion for her to come all the way in. "We are acquiring The Seattle Titans by the end of the day. I want you to oversee the deal."

"The hockey team?"

I don't answer, but rather look up from my stack of papers and make eye contact with her.

"Don't you think that Liam may be a better fit to take on this project?"

"Why?" I lock my jaw and lean back in my chair. "Because he's a man?"

Toria's eyes widen, and she quickly opens her mouth to reply, but pauses, recomposes herself. "No, of course not. Consider it done."

I nod my approval and watch Toria leave my office, pleased I don't have to fire another weak-minded woman.

My secretary buzzes in. "Your brother, Phoenix, is on the line."

"Thank you," I reply, prepared to take the call even though I have a million things to do today.

Phoenix hasn't been himself lately. He's been obsessing over these damn journals he found of my mother's. My brother has never been stable to begin with, which makes me worry what going down this rabbit hole could do to him.

She killed herself. We need to accept that fact and move on. Actually, we should have accepted that fact years ago. But sadly, Phoenix struggles with this, and I feel I need to be his support system simply by default. My father sure as hell isn't going to be. Our brother, Apollo, has the sensitivity of a gnat—though I'm not much better—and my other brother, Ares, is dead. So, that leaves me.

"Athena," Phoenix says when I answer the phone.

"Is something wrong?" I can always pick up on my brother's emotions.

"It's Mother." He takes a deep breath. "I don't think she killed herself."

I release a heavy sigh. "We've discussed this. Does it really matter if she was the one to jump off the cliff or if someone actually pushed her? She's dead. And this happened a long time ago. It's long due we let this go."

There's a long pause. "Athena... I think our mother is still alive."

"Phoenix—"

"You need to read these journals," Phoenix blurts out. "She says that Father helped her leave the family."

"You know as well as I do, that Father would never let her go. Godwins don't divorce. It's some dictate our fucked-up ancestors made or something."

"If you read these journals—"

"I'll look into it, okay?" I say, not wanting to tell Phoenix that I already hired a private investigator to dig more into the mysterious events around my mother's death. Or the fact that I am scheduled to meet up with him today.

My brothers and I were never convinced that she simply jumped to her death off the cliff in the back of Olympus Manor. It's what we were told. It's what we were supposed to believe. But deep down not one of us truly believed it. In the darkest shadows of our hearts, we feared our father had something to do with it.

Not suicide. Murder.

"I want you to read these," Phoenix presses.

"I told you I'd look into it, and I will, but right now, I have to go. I have a meeting."

I hang up the phone before Phoenix can say

more. I don't have time to get wrapped up in these thoughts and emotions. I need to make decisions and act based on facts. Hard facts.

Hopefully, after my next appointment with the PI, I'll be closer to knowing what exactly happened to my mother. She died when I was fifteen, supposedly by her own hand, but that just doesn't sit right with me. The woman I knew was vibrant, full of life and, like most of my family, was far more likely to commit homicide than suicide.

Did she have demons? Sure. We all do. Godwins are swimming in them, but that doesn't mean we'd jump to the crashing waves beneath a jagged cliff.

Either way, she's dead—regardless of what latest freak-out moment my brother is experiencing. Part of me thinks that's all I need to know, but another part says there is more to the story, and my curiosity is getting the better of me.

My cell phone vibrating on my desk pulls me out of my thoughts. Of course he is calling now. No doubt the little worm ratted me out to my father.

"Hey, Daddy," I say when I answer.

"Athena, I hear you're busting my favorite client's balls." There isn't even a hint of disapproval in his voice. I hate how much I love making him proud.

"He thought I was going to be an easy target. I had to correct that misunderstanding immediately."

"You threatened to frame him for insurance fraud?" There is a touch of laughter in his voice.

"Honestly, I would have done more than that. If I felt the need to get the law involved to do my dirty work, I might as well pin a few of our sins on him, too. Several birds, one boulder, all that jazz." I have to get him off the phone fast. My next appointment is one I have been looking forward to all day, and after Phoenix's call, a needed one.

"I know what you're doing, and who you're meeting with. Stop." His voice loses all its humor.

"I'm doing a lot of things. I need you to be a bit more specific." The lie rolls off my tongue, not giving away how my heart is racing. How did he find out?

He's Troy Godwin. That's how. The man knows everything.

"Your mother is dead. Has been for years. Stop digging into something that doesn't exist."

"If she's dead, why does it matter if I'm looking around?"

"Because I told you to stop," he growls through the phone.

"But you won't tell me why, which makes me believe I may be onto something. If it's truly nothing, you wouldn't even be wasting your breath trying to forbid me to do something," I bite back.

"You're starting to act as crazy as Phoenix."

"Family genes," I counter.

I love my father, I even respect him most of the time, but I will never be a doormat, not even for him. My mother is gone, but if there is a chance I can get answers to questions I've always had since her death, then I will. And if it can help Phoenix heal his deep wounds, then I won't question trying for a second.

"I said drop it."

"And I said no. If you want children that will do your bidding without thought or complaint, call your sons." I hang up, knowing I'm going to pay for that later, but fuck it. He can add it to my tab.

My phone rings again. I picture his angry eyes and square jaw with a graying beard that sharpens the harsh lines of his face instead of softening them.

I hit ignore just as someone knocks on my door.

"Come in," I call, already knowing who it is.

"Ms. Godwin, I am afraid I have some delicate news." The PI I hired steps into my office. His blue baseball cap is in his hands, and he is twisting the bill.

"Have a seat." I motion to the chair in front of my desk. It sits lower than my own, not that the PI needs to be put in a submissive position. He doesn't treat me like a stray woman that escaped the kitchen. He just isn't worth me adjusting my furniture for before our meeting.

"I'm not really sure how to say this," he begins.

"I have little patience," I begin. "Get to the point."

"Your mother didn't die seven years ago." His gaze isn't locking onto anything in the room. Interesting, he is nervous, but why? For all he knows, he's giving me good news.

"She didn't?" My wariness bleeds through on my voice. "So she is alive?"

Jesus Christ. Phoenix is right. Am I living in a goddamn soap opera?

"No." He stares at the ceiling over my head. "Your mother died about a month ago."

"What?" I have no idea what to say or even feel about this slew of insanity. She's dead. She's alive. She's dead.

"I think had you not hired me, someone would have still been contacting you. There is a reading of her will in a few days. Her lawyer said that you are mentioned and should attend. Only you. Not your brothers or your father." He places a piece of paper on my desk. I don't have to touch it to see the address on it is just outside Seattle.

"Is that the address of her lawyer's estate?"

"No, it's the mansion your mother was living in."

She had a mansion in Seattle. *Seattle!* She was living so close this entire time, never telling any of us. Why? Why stay so close if she never came back to Olympus Manor? And if for some reason she didn't want to return to our home on the island of Heathens Hollow, then why the fuck not reach out to us later? We all live in Seattle now!

"She's dead," I repeat to myself.

"Yes. She is now, but she didn't die in Heathens Hollow like you all believed."

I sit in silence, trying to absorb everything being thrown at me. I want to call my father. My brothers.

But at the same time, I don't. I'm not ready to ignite the bomb onto my family.

"The estate lawyer said—"

I raise my hand to silence the PI. I don't want to hear anymore right now.

I want nothing of hers, but maybe if I go to the reading of the will, I can speak to someone she was close to. Maybe get some answers, if not all of them.

"Okay. I'll go to the house. I'll contact the lawyer. See my assistant for your payment."

"Ms. Godwin, there's more." His voice is stiff, like he's trying not to run out the door.

"Make it quick." I wave my hand at him. The reality is I'm on the verge of a meltdown, and I don't want him to see it.

"Your father." His words come out stronger and he meets my eye. "I have reason to believe he is the one who bought that property and banished her to it."

"Are you saying?" Heat rises to my cheeks as an icy chill settles into my gut.

"Your father knew she was alive and where she was the entire time. He put her there and turned his back on her, faking her death to take her away from her children."

CHAPTER TWO

Athena

I pull into the long, curving driveway of a rundown Victorian manor. It was probably beautiful in its heyday, but I instantly hate everything about it. It's like a decrepit, dirty version of the Olympus manor, our family home. I wonder if my mother picked them both, and they were to her taste and not my father's. Or maybe he chose this place to make her feel like she was living in a lesser version of what she had?

Either way, it is a far cry from my sleek, modern penthouse in downtown Seattle. I live for the vibrant, clean, efficient vibe of the city. Not this slow, dusty, old-money energy of whatever HGTV show was about to show up and DIY this thing into this century.

I approach the door, each step creaking under my Jimmy Choos.

This is the Gothic monstrosity my mother hid in after she abandoned me? Why? What could this place possibly offer that is more important than me and her sons? Not that I will ever be able to find out. No mother-daughter union is in my future. She really is dead this time. Knocking on the door, I remind myself to be strong. To never show weakness. I am going to enter this house, maybe talk to a few people about my mother, see what information I can find. Maybe someone here knows why she left and remained hidden away this entire time.

"Yes, can I..." An older woman with gray hair tied in a tight bun and wearing a maid's uniform opens the door and stares at me, her eyes getting enormous, then filling with tears. "Oh, you look just like—"

"I'm Athena Godwin. I was hoping I could speak to someone about Freya Godwin?"

"I'm sorry to say she passed." The old woman's eyes fill with tears even more. "You're too late."

I'm late?

I'm the one late?

Rather than correcting her, or losing my shit, I say, "Yes, I have heard of her passing. I was hoping I could speak to someone who knew her. I have a few questions about Freya that I would like to be answered."

Dear Lord, I hope this isn't the only person here

I'm able to speak with. Only one maid who, by the looks of the dirt and cobwebs on the front porch, isn't very good at her job.

"Oh, you should speak to her son. Come in, come in. I will fetch him for you." She grabs my arm and pulls me into the house.

Her *son*?

What. The. Fuck?

Suddenly, I feel very self-conscious as we walk through the halls. It's like my mother's ghost is inside waiting. Her eyes on me are making my skin crawl, but I tighten my stomach and straighten my spine, just dealing with it. I have come here for answers, and I intend to get them.

"If you would like to take a seat in the library here." The older woman places her hand on my elbow to guide me into the dusty room with bookshelves lining the walls and furniture made from wood and upholstered in velvet. "I'll get Perseus."

Without making a sound, she leaves the room. I have no idea what to do. This all feels so surreal. I feel like I am floating in a dream, and I am desperate to anchor myself to something real. Something in my life, not this weird alternate dimension where my mother was breathing only a month ago.

I grab my phone from my purse to call my father. I'm livid at his lies, but it's not the first time he's lied to me, and most definitely not the first time I've been pissed at the man. Maybe I can use that anger to center me.

"Athena. Where are you?" my father barks into the phone. "I've been looking for you all day."

"Apparently, I am in the home of a ghost. You lied to me."

"I don't have time for your riddles."

"Okay, I'll be blunt, Daddy. I know you lied about my mother committing suicide when I was fifteen. I want to know why."

"I don't know what you're talking about."

"I'm in her house! Standing in her library! So, for once in your life, stop lying to me."

There's a pause. No doubt my father is regaining his composure before he speaks. He'd never respond until the pitter patter of his heart is back to normal cadence.

"I didn't lie. Your mother no longer wanted to be a Godwin. She chose to leave our family, so she was dead to us. Dead. The Godwin legacy comes first. It's bigger than all of us. You know that."

"Dead to us is not the same as dead," I reply, biting the anger back. No doubt he knows how furious I am. There's no telling who else is listening in, and there is no need for anyone else here to be privy to my emotions.

With a few steps, I move to the window and gaze out at the sprawling, unkempt grounds. This place is in desperate need of a gardener and a team of maintenance workers.

"So you refused to stop looking for her. I take it you found her?" he says in a low tone.

"I did," I admit as I watch a stray cat slink across the overgrown grass to disappear into the shapeless shrubs. "I was too late, though. She died a month ago. I'm in her home now, hoping someone here can give me some details of what my ghost of a mother has been up to."

I decide not to mention the apparent son my mother had. My father is a jealous, possessive man, and something like that is enough to set him off on a rampage. I don't have the time to clean up after one of his tantrums, and he'll probably destroy any chance I have at answers.

There's a pause, and I wonder if my father is processing that his ex-wife is dead. Truly dead this time. Is he feeling any pain? Any sadness?

Doubtful.

"She left you just like she left me and your brothers. What more could you possibly want to know?" His words hurt more than I want to think about right now. I don't understand the mix of feelings I'm having. I just know that I need to be here and face the truth, whatever that looks like.

"I'm here for answers that you could have given me and simply chose not to." I turn away from the window just in time to see the most stunning man on the planet enter the library. I guess he is about my age, at least 6'4 with broad shoulders and light blond hair hanging down to his strong jaw and the coldest blue eyes on the planet. "I have to go. I'll call you later, and when I do, I expect a different story to the history you wrote us." I hang up the phone, not waiting for my father's reply.

"Who the fuck are you?" He curls his lip in disgust, looking at me.

Oh, hell no. I don't give a fuck how pretty this man is. No one talks to me like that.

"Athena Godwin. Who the fuck are you?"

"I'm Freya's son." His words come out between clenched teeth. "Her *only* child."

"Well, buddy, looks like I have some news for you."

I arch my eyebrow as I take a closer look at him. His frame is leaner than my brothers. His muscles are prominent but lean like a swimmer, not bulky like Phoenix and Apollo. He has darker, tanned skin. The Godwins all burn, then end up whiter than before. He looks nothing like me or my brothers. His eyes are the wrong shape, his nose too long, his cheekbones too high, and his hair is a striking almost white blond, not dark brown like everyone else in the family.

The only thing we have in common is the color of our eyes. But my mother's eyes weren't blue, like mine. I have my father's eyes.

Freya Godwin had green eyes.

"Not only am I her daughter, but I have two brothers, and a deceased one. And I'm guessing you are about my age, so there is no way she could have been your mother."

"You lie."

"Frequently, about a lot of things when it suits me, but not this." I cross my arms over my chest. "So, I'll repeat. Who the fuck are you?"

"Perseus, Freya's *adopted* son." He pauses, studies me, and as if I have suddenly developed a stench, he grimaces. "You should leave. Now." He leans over me like he's trying to intimidate me. I usually hate it when men pull the macho crap or try to use their size and strength to cow me, but the heat rushing through my body isn't anger. It's desire.

He's too good looking, and I hate him instantly for it.

"Not until I get what I am owed."

He's thrown off. I can see it all over his face. I'm a surprise to him, and though he's struggling to not show his cards, his feelings are obvious to me. Mommy dearest clearly kept secrets from him, too.

"Owed? You want money? And you think I'm just going to let you come and take my inheritance?" His shapely lips twitch, and part of me wonders what they feel like when they aren't twisted in distaste.

Now I hate him even more for having me think this way.

"You know what?" I put my hands on his firm chest and shove him back, getting him out of my personal space. His spicy sweet scent still lingers around me, but it's a little less distracting. "All I wanted was answers. I just wanted to talk to some people that knew her. But now, I think I need to speak to the lawyer handling her estate. Question any will that gives her only heir an inheritance. Especially since *you* are not the only heir."

"I told you to leave," he growls before grabbing me by the throat and pushing me against the wall. He doesn't squeeze, he just holds me there, pinning me to the wall with his hand and his body pressed against mine. "You don't know who you are playing with."

Most women would be terrified if they're being threatened like this. Most...

I should be livid, but all I can think about is the way his lips are so close to mine. I can taste the mint toothpaste still on his breath. I can feel his heart pounding against mine.

His eyes darken as he leans in closer. "Leave now, and I won't destroy you."

"That was cute." I give him my best condescending smile. It gets brighter as his brows furrow in confusion. "Threatening me was probably the dumbest thing you have ever done. And by looking at you, I would guess it was already a pretty impressive list of stupid shit."

I grab one of his fingers from around my throat and pull it back, forcing him to release his grip or let me break it. Truthfully, he could have easily stopped me, but he is trying to intimidate me, not hurt me. Not yet, anyway.

"You don't know who you are playing with," he repeats.

I roll my eyes. "No, *you* don't know who you are dealing with. This could have been easy, but now?" I push him back another step. "It's going to be fun."

CHAPTER THREE

Athena

Three days later, and I am back on the doorstep of this run-down Addams family mansion. It turns out I didn't need to have my PI hunt down anyone. When I got home, a message from my mother's estate lawyer was waiting for me.

So here I am, dressed to kill in a tight black dress that shows off my slender legs, shapely curves and ample chest. I'm sure to see the asshole my mother adopted, and I intend to distract him, or at least take note. Perseus's attractiveness caught me off guard last time. That will not happen again.

I don't expect my mother to leave me much, or anything, really. It's not like my brothers or I need her money, or even care. However, I'm prepared to fight her will just to piss off Perseus.

"Ms. Godwin, please right this way." A mousy brunette with large glasses greets me at the door. "I'm Mr. Carion's assistant. He just stepped out back to make a call, and we are waiting for the others. Can I get you a coffee or water while you wait?"

"Coffee, please," I say with a slight smile. She leaves me in the library again while she scurries off to get the coffee.

I take my seat and wait. My phone dings with another text from my father, not sharing concern over the will or even acknowledging the rift between us.

Nope, it's all work related. Classic Troy Godwin.

We haven't even discussed my mother since our last call, nor have I mentioned this to my brothers. Apollo and Phoenix are both busy getting their lives together, and for the time being, they both seem happy. They're in love, living their lives out of the Godwin shadow of doom, and I don't want to take that from them. At least not yet. Plus, the estate lawyer made it clear it was not required for them to attend. My cowardly mother has seemed to forget her *real* sons in the will.

I'm about to send a text to my father when the library door opens and Perseus comes in with three other mouthwatering, sexy men. The biggest one right behind him looks like he is ready to step into a heavyweight wrestling ring and take on the Rock. He's about the same height as Perseus, but thicker.

His dark hair is a mess of soft curls, and he is practically radiating power and rage.

I like him.

The one next is taller and thinner but looks more sinister with piercing green eyes, longer hair that brushes his back and tattoos across his knuckles and hands disappearing under the cuffs of his black shirt, just for the ink to peek out of the open collar at his neck. He also has a ring in his lip and brow, a stud in his nose and a chain hanging from a piercing in the top of his ear down to one in his lobe. It's enough metal to make me wonder if he has any piercings not easily displayed.

The last man to enter doesn't quite fit in with the rest. He is just as attractive but cleaner cut in his Burberry coat staring at a tablet. His thick-rimmed designer glasses slide down his nose every few moments.

Interesting... Did my mother become a cougar, or start a boy band in her final years? Are all these hot men my new *brothers*? The absurdity of the idea has me smirking.

"What the fuck are you doing here? I thought I said you weren't welcome," Perseus practically yells as he stalks toward me.

"Down boy." I stand to face him, my sky-high stilettos putting me at almost his eye level. "I was invited."

"By who?"

"It wasn't me, but I am kind of wishing it was,"

the one with the serial killer glare and tattoos says, while undressing me with his eyes.

It's not an entirely unpleasant feeling. I shoot him a quick playful wink and love the thrill it gives me when Perseus moves to stand in between us, his nostrils flaring and his jaw clenching hard enough I can almost hear his teeth crack.

"Who're your hot friends?" I ask, blinking innocently up at him.

The muscles in his jaw tick. Making him angry is so easy and so much fun.

"The one looking like he wants to snap you in half, and not in the fun way, is Heph," the serial killer says. "The one tapping away on his computer is Paris, and I'm Eros. Now, who are you? Are you lost, pretty little thing?"

"I'm Athena," I answer. Before I can say more, Eros is shoved back and Perseus is in between us again, his fists clenching at his sides like he is aching to take a swing at something.

"Who invited you here?" he snarls.

"The lawyer, my mother," I slow down and over enunciate every syllable of *mother*, "hired for her estate."

"This is the girl who says she is—" the man, I think it is Paris, says.

"I am Freya's daughter. Would you like to see my birth certificate? Or perhaps my baby pictures where I am in her arms? But I think by looking at me, you all know I'm flesh and blood." Like mother like daughter.

"This is *my* home. I may not have been her blood, but I was the son she chose. You are the daughter she abandoned."

His words cut into me deeper than I will ever show.

"No, I am the daughter whose father kept her away. You are nothing more than the street rat she cared for in some attempt to fill the void that was left from losing her actual children. Not just me, but her actual sons Apollo, Ares, and Phoenix." We stand practically nose to nose, glaring at each other, the tension in the room palatable.

"Get the fuck out of my house." His words hold promises of violence, but he has no idea who he is fucking with. I might look like my mother, but I am my father's daughter, and he will bend to *my* will, not the other way around.

"Is that the best you have?" I ask. "Your usage of vocabulary is limited. Good thing you're pretty."

"Out. Now."

"Make me." The words fly from my lips barely more than a whisper, but I know he heard me. I'm clutching at the taser I have tucked in my purse, waiting for him to lay his fucking hands on me, practically begging him to do something. "That's what I thought. I'm not going anywhere."

The library door opens, and someone clears their throat.

"Good. You two have met." The speaker has a deep, masculine voice.

Perseus and I each step back from each other.

"Something like that," I mumble under my breath.

"Ms. Godwin"—the man reaches out his hand for me to shake—"I'm Mr. Carion, your mother's lawyer. This case is a bit... unusual, so let's get started."

Perseus and I make a move for the same arm chair, but I drop my purse into it before he can sit. It opens just enough that he can see the taser. He gives me a look, then moves to sit on the couch with the other mouthwatering misfits.

Paris's tablet flips into a laptop, and he is sitting on the couch typing way. Eros is sitting on the floor by the couch spinning a knife, eying me like he wants to eat me for lunch, and Heph is staring at me like I kicked his dog, which if I consider how close he is sitting to Perseus, maybe I did. Maybe I'm going to do it again, and that arrogant prick realizes who the fuck he is dealing with.

CHAPTER FOUR

Athena

"Right, so the assets are to be divided as follows." The lawyer removes papers from his briefcase and settles back into his chair to read. "I, Freya Godwin, being of sound mind and body, have divided my assets between two, and only two, of my children. To my son, Perseus—"

Perseus sneers at me as the lawyer continues to read.

"—I leave the sum of fifteen million dollars."

His face drops.

"And what else?" Perseus demands.

"That's it. Please let me continue." The lawyer clears his throat. "To my daughter, Athena, I leave this house, my worldly possessions, and what is left in my bank account after settling whatever end-of-life costs I have accrued."

"No. She doesn't get my home." Perseus stands and paces the room. "That spoiled bitch doesn't get a single fucking cent, let alone my home."

"That bitch is Freya's daughter, and we will honor my mother's will," I bite out.

Seriously, this is a grown-ass man throwing a temper tantrum that he only got fifteen million dollars. Only. He could live his entire life in the lap of luxury, but he is mad. It's only a fucking fortune, and I am the spoiled one? Not to mention that my mother failed to acknowledge her other sons.

The lawyer raises his hand and says, "Let me finish, please." He glares at Perseus before adding, "To Apollo, Ares, and Phoenix, I leave you my well wishes and love because I know you don't need my money. I know that your father will have your best interest at heart, and Medusa Enterprises will be left to you. You three will be wealthy men if you aren't already. I can't say the same about Athena, since she is not a male Godwin, hence why she is in my will. And to my other boys: Heph, Paris, and Eros. Though you are not my sons by blood or legally, you will always be in my heart. I have a trust set up for each of you for a million dollars if you are willing to follow the terms."

Perseus spits on the floor in front of my shoes and storms out of the room, leaving us all stunned.

"Really?" I ask no one in particular.

"I'm afraid there are stipulations Freya left with the will that I need everyone to hear," Mr. Carion says. "As I said, it's a rather odd case. And if you don't meet the requirements, I'm afraid none of you will get anything."

I roll my eyes. Of course she attached strings.

We all sit in silence for a moment.

"Will one of you please go get your friend?" I finally break the silence.

"Heph, go get him and bring him down here. You're the only one he will listen to," Paris says without looking up from his computer.

Heph gets up, glaring at me like it is all my fault, and leaves.

Eros moves to sit on the edge of the couch closest to me and leans over the arm. His tongue must be flicking the inside of his lip ring because it keeps rocking back and forth, pulling my attention to his lips.

"Tell me why you're here," he demands.

"Well, apparently this is my house," I deadpan.

"No, you showed up before. I want to know why."

"Does it matter?" I counter.

"I don't know yet. That's why I want to know."

"Get used to disappointment."

He sits back, his lips tilt in a sexy half grin. "It's such a shame, so pretty, and I bet you're a wildcat in the sack, but you're empty inside, aren't you? All fight to cover up the pain of how fucking empty and alone you really are."

I hate how he can see through me. I'm so overwhelmed by everything going on, that I'm clearly letting down my guard. I'm readable. I hate being readable.

The telltale prickle of tears starts in my nose. I hold them back through sheer will and glare at the man sitting in front of me, covered in ink and piercings. "I bet it's like looking in a mirror, isn't it?"

"No, see, unlike you. I'm not alone. Perseus isn't alone. You should just leave now, princess. Leave, don't come back, and we won't come for you. But you try to take what is his, and we will make your life hell."

The threat in his eyes make me laugh. I couldn't hold it back if I wanted to.

"What the fuck is so funny?" he bites out.

"You." I laugh harder, then imitate his voice. "Leave now, and we won't make your life hell." I laugh harder. "It's just so adorable. You think I am some little girl on the playground who will cry and run away just because you pulled my pigtails? Oh, sweetheart, you don't know a damn thing about me. You have no idea who you are threatening."

"Athena Godwin, daughter of Troy Godwin and Freya Godwin, sister to Phoenix, Ares and Apollo Godwin. Although your family just suffered a devastating loss with the death of your brother, Ares. Despite your brothers' size and fondness of violence, you are the heir apparent to your father's company and the one to be feared. You have never been arrested or even implicated in a crime officially. But unofficially, you are suspected to be behind a few missing people, several acts of felony-level vandalism and arson, some of which you just gave the order for, others you handled personally. It is also believed you have several politicians and police chiefs on your payroll and a few others you are blackmailing," Paris says, not looking up from his computer. "Some people think you are a vile shrew. Others just think you are a strong business woman having to work twice as hard to be thought of as half as good. Personally, I think you are just a thug in a skirt and fuck-me pumps."

"Oh, you like my shoes?" I taunt as I extend my leg to show them off. "Thanks, they're my favorite. Is that all you found?"

"No. Some think you're a lesbian because you have never had a steady boyfriend, but I can't find any evidence of a steady girlfriend either. But I didn't see how your sexual orientation is relevant."

"Personally, I find that very relevant," Eros says as his eyes travel down my body again.

"My sexual orientation is picky. And sorry, sweetie, you don't make the cut."

"We'll see about that," he says with a wink.

Paris continues to read from his computer, "Your family owns a manor on an island called Heathens Hollow, which apparently the Godwins also own." He glances up from his computer to look at Eros. "Who the fuck owns an island?" Paris shrugs and returns to reading off his computer. "But you rarely go there and prefer the buzz of Seattle. Not that I blame you, since Heathens Hollow is cold, foggy, and filled with a lot of mysterious stories and secrets. Frankly, the island appears as if it belongs in a horror movie rather than in a billionaire family's portfolio. It looks like you enjoy a fine wine and expensive parties, even though you never have a plus one."

"Someone clearly has been doing his research," I say. "Do you know my blood type as well? My first-grade teacher?"

I'm about to say more when Perseus returns and sits down, his arms crossed in front of his chest. He really does look like a pissed-off toddler. Heph stands behind him, like his bodyguard or something. Weird.

"Great, so Mrs. Godwin has a list of conditions that must be met before either of you receives your inheritance." Mr. Carion reads my mother's words again, like nothing happened. I've honestly been so caught up in taunting Eros that I forgot he was still in the room.

"First, dear Athena, you must take a six-month sabbatical from Medusa Enterprises. I believe you must take time to find yourself outside of your father's influence."

I don't like the idea of taking time off work but will make it happen if it means fucking with these pricks in the room. My father is going to lose his mind over this idea, which fills me with some giddy excitement. I give a curt nod, and the lawyer continues reading my mother's words.

"You must host lavish parties in this mansion. At least one a month. Part of the deal your father and I struck was that I would spend the remainder of my days as a recluse and never be seen outside this house. You are to use this home to live the life that I was denied. Be social, make friends, have fun. Life is about more than work. But that does not mean you can turn this home into a bacchanal. Any media scandal with merit will mean an immediate forfeiture of the inheritance."

Really, Mom? Have fun, but not too much fun. If she only knew. I may technically be a virgin, but that doesn't make me a fucking prude. But fine. No media scandals.

"My boys—Perseus, Heph, Eros, and Paris, if he chooses—are all to remain in this home, and you are to live here full time until you reach the age of thirty." The lawyer stops to take a sip of water. "The boys have been my protectors in my darkest days, and I want the same for my only daughter."

The lawyer pauses and studies each one of us. I think we all must be too stunned to speak.

"So, I have to live with them?" I ask. "One big family under this roof? Is that what I'm hearing?"

"That's it. She gets my home, but she has to allow us to stay," Perseus says.

"No," the lawyer continues, "the six-month sabbatical is the only thing limited to Athena. If you want your money, you and the others must continue to live here with Athena. You are to protect her. No harm is to come to her while she is living in this house, by your hand or any other. Failure to do so, will mean you all forfeit the entire fortune."

No harm to be done to me?

Who the fuck are these guys if that stipulation even has to be made?

CHAPTER FIVE

Athena

Perseus is the first out the door in a huff, and frankly, I don't blame him. This entire situation is bullshit.

I could walk away.

Maybe I should walk away.

I have a good life. I have more money than I care to discuss. I don't need this, I don't need this house, and I sure as hell have nothing to prove to my dead mother.

But I saw the challenge in every single one of my mother's *boys'* eyes. And I've never been one to back down. They think they can bully me. Ha! Think again.

The lawyer hands me a few forms to sign, and I do. Then I tell the maid who opened the door for me the first time, a Mrs. Medea, I will be going to my penthouse to collect a few things and to please prepare my mother's room for me.

"Please don't clean out her things. I want to do that myself. But if you could dust, vacuum, and put fresh linen on the bed."

"Of course, Ms. Godwin."

"Athena, please," I correct. I don't mind being addressed as Ms. Godwin in business, but I don't like it in my home. And since this gothic, vampire den is going to be my new home, I had better set the standard now.

I take all of two hours to make it back to the mansion with a single suitcase packed. I just need enough for right now. I'll hire movers as I figure everything else out. I also asked for the PI to do some digging on these psychopaths my mother somehow trusted. They seem to know all about me, and I know nothing about them. Not that I care to know every detail, but at least the basics. It's likely I'll be having to live with the enemy. I should at least know what that means.

Being in my mother's room brings out a torrent of emotions I'm not sure how to handle. So I don't. I force them down. Right now, I have things that need my immediate attention. The parties will be easy enough. The mansion is huge; it needs some work, but it's suitable as a venue for any kind of society party. Or it will be as soon as I hire gardeners and maintenance workers. As for the parties themselves, Seattle is full of event planners who will jump at the chance for steady work and fat commission checks.

Withdrawing from Medusa is going to send my father through the fucking roof. But I am owed some vacation time, and it will give him a chance to see that no, Apollo and Phoenix would not be better suited as men to run the company. Six months should be just enough time for him to figure out my absence is not worth pissing me off. I type out a quick email telling him of my intentions to step down for now, and how Apollo should know my job well enough to handle it. I laugh as I turn off my phone, not wanting to deal with the backlash.

One overgrown man child down, one to go.

I'm also not ready to have the conversation with Phoenix and Apollo that our dead mother was actually alive. But dead now. And oh hey, guess what? She left you guys out of the will but gave money to some adopted son and her lost boys. That conversation is sure to go over really well.

It takes far longer than I like for me to find Perseus. When I do, he is swimming laps in a heated pool under the house. There is a full gym down here. Good to know.

I take a seat and wait for him to finish his laps. I have a plan, a logical plan where we can both get what we want with minimal interruptions to our lives. Any reasonable person would see the value of what I have to propose.

"What the fuck do you want now? Come to steal

the clothes off my back?" he says, climbing out of the pool in nothing but tiny swim shorts. I try and fail to not rake my eyes down his body.

Fuck, this man is gorgeous, too bad he is a raging asshole.

"As tempting as it would be to see you without those shorts to see if your dick is as big of a dick as you are, no. I'm here with a truce." I hand him a towel, which he takes and then throws on the seat next to him before crossing his arms in front of his chest, and I'm pretty sure he is flexing.

"So, are you are going to leave? Give up your claim to my home and my money? That works for me."

"Not quite." I resist the urge to roll my eyes, barely. "And it isn't your money. It was my mother's."

He huffs. "Funny this is coming from spoiled rich girl. Little Miss Godwin princess."

"I'm not leaving so—"

"Then we have nothing further to discuss." He stands there staring at me, still dripping. It's a struggle to keep my eyes on his and not following the trail that drops of water make down his tight, toned abs.

"Look, it's a big place. I'm sure we can co-exist peacefully," I try. "I'll stay out of your way. You stay out of mine. Really, we can be roommates with the added benefit of this place being so large. The only space we actually have to share is the kitchen."

"That's not going to work for me."

Asshole.

"You know what? Fine. I tried to be an adult, but you are just fucking determined to make this difficult." I turn to leave, and he grabs my arm, whipping me around so fast I almost lose my balance.

"I'm making this difficult? This is all your fault."

"I didn't write the will, jackass!" I scream in his face. He doesn't even flinch.

"No, but it's a pretty big fucking coincidence that she dies right before you come looking. How fucking dumb do you think I am? I know you're just here for her fucking money. What's wrong? Did Daddy cut your allowance?"

"You think *I* did this? You think *I* killed my mother for this ugly-ass house?"

"Of course I think you did it. Why else did you show up when you did? I don't believe in coincidences."

"Because I was looking for my mother. I was told she killed herself when I was fifteen. I was looking for answers!" Tears of frustration are building behind my eyes, but he won't see them. I pull my hand out of his arm and walk away. Before I reach the door, I stop, not turning to face him. "The funny part, if you had just talked to me like a person, if you had answered the questions I have about her, I might have let you take it all."

"Do that now. Move out, give up your claim on

my home, and I'll give you all the answers you want." He stands just behind me. I can feel the warmth of his body on my back. I hate how fast my heart beats and how in tune my body is with his. "All you have to do is leave, and I will tell you anything."

His breath ghosts against my neck, sending sparks of electricity skipping across my skin. Looking up, I can see our reflection in the glass door separating the pool from the rest of the basement. His head is bent down close to my neck, he is leaning over me, his hands move to my hips, stopping just before touching me. I catch his eye in the reflection. His eyes are dark, his lips parted. He wants me as much as I want him.

Too bad he would never be enough for me, even if he wasn't a raging asshole.

"You didn't know I existed until after my mother was dead. Clearly, you didn't really know anything about her. What answers could you possibly have for me?" I say.

His eyes go from dark, full of need and heat, to ice cold in a flash.

"I know everything about Freya. It wasn't just a piece of paper that made me her son."

"Then she lied to you. She had three real sons, she had a daughter, a family she abandoned. You didn't know the first thing about her. I'll find my answers on my own. Get used to me being here, or leave. Your choice."

I throw my elbow into his stomach. He lets out a

grunt, but I doubt I hurt him. He allows me to go without saying another word, and I leave him there to find the answers I need.

Something about what he said doesn't sit right.

The timing. It is odd.

Thinking about that, I head back to my mother's, now my room, praying she kept a diary here as well. I could simply ask Phoenix for the ones he's been trying to push on me, but I'm not ready to unleash that chaos. Not yet.

Thirty minutes looking in drawers, on shelves, under mattresses with no luck. I'm about to give up when my door opens, and Perseus is standing on the other side, sadly now fully dressed. He glares at me from the door.

"Why are you in her room?"

"It's my room now," I say, sitting on the bed.

"There are dozens of other rooms to choose from. Why this one?" He braces his hands on the top of the door frame. I'm not sure if it's to cage me in or keep him out.

"Because I can." I sit back, bracing my hands on the bed behind me. "Please leave."

"You can't be in here."

"This is my house, and this is the room I chose. Get over it, or move out." I absolutely do not look at the way his defined arms are stretched out, and I have no desire to know what it would be like to be under him while he works out all his pent-up anger issues.

Nope, not interested. My heart is pounding because he is annoying, not because he is looking at me like he wants to eat me alive.

"This isn't your house yet." He means it as a threat, but why does it make heat race down my spine?

"What are you going to do, Perseus? You can't touch me. You don't have the balls. If anything happens to me, you end up with nothing. So either man the fuck up and do something, or go back to your room, turn your stereo up and blast angry emo music while you massage your small dick like the petulant child you are."

For the first time since I've met Perseus, he smirks. "I can assure you one thing, princess. There's nothing *small* about my dick."

CHAPTER SIX

Perseus

"We need to get rid of this girl now," I say as I enter the billiards room. Eros and Heph are playing, and Paris is like always—focused on his laptop.

"Come on man, she isn't that bad, is she?" Eros lines up a shot. "She's kind of hot. I bet she would look better naked and panting between us." He slides his cue back and right as he takes the shot. Heph hooks his cue under Eros's legs, making him stumble, and his shot go wide.

"She isn't welcome here," Heph growls in Eros's face. "She's a thief stealing Perseus's inheritance. This is his home. Our home."

Eros doesn't back down, and to be honest, I wouldn't expect him to. He shoves Heph back, and they square off against each other. They could come to blows. They have before, mostly when Eros is being a little shit, and Heph can't tell when he is joking.

Normally, it's fine. If they fight, it will be over after a few solid hits and then acting like it never happened within the hour.

Tonight, however, I just don't want to deal with them.

"I didn't say we hand over anything. I'm just suggesting that maybe we have a little fun while she is here." Eros shoves Heph back again. In an instant, Heph is in his face again.

"Fun?" I ask, pulling both their attentions back to me.

"Yeah, fun. Like we had with the little redhead at the party last week." Eros's eyes light up, and I know he is thinking about the woman we had kneeling on the bathroom tiles at the governor's mansion. She was pretty, and we were bored. And she just wouldn't stop talking, so we gave her the opportunity to put her mouth to better use. She went back and forth between sucking me and Eros off, and she did such a good job, we brought her home and shared her with Paris and Heph.

We don't always share women, but when we do, it becomes a game. None of us has the time or even desire for a steady girlfriend. But that doesn't mean we don't have needs that must be met. And we learned a long time ago, sex can be so much more fun if it's a game. Whenever we share a woman, it becomes a sport. Who is the better lover, who can make the girl come hardest, who can make her come more, and whose name will she scream first?

Eros can almost always make them come the most, but he is aided by his piercings and love for eating pussy. Paris can make them come the hardest. The redhead came so hard for him she squirted and drenched the bed. Heph makes each one scream his name while he brutally fucks them with that thick, coke-can cock of his. But when they are asked who the better lover is, my name comes from their lips. Every damn time.

I make them earn my cock.

I whisper the filthiest things in their ears until they beg me to fuck them. I edge them over and over, telling them how amazingly tight their pussy is, how beautiful they look sucking down Paris, or riding Eros's face. I tell them how well they take Heph and how much of a good girl they are being for me.

By the time I slide into them, they're shaking and on the verge of another orgasm. Some nights I give in and give it to them without much of their pleading. Others, I pull their hair and make them stare at Heph, who loves to watch me work. I will lie to these girls and tell them how he only watches the most beautiful of women. That he thinks when a woman comes, you can see her soul, and it is stunning.

That poor girl walks out of here the next morning a little bow legged and completely ruined for the next man.

We even manage to get Paris off his computer for a solid two hours.

Heph argues with Eros again, but I think he might be right. "I think you could be on to something," I say, pouring myself a few fingers of whiskey.

"You can't be serious," Heph scoffs.

"I am very serious." I pour the others a drink. "I want her gone. We all want her gone, but we can't hurt her, and we have to handle this... delicately."

Eros and Paris both make a noise in the back of their throats, so I add, "Not that we would hurt a woman."

Both men nod, but Heph looks like he might consider it, if the situation is right. We've had to hurt people in the past. Rough some people up who owe money. It's hard to keep your hands clean when you're a high-end loan shark as a career. But women have always been off limits—both lending to and collecting. Our cocks rule our minds. We know this. It's our weakness. So we keep it clean.

But maybe... an exception can be made for this *see you next Thursday* who just burst into our lives.

"So, what are you thinking?" Eros takes a seat on the leather couch. I go sit next to him, and Heph and Paris both move to the seating area as well, with their drinks.

"The will has all these rules. Let's drive her to break them. She isn't allowed to live outside of this house. Heph, I want you to make her miserable.

Follow her, embarrass her in front of the staff, anything to piss her off. Make her want to leave."

"Done," he says without a single hesitation, and I know he means it.

"Paris, can you keep an eye on her comings and goings? Can you find out if she is still working for Medusa Enterprises in any capacity? The second she does anything work-related, I want to know, and I want proof to go to the lawyer with. She can't work for six months, and my guess is that rule will be very hard for her to follow. I can see it in her eyes. The girl has something to prove, and she's going to get nervous knowing her brothers are stepping in and could replace her completely."

"I already hacked into her bank accounts, and her work e-mail and accounts. So far, all she's done is tell her father of her hiatus, set up an auto email saying she is going to be gone for the next six months, and to e-mail her brother, Apollo, letting him know what he needs to take over while she's away," Paris answers, looking up from his screen. "Did you know that Medusa is buying The Titans hockey team?" He shakes his head and returns to his computer screen. "I also hacked her phone, have her real-time location, and all her text messages and records of her calls."

"Good. Eros, she also has the morality clause. I want you to shatter it. Gain her trust, make her want you, and then I want our friends in the media to catch a few scandalous pictures. It has to be huge, though, so make them run it instead of just selling the pictures to her. You need her doing something shockingly kinky for it to create the kind of buzz we need."

"Boss," Eros looks at me with a stern face, his jaw set like he is about to tell me no, "I just have to say, this is the best assignment you have ever given me. I will not let you down."

I don't even try to hold in my laugh.

"I know you won't. None of you have ever let me down, but I am not your boss. We are equals." I grab his arms. "We have always been equals. Our business may not compare to Medusa, but we are all powerful men who can get shit done. There is no one else I could ever trust with this."

I mean every word. These men have been by my side since we were kids. Heph and I were together on the streets since before I can remember, and it wasn't long until we found Eros scamming cougars outside bars when we were barely fourteen. Freya found us. She pulled us out of the dirt and gave us a home and an education in a fancy school full of entitled assholes. Assholes except for Paris. The second we saw him, we recognized him as one of our own, a man who was already older than his years and had seen some shit. We instantly pulled him into our circle, and we have been together ever since. With Freya's help, we went from juvenile delinquents to powerful, educated men with the ability to rule the world. Sure... we still hustle in our own way. But the difference is we now have money and aren't just street rats.

I trust these men with my life. With the four of us working together, Athena will be a distant memory before the first year is up.

"Two hundred dollars says we drive her away before the end of the month," Heph says.

"I give her the year," Paris says. "She is Freya's daughter. I don't think she will be easy to crack. Also, from what I've dug up on her... this chick is dangerous. We need to be smart about this. Messing with a Godwin isn't the wisest move."

"Six months," Eros bets. "Godwin is just a name. Nothing to fear."

"I give her three months until the deed is in my name." I smile. "Between the scandal, monitoring, and the harassment, three months easy. She's nothing but a spoiled rich girl."

"What about you?" Eros asks. "What are you going to do?"

"I am going to undermine everything she does. She has to throw a party every single month. I am going to make that extremely difficult. I'm going to humiliate her constantly, and I will push her over the edge. I'm going to become her enemy in every way. She will hate it, but I will love it. She will break so beautifully for me."

"As long as I get to break her in first." Eros laughs. "She has a sexy little body that is going to look so perfect tied to my bed."

I snap my head to look at my friend and have to fake a smile.

For the first time, a burning sensation rips through my chest, and my jaw clenches. A single thought screams in my head. Could it be?

Jealousy?

I saw her first. She should be mine.

Nah... fuck that. Let's all share in breaking this woman.

CHAPTER SEVEN

Heph

I wish Perseus would just let me drop this dumb bitch off a cliff somewhere and be done with it. It'd be so easy to frame one of her father's many enemies. It'd never come back on us, and Perseus would get the money he is owed. Just one word, that is all I need, and I will take care of this the easy way. Hell, I don't even need a word, just a nod. One nod, and all this bullshit will be over.

But Perseus loved Freya. Even in her death, he will remain loyal to her, like I will remain loyal to him. So it's time to get to work.

It only takes me a few minutes to find Athena. She is sitting at the kitchen table eating one of Mrs. Medea's signature omelets. I shoot Mrs. Medea a glare. She shouldn't be feeding the traitor. She should be starving her out.

"Good morning, Heph, isn't it?" Athena's cheery voice rubs me the wrong way.

"It is. So what's your plan today, princess? Going to rob anyone else of their inheritance? I mean why should they just be grieving the loss of a loved one when they can also be grieving the loss of their home and livelihood?"

"Well, we all need hobbies." She smiles sweetly before taking a sip of her coffee. I can see why Eros is so into her, but I'd still rather see her silky brown hair sinking under the surf.

"You didn't answer my question," I say as I nod at Mrs. Medea, who is offering to make me an omelet.

"Was it a question or an accusation?"

"Both."

"I have to get this place ready for a party." She sighs. "I don't suppose you are willing to be helpful?"

"Depends on what you need?" *I'll help you jump in front of a bus.*

"Well, I need to hire a planner, start getting the grounds ready, and talk to the staff about what I need done inside, and—"

"Oh, poor little princess, so much work to do to plan a simple fucking party. Life is so hard, isn't it?" Ridicule is dripping from my words, and I know she hears it. Her back straightens as she glares at me.

Mrs. Medea puts a plate in front of me, and I take a few bites, not really tasting the meal. Being this close to this... *thing* has put me off my appetite. Mrs. Medea steps out of the room to no doubt get out of the line of fire. She already told Perseus that she was staying out of it. Her job is to care for the house and the people in it. Nothing more.

"Throwing these events, especially on such short notice, is a lot of work," Athena says as she texts something into her phone. I hope it's Medusa-related, and Paris will catch it.

"I know you have to go order other people around all day." I roll my eyes. "You wouldn't know a hard day's work if it bit you in the ass."

She looks up from her phone, an eyebrow arched. I haven't frazzled her one bit, and I'm growing annoyed and frustrated by the steel wall that surrounds this woman. "You don't know anything about me." There's a challenge in her voice.

"Don't I? I know you have only ever worked for your daddy. And I am sure the shit that whatever he makes his daughter do to earn her pocket book money is rough. I'm guessing he offers *you* as a signing bonus to clients. And I'm sure that takes a lot, but don't compare what you do on your back with what the rest of us do."

Her chair scrapes against the tiles as she stands. I expect her to go run off because I've been mean. What I don't expect is her closed fist slamming into my nose hard enough I hear a snap.

I'm up in a second with her throat in my hands, holding her against the wall. I'm not hurting her, I'm under strict orders from Perseus not to, but that doesn't mean I am going to let this little bitch get away with breaking my nose. Blood is dripping down my face, and I intend to use it to help drive my point home.

"You do not belong here. Pack your shit and leave before this gets any uglier."

She smiles. The little bitch gives me a wicked grin that makes my cock twitch with interest.

"I drew first blood. Why the fuck would I leave now?" She has more fight than I gave her credit for. It's no matter, I'll stamp it out quickly enough.

"Because, princess, this is no place for little rich girls. I don't play nice." I press my body against hers in an obvious threat. It's empty, but she doesn't know that.

"I don't *play* at all. Get your fucking hands off of me." Her knee comes up, but I block it before she makes contact with my balls.

"Bad, girl," I growl, and for just a second, I swear her body responds to mine. She likes this. I'll be sure to let Eros know, but my job is to torment her, not seduce her.

"Fuck you," she bites out.

"Nah, brat isn't my type. I like my women a little less desperate." I let her go and take a step back, before turning and grabbing a towel for my nose.

It smarts, but it's not too much blood. Maybe she didn't break it. Perseus enters the kitchen before she can say anything.

"What's going on here?" he asks.

"I want him gone." Athena points at me.

"Nothing," I answer Perseus, ignoring Athena as I pour a cup of coffee for him and one for myself and make his coffee just the way he likes.

"You need to leave my house. Now!" Athena demands.

I set down my coffee, about to lay into her again when Perseus turns on her.

"No," he says simply.

"This is my house."

"Not yet, it isn't." Perseus is in her face, his fists clenched at his sides, but he's controlling his temper. "This house is still half mine until you screw up and lose it. Freya also stipulated that *all* of us get to live here. All of us have free rein in this house. I live here, Heph lives here. Eros lives here, and Paris will always be welcome to come and go as he pleases. If you don't like it, then give up your claim and leave."

"I'm not going anywhere." She pushes him back, and I am on my feet in an instant in case she tries to take a swing at him. Athena doesn't attack him. She doesn't even leave the room. She steals my cup of coffee and sits back at the table, pulls a planner from her bag and a tablet, and starts typing away on her phone like I found her. "I will be spending the day planning this next party. If you have any allergies, please let me know now so I can make sure the caterers can put it in everything." She levels a look at Perseus and me.

"I have shit to do," Perseus says to me. "You good here?"

"Yup." I take a seat at the table in front of Athena. "I'm just going to help the princess plan the party. Make sure she doesn't kill you with shellfish."

"Awe, no shellfish? What a shame," she says, staring at her screen. I look behind her and Perseus winks at me. Normally, driving someone crazy isn't my idea of a good time. But maybe this could be a little fun. There isn't really anything I won't do for Perseus. I owe him everything.

The rest of the day I make sure I am wherever Athena is like an annoying fucking shadow.

She wants to hire a grounds crew. I tell her no. We have a grounds crew. They just need a list of what needs to be done.

"Just give me the list, and I will get it to them," I say with a smirk.

"No, you won't." She doesn't even look up at me. "You will toss it away, and nothing will get done."

"Are you saying I'm lazy?" I lower my voice issuing an obvious challenge. She takes the bait just like I knew she would.

"No, I'm saying you're dishonest. I'm saying you're a dick who doesn't give a fuck what happens to anyone but himself. So no, I will not be accepting your help."

I cross my arms and wait just a beat. The grounds crew are here and just outside the door. It's their morning routine to fill up their water bottles and get some coffee before they start the day. I know this, but Athena doesn't.

As soon as I am sure they can hear us clearly, I say, "Look, princess, this house has a full staff. The grounds crew we have will take care of everything you need. They are the best at what they do. You just need to let me know what needs to be done."

"Everything," she snaps. "Everything needs to be done. And the best?" She huffs. "Hardly. Best at being incompetent maybe. The grounds are a mess. The hedges are overgrown and shabby looking, the lawn desperately needs to be mowed and—"

"I'm sorry Miss, but Freya preferred the grounds to look wild. She had us tending to the plants to see they were healthy, and the gardens in the very back," Myra, the head of the ground keepers, says, her daughter Polly behind her grabbing her skirts and hiding from Athena. "But if there is anything you would like changed, we just need to know, and we will handle it. My crew has been tending this house for almost five years. There is no better crew for this estate."

Athena turns her eyes on me, her face growing bright red and her teeth grinding as she realizes I set her up. I knew they were there, and I let her walk right into that.

"I'm sure that won't be necessary, Myra," I butt in before Athena can say anything. "Athena is just new and over her head. Keep doing what you are doing. We will let you know what needs to be altered. Don't worry, you are not losing this job."

"N-no, of course," Athena stammers. "I'll let you know as soon as I have that list, but can we start with the back patio area. I want to have it open to guests for the first party in a few days."

"Of course." Myra takes her daughter and practically runs from the room.

"You know I hate you, as does everyone else in this house," I say as I take a seat on the counter. "And you just made Myra's daughter, Polly, cry. Once that gets around, the staff will hate you, too. Why don't you just leave now and save yourself the trouble? I can't imagine anyone is going to want to come to your little party, anyway."

Athena takes a step toward me and leans in. Her eyes are locked with mine. "I'm glad you hate me." She glances down at my lap, zeroing in on my cock beneath my pants that suddenly hardens as if this vixen is Medusa herself and can turn anything to stone. "But something tells me that hatred makes your dick hard."

She then turns and stalks out the door.

CHAPTER EIGHT

Athena

"Thank you for coming early." I glance at Phoenix wearing the rare tuxedo perfect for tonight's party. "And for agreeing to come to the party. I know it's not your thing."

"We aren't staying long," Phoenix says, his arms across his chest. He appears angry, but it isn't directed at me. Being away from the four walls of his attic puts him on edge. I know this, which is why I appreciate him making the effort.

"What is this place?" Apollo asks. "You bought a mansion outside of Seattle? This doesn't fit your style. And why the fuck did you just decide to quit Medusa?" His eyes go to my stomach. "Are you pregnant or something?"

"No, of course not," I say, running my hand over

my belly and wondering if there is reason for him to say that. Do I fucking look pregnant? "And I didn't quit Medusa. I simply took a leave of absence."

"You told us this was urgent," Phoenix adds.

I release a deep breath. The only way to say this is by spitting it out. Godwins don't sugar coat things, and there is no reason for me to start now.

"This was our mother's house," I begin.

Apollo and Phoenix both look around the room with fresh eyes now knowing it isn't my new house. The confusion washes over both their faces.

"She was alive. The entire time." I look to Phoenix. "Just like you thought. She didn't jump off that cliff and commit suicide like we were led to believe."

"What the fuck are you talking about?" Apollo asks. "Alive?" He looks at Phoenix. "And you knew this? You knew Mother was alive this entire time?"

Phoenix shakes his head. "I didn't know anything, but I've been reading her journals, and there was a line in one of them that made me think there was a possibility."

"So I dug into it," I say. "And long story short, I found out she lived in this house."

"Lived? As in she's not alive now?" Apollo asks.

"She died about a month ago," I say. "She left me the house in the will."

"Will?" Apollo shakes his head and runs his fingers though his hair. "She was alive, now dead, and there is a will? Journals? And this is the first I'm hearing of this? What the fuck, Athena!"

"Does Dad know about this?" Phoenix asks.

I nod. Our father knows everything. Stupid question.

"And no one felt the need to share this information to her fucking sons?" Apollo's face is reddening, and I can't say I blame him.

"I know it's a lot," I begin in a soft voice. "I'm still trying to process it all myself, but she wanted out of the marriage or something, and our father decided to banish her from our fucked-up kingdom instead."

"So, she's been living here the entire time? While we all believed she died?" Phoenix takes a seat on the nearest chair. I can almost hear the wind being knocked out of him.

"It appears so."

We aren't a huggy type of family, but a part of me wants to console Phoenix by taking him into my arms. Instead, I open Pandora's box fully and tell my brothers everything I now know. I rattle off about the ridiculous rules of the will, the terms of madness, and the assholes that I now have to live with. I tell them every little detail of every single thing to help ease my guilt for keeping it from them for so long. There's pain in their eyes, rage in their movements, and the stench of betrayal is thick in this room once I am done.

"I don't care what that will says," Apollo finally says after pacing the room in silence for several long moments. “We’ll contest it. We can argue she wasn’t sane. Or she was held here against her will and forced to make it. Frankly, who cares? It’s not like any of us want her money. We’ll do it just to fuck with that Perseus guy and his band of shitheads.”

“I considered that option,” I say.

“Then pack your shit. Let’s go.” Phoenix rises from his chair. “Come to Heathens Hollow. Some time on the island could be good to clear your mind. All of our minds.”

I shake my head. “There’s a party about to start.”

“Your point?” Phoenix asks.

“Don’t ask me why, but for some reason I want to follow the terms of her will. I want the house,” I confess.

Apollo extends his hands at his surroundings in disbelief. “This is like some haunted mansion out of a bad horror movie. Why the fuck would you want this house?”

I shrug, not knowing the answer myself.

“To win,” I finally say. “I won’t walk away and let those men think they got the upper hand on me. I refuse.”

Phoenix reaches for a bag I hadn’t noticed before. “Her journal I mentioned is in here. If you read it, you’ll see just how fucked up our parents were. We need to step away from this. Not dive into it.”

I take the bag, unsure if I’ll read the journal. “I’ve never been afraid of the dark before.”

Apollo and Phoenix exchange a look. “All right.

We'll stand by you. Not like we have a choice," Apollo says. "But tell me more about these men."

"Just your basic thugs," I say. "My PI dug up that they have some money, they act as investors, but really are just low-level sewer snakes. Nothing I can't chew up and spit back out."

Phoenix smirks. "I have no doubt you can handle yourself. The question is, why bother? Our mother stayed away for a reason. You want my opinion? Fuck her. Fuck her for making us believe she died for all these years."

"I get it," I say. A part of me feels the same way as Phoenix. "But something inside of me tells me I need to finish this. I don't know how this ends, or what is in store, but I don't want to just ignore this one."

"What does our loving father say about all this?" Apollo asks.

I roll my eyes. "What you expect. Very little. He's not ever going to tell any of us the truth, and you know it. We could get angry, make demands, and then what? He's not going to change."

"Fuck him, too," Phoenix adds.

"Fuck them both," I agree with a nod, "but that still doesn't answer questions I have. It doesn't take away this feeling in my gut that I need to remain in this house and follow her stupid rules."

Apollo sighs. "What can we do to help?"

"Run Medusa while I'm away. I can't check in. I can't do anything. I know they are watching. One of the asses is savvy on the computer. I know he's hacking into my shit."

"I'll stop it," Phoenix snaps.

"Yes, get on it, but regardless, I'm not going to give them anything to use on me. Especially something as simple as that. I see through their weak plan to break me, even though they think I'm blind. They are digging, they are trying to push me to hate them, and I know they are going to try to seduce me as well. They think I'm a weak-willed girl who will cave to their every desire if my pussy is pleased."

"If they so much as touch you," Apollo starts.

I smile and try not to laugh. "My dear ol' brother, I've gotten this far in life taking care of myself." I wink. "Maybe I'll seduce them right back."

Phoenix groans, clearly being pushed to his comfort line.

I inhale deeply. "I need a vacation anyway."

Apollo smirks. "This place is far from a vacation."

I give an evil giggle. "I don't know. I think I may have some *fun* while here."

CHAPTER NINE

Eros

The past few days, Heph has been driving that little Athena mad. He has made every single step she has taken towards this party, and even literal steps, an absolute nightmare. It would be funny if I wasn't just a little afraid of him now. The man truly is relentless, but I also see something else in his eyes. Lust. There's no denying that fact.

But despite all of Heph's best efforts, and they are impressive, it's time for the party. Which means it's my turn. I can't help the smile that's been on my lips all day. The party is a masquerade, which makes my job that much easier. The false anonymity gives the party a titillating feel. The liquor is flowing, and my job is going to be a piece of cake.

Our plan is simple. Perseus and Paris made sure

every single tabloid will be in attendance, and I am going to lure the fair maiden away from the party. Then with my charm and wit, I will seduce her and get her into a particularly scandalizing position just in time for the doors to open and each tabloid to get the perfect money shot, as it were.

The only question now is what kind of position will I put her in? I can't just bend her over the desk. That won't be salacious enough. Getting those perfectly juicy lips around my cock, is on my to-do list, but that is still too tame. The tabloids would make more money selling those pictures back to her than publishing them. It has to be something really dirty.

I considered having them walk in on my going down on her, but honestly, that would probably just make her a hero to unsatisfied women everywhere.

Though it would do wonders for my reputation.

No... It must be something kinky.

Naked and tied in Shibari knots would be fun, but I don't have that much time. If there was a chance in hell I could get Perseus's help and tag team her, that would work, but it will never happen. They hate each other too much.

Then it hits me as I'm tying the bow tie on my tux and adjusting my mask. It's all about perception. Maybe I could convince her to test out a new toy for me. A remote-control vibrator. Then I could use it to turn her on, play with her, make her delirious, and just as she is about to come, I will make a hasty exit just as the photographers come in. It will look like she is masturbating at the first party in her deceased mother's house. It will show everyone how little Athena cared for the mother who suddenly died and left her almost everything. Who masturbates at a party you are hosting, anyway? It's devious, and I am so proud of myself for coming up with it.

With the toy in my pocket, a new one that I have been looking for the right time to use, I head downstairs to a party that's in full swing. I have to admit, the place looks good, and the crowd seems to be having fun. I snag two flutes of champagne from a server so Athena and I can toast her success. I look around, but I don't see her.

I know she came down. She greeted her guests. She has to be here somewhere. I search the ballroom and the patio, even the kitchen. She is nowhere to be found.

In a last-ditch effort before calling for backup, I look for her in the library. She is there with a book on the desk I plan on spreading her out on for all to see. I send the text to Paris letting them all know where I am, and to give me thirty minutes.

"Hiding from your guests?" I ask, sliding up to her.

"What do you want?" She doesn't even look up.

"I wanted to congratulate you on a grand party, but you don't seem to be enjoying the fruits of your labor."

"Well, your little buddies made throwing it such

a pain in the ass that it's ruined the entire thing for me."

"Yeah, Heph is a little protective of Perseus, and I think Perseus is just grieving Freya and hurt by her betrayal."

"That has nothing to do with me," she argues, looking up from the old book.

"Doesn't it, though?" I ask. "He thought he knew Freya, and he trusted her, but then he finds out that not only does she have other children he didn't know about, but that she gave the bulk of her assets to her only daughter. This mansion isn't just a house to him. It's his home. The only home he's ever had and known. Until you live one day homeless on the streets, you can't understand the importance of that."

She looks up at me, the cutest little crease between her eyes. "I'm not kicking him out."

I set the champagne flutes on the desk. "But you're planning to, baby girl. Don't try lying to me."

"I'm not your baby girl," she says immediately, but there is no fire behind it.

Deciding we need something stronger than champagne, I cross over to the good stuff. I pour us each a glass of bourbon from the crystal decanter on the side table and hand her a glass.

"Look," she says, taking the glass. "I know this is a lot for him, and all of you, I guess, but that isn't my fault. I didn't write the will. I didn't do this. She did.

Maybe he should sort out his mommy issues then start acting like a grown-ass man."

I can't help the laugh that comes from my lips. She surprises me at every turn, and I like it. She's full of fire, and it's a damn turn-on, but I have to remember that I'm here for a reason, and I am working on a clock.

"You're not wrong but give the man a break. He wasn't expecting anyone, and then to have the most devastatingly beautiful ball-buster kick in his door. Baby, you got the poor guy on the ropes."

I toss back the bourbon and she does the same, then as I put down my glass, I see what she is looking at. It's a diary, and I recognize Freya's handwriting.

"I didn't realize Freya kept a diary."

"It appears so. Apparently, there's a lot about this woman we don't know."

I stand behind her, placing my hands on the desk on either side of her so I am caging her in while looking over her shoulder.

"Anything good in there?" I lean down so I know my breath is caressing her skin. I press myself up against her, and her breath catches.

"I don't know," she says.

"Not going to read it?" I ask.

"Maybe I plan to give her her privacy."

"Speaking of privacy," I say, my lips right next to her ear. "I've been wanting to get you alone since the minute you walked into this house."

My dick is hard and pressing against her. There's no way she doesn't know what my intentions are.

"I'm a virgin." The words come from her lips so causally, but they take me off guard. I see a hint of smile on her face. She knows what she just did. It's her weapon.

"What? How? Why did you just blurt that out?" I can't rebound. Not only am I shocked by her announcement, but I'm also surprised she's being so open and honest about it. At her age... is virginity even a possibility?

She turns her head to look up at me, meeting my eyes. "I am a virgin by choice, because it gives me power. It's part of who I am. I make the choices with my body, and I decide if someone is good enough to please me. So far, no one has measured up." She shrugs. "I have no shame in admitting that fact."

Rebound. I need to rebound quickly.

"How do you know if you won't give them a chance?" I ask before I gently kiss her neck. Her head tilts to give me more access, so I place a few more kisses as she thinks about her answer.

"Because every single man I have ever met is egotistical and self-serving. They see women as objects to use. And if the woman gets off in the process, great, but if not, they don't really care. I have no desire to just be a vessel so some asshole can shoot his cum in me and then walk away."

"Seems to me then you need more than one

lover," I say, kissing my way up to her ear. Her pulse is fluttering against my lips.

She smiles. "Possibly. But until I can find my own personal harem of men willing to work together to please me, then I guess I am just left with my imagination and my fingers... and maybe a few toys."

My cock is rock hard, pressing against her ass that is so beautifully shown off in the tight, floor-length gown.

"Tell me more," I growl, moving my hands to her hips and pulling her body into mine.

"Tell you more about what? How I like to tease myself at night. How I edge myself over and over, spending hours exploring my body?"

"Yes," I say, as one of my hands moves up her dress to just under her breast. "Tell me what you think about when you come all over your fingers." I lift her right hand and bring it to my lips, kissing the offending fingers.

"No." She pulls her hand out of mine but doesn't step away from me. "I want you to tell me what you think of at night when you're alone."

"I'm rarely alone," I say.

"Bullshit, you've slept here every night since I got here, and you haven't had anyone over."

"Are you checking up on me, baby girl?" I can't believe a woman so inexperienced can radiate such sexual prowess. I need my dick inside her now.

"I like to know who is in my home. Now tell me."

"Lately, I've been thinking about how fucking

sweet your pussy would taste when I have you tied to my bed."

Her laugh is a deep, sexy sound that makes my cock ache.

"Well, that would never happen." She presses her ass against my cock. "If I was going to let you taste me, then you would be the one tied to my bed while I rode that pretty face."

"I might let you ride my face," I say, "but only if you put that sexy mouth to work on my cock."

"Maybe." She smiles at me. "If you were a good boy."

I place my hand into my pocket, fingering the vibrating balls I brought for her. I'm pretty sure I can get her to wear them for me simply by daring her. The chemistry in the air is thick, and I know I can use it to my advantage. But I suddenly don't like the idea of other people getting to see her come. At least not yet.

No, I am going to earn each orgasm I coax from her, and there will be many. I am the only one who gets to see her come apart. Only me. At least to begin with...

She looks down at the diary again, her deep neckline giving me a perfect view of her large perky tits that I just know will be sensitive and a dream to slide my cock in between.

"Why don't we go up to my room right now, and I will show you exactly how good I can be?" I say as I look directly into her beautiful blue eyes when she twists her head to look at me again. "Let me give you a taste of what it will be like when you find your harem of men."

"And why would I do that?" She picks up the glass of bourbon and takes a sip while arching a perfectly shaped eyebrow at me.

"Because you want to, and I promise my mouth is better than your fingers. I might have a few other things you would like to try as well."

Before she can reply, the doors open, and several men walk in snapping photos of me and Athena both leaning over the table looking at an old book.

Paris, Heph, and Perseus are there, giving me bewildered looks.

"Can we help you, gentlemen?" Athena's voice is cool, the heat and passion coloring it a moment ago gone.

"Well, I guess we will have to finish our conversation later," I say, as she turns her head to meet my gaze. "Let's pick up our discussion later tonight, after the party."

"Maybe," she says as she strolls out of the room and back to her guests. I don't even try to hide how I am watching her ass sway.

The photographers all follow her out, leaving me with my pissed-off friends.

"What the fuck?" Heph shoves me back into the desk.

"What?" I ask. "We had an enlightening conversation. Sorry, boys, I think my powers of seduction aren't going to be as useful as we thought." I push past Heph, who is glowering at me. "Maybe try annoying her some more?" I add as I head back to the party.

I mingle for the rest of the night, talking to socialites and millionaires while mostly trying to catch Athena's eye, but she ignores me. It's as if our conversation didn't affect her the way it had me.

She's cool.

She's collected.

She's a goddamn goddess.

The other guys keep looking at me funny. Perseus looks confused. Paris looks worried and, well, Heph looks pissed. But Heph is always pissed. It doesn't matter. The only thing I am thinking about is getting her alone again.

Athena won this round tonight, but my dick doesn't care. Right now, I'm prepared to admit defeat. My eyes follow her every move. I'm waiting. Waiting. This party needs to end.

CHAPTER TEN

Eros

It feels like years before the guests finally leave, and I can sneak off to Athena's room feigning guilt about not being able to get the job done.

I don't knock, not wanting Perseus, who has a room nearby, to hear. I slip into the room just in time to see Athena step out of the bathroom wrapped in a towel. I almost drop to my knees at how beautiful she is. Her skin slightly pinked by the hot water, the towel wrapped around her appears so soft and like with one simple little tug, it would fall to the floor, showing me what I just know is the sexiest body that has ever existed.

"What do you want?" She doesn't seem surprised to see me.

"You know what I want." I take two large steps to

close the distance between us. I grab her by the back of her head, lacing my finger in her wet hair, and pull her lips to meet mine in a searing kiss that has my cock hard as steel in seconds.

She pushes against me when I let her go. Panting, she says, "I'm not going to fuck you."

"Tonight isn't about me, baby girl. It's about you."

I pull her back to me, and this time, she presses up on her toes to kiss me first, her hands instantly in my hair. With one swift tug, I pull off the towel and let it fall to the ground.

Her breath hitches, her chest rising and falling rapidly.

I feel her hands slide down my back to my waist, then she pulls away.

"Is this what you want?" She snakes her hand down beneath my pants to grip my cock.

"Fuck, yes," I tell her, my voice low and hoarse. "But I'd rather taste you first."

She wraps her hand around me and squeezes before she releases her hold on me.

"Get on your knees," she says. It's a command, not a request. I like when Athena is bossy. It's fucking hot.

I obey, my heart racing as she stands completely nude before me.

"Tell me," she says as she stands before me, her small hand between her legs, rubbing her clit. "Tell me what you want."

"I want to suck that pussy of yours until you come, and then I want to lick it clean," I confess.

Her hand stops rubbing her clit. She looks down at me, her lips parted, her eyes wide.

I open my mouth to say something else, but she says, "Then do it." Without pause, she straddles my face.

Her taste is sweet. It's addictive.

I groan, the first of many sounds she's going to hear me make tonight.

I spread her open with my fingers and lick her from her clit all the way up to her fucking perfect tight little hole. I press a kiss to it, and she shudders.

She's moving her hand between her legs again, stroking her clit as I lick and flick my tongue over her pussy lips.

"You have the sweetest fucking taste in the world, baby girl."

Her hips buck up, and she moans. "Oh, God," she cries out.

I wrap my lips around her clit and suck hard. Her little cunt gets wetter beneath my tongue as her knees start to shake.

I release her clit, and I press my tongue past the silky folds of her pussy. "Come for me, baby girl," I demand.

"Then you're going to have to do better than that," she says, but it's obvious it's all for show. My little viper is about to come all over my tongue.

I grab her hips and hold her steady so I can get in

there deeper as I suck her clit. I then move my tongue in a circular motion as I insert my finger into her virginal hole, loving the idea of keeping her cherry intact... at least for tonight.

I feel her tighten all around me as her pussy starts to quiver beneath my tongue. I continue to finger fuck her as I lick, careful to not go too deep. Though I want to add a second finger and hear her cry out in delicious pain, I decide to only give her pleasure for now. I'll save the erotic affliction for another night.

She's panting, her body arching up as she squeezes her thighs around my head, and I lick and suck that hot fucking pussy as her juices drip down my chin and into my mouth.

I can't get enough of the taste of her. I want to bury my face in her cunt and just fucking eat her until she's spent and until I can taste the last of her sweet fucking cream.

Her legs are still shaking as she tugs on my hair. I look up at her, and she's staring down at me, her chest moving up and down as she tries to catch her breath.

Not wanting to even give her a second to regain her senses, I lap at her little cunt, devouring her pussy like a starving man. And just as she's about to come, I move back up to her clit and suck hard.

"Eros!" she screams, her fingers digging into my shoulders.

I continue to fuck her with my mouth, pressing

my lips around her clit and using my tongue to stroke her until she explodes, her pussy juices coating my lips.

I release her clit and take a deep breath, her sweet taste still on my mouth.

She looks down at me, smiles, and moves her hand to my head so she can gently stroke my face. "You're really something."

I smile up at her. "That was just the prelude to what I have planned, baby girl. But that's enough for one night. I have to keep you wanting more."

CHAPTER ELEVEN

Paris

Athena is running a little slower today than normal.

I check the tracing data on Athena's phone. She went on her run about an hour ago, and she always stops here for a coffee before running back. I sit, getting some work done on my laptop, just waiting for her. In the meantime, I'm checking her work correspondence. So far it looks like she hasn't even logged in since she set up the away e-mail.

Honestly, I am a little impressed. I pegged her as a workaholic. A rule-breaker. I was sure when Eros couldn't get it done, this would be the way to take her down.

I'm going to keep monitoring, of course, but I don't know what I'll be able to find like this, so I am going to have to get to know her a little more.

The bell above the door chimes as Athena steps in.

"Your usual?" The barista calls out to her, holding up a medium cup.

Athena shakes her head no. "I need a large today, and can you add an extra shot? I had a long night and not much sleep."

"Athena?" I pretend I'm not expecting her, and I close my laptop.

She steps up to the counter, pretending she doesn't hear me. I'm not letting her off the hook that easily. I stand up to bring my cup to the counter for a refill of the drip.

"Hey, I thought that was you." I offer her a smile, effectively cornering her.

"Paris, hi." She gives me a wary but polite smile.

"Would you care to join me?" Before she can make an excuse, I add, "I was actually hoping to catch you outside of the manor so I could talk to you about a few things. About Perseus, and why he has been—"

"A huge asshole?"

"Yeah." I rub the back of my neck. She is blunt. I'm not used to women being so upfront.

"Sure, I have a few moments."

We get our drinks and head back to my table.

"Come here often?" I ask.

"You had something you wanted to tell me?" She takes a sip of her coffee. "About why you and your buddies have decided that being giant dicks is the best way to honor my mother's wishes."

"Well, I honestly don't think that, but it's not my inheritance on the line. And you have to understand—"

"Do I though? Do I have to understand?"

"Okay, well let me explain why Perseus is the way he is, and maybe it will make more sense."

"Sure," she says, sitting back. I can't help but notice the way the light is catching her hair, giving her a halo, making her blue eyes seem bigger and brighter. She looks so innocent, like an angel.

"Perseus met your mother when he was a young teen. He had been living in a box with Heph. Literally a cardboard box. Anyway, one night he was attacked by some asshole who thought Perseus was moving in on his turf. He was just a scrawny underfed kid at the time and was pretty much getting the shit kicked out of him. When your mother stumbled out of a bar, drunk with some fresh bruises of her own on her jaw, she saw what was happening and pulled a gun. Without a warning, she fired four shots into the drug dealer. Then she panicked, screaming and crying. So Perseus grabbed her and ran. He took her back to his makeshift *house*, and they hid there next to some dumpsters while the cops searched the area."

I stop to take a drink of my coffee and see how Athena is taking all of this. She is chewing on her lip, so I keep going.

"They fell asleep in that box, but when Perseus

woke up, she was gone. He was sure it was a dream, and she would never be back. He just lay in that box nursing his broken ribs for who knows how long when Freya finally found him again. Heph tried to scare her off, but he was skinnier that Perseus was. She gave Heph a few hundred dollars and told him to go shopping, get food, and head to this shitty little motel. She handed him a room key. She said she was taking Perseus to the urgent care, and then she would meet him there. Heph didn't want to, of course, but Perseus told him to go. It would be okay."

"Then what happened?"

"Well, the way Freya told it, Perseus looked her in the eye and said, just to do it. Just kill him and get it over with. He thought she was there to kill the only witness to her committing murder. She pulled him to his feet, put him in the back of a Town Car, and took him to the hospital, paying a lot in cash to make sure there was no record of either being there."

"So what? She saved him, then he saved her, then she saved him again?" Athena is leaning forward in her chair like she is hanging on every word.

"Pretty much. That was the start of a long friendship. He actually didn't see her again for a few months. She would send money, keeping both the boys in that motel room, and they were able to start taking care of themselves a little. Eros had moved in with them a while after. Then one day a man shows up. They think they are finally getting the boot, but he tells them Freya is in trouble and needs them."

"When was this?" she asks.

"About ten years ago," I answer, having already put the dots together in my head. I wait for her to come to the same conclusion.

"After my father banished her."

"Yeah, apparently, she was a mess, but having her boys there to take care of gave her purpose."

"Okay, so where do you fit in?" she asks, catching me off guard.

"I met them at school."

"There is more to that story." She narrows her eyes at me.

"A lot more," I admit, "but I agreed to share all Perseus's secrets. Not mine."

"Well, that's not fair."

"It has been my experience that life is usually not fair."

"Which side of that equation are you on?"

I set down my coffee, trying to figure out what she means. "I'm not sure I—"

"I mean, do you get more or less than your share? Is life kind to you, or a raging cunt like she is to so many?"

Talking to Athena isn't what I expect. She has the face of an angel, the mouth of a sailor, and the brain of a shrewd businesswoman. All strategy and seeing more than most would like. It's clear she reads people the same way I read code. I have no doubt that for her, it's incredibly easy, but it baffles lesser people.

"Depends on what we are talking about. I have always been lucky that money has never been lacking in my life."

"But something else has been." Her bright blue eyes seem to see through me, something I should find incredibly off-putting, but for some reason, I don't.

"It has."

She looks like she wants to press, and part of me wants her to, but she sits back and just watches me.

"Trust," she finally says. "Freedom. Love. A Home."

"Those used to elude me, the freedom one is still kind of iffy, but with those men you hate so much, I found my home with a family I trust."

She nods like that is an acceptable answer, and I can't help but watch the way her little tongue darts out of her mouth to lick the bit of foam her coffee left on her lips.

I want to kiss her.

I have no idea why. I shouldn't want to. But I do.

"What about you? Has life been generous or a cunt?" I ask, hoping I can wash away the thoughts of tangling my fingers in her hair as I dance my tongue with hers from my mind.

"A bit of both. Like you, I don't know what it means to struggle financially, and I know I am lucky for that. But everything else has been a scarce commodity."

I nod. I know exactly what she means.

"What's with you and that computer? I think this is the first time I have seen you put it down."

"Hacking is a hobby." I shrug. "Nothing too serious or illegal," I lie.

She shifts a little and tilts her head. Something tells me she knows I'm lying, but she decides not to push me on it.

"You don't live at the mansion, why?"

"How about this? You answer a question for me, then I will answer one for you," I offer, not wanting her to take control of the conversation. I know one thing about Athena—she's used to taking control.

"Sure, but if we are going to hang for a while, I need more coffee and food." She rubs her stomach, and I look at the clock. We have already been talking for awhile. "They make great bagel sandwiches here, you want one?"

"Sure, but let me get them. What are you drinking?"

"Mocha latte," she says.

I nod and get up to grab our food.

I half expect her to be gone by the time I return, but she is still sitting at the table with her phone out, scrolling through social media. She seems so carefree and at ease. I am in awe of this woman. I can't pinpoint exactly why, but it's as if she's a siren or has some spell cast on me. Part of me feels I'm betraying Perseus and the others by not hating Athena. Actually, hatred isn't an emotion I'm feeling at all.

We dig into our food, trading questions, some

serious but mostly light. I know she is smart; she has to be in order to run Medusa like she does. And I know she is stubborn, but I had no idea she is so charming and witty. At one point, she makes me laugh so hard I can't swallow my drink until I calm down. I don't remember the last time I laughed this hard. We just sit talking for a little over an hour when an alarm on her phone goes off.

"Shit. I have to go. I'm going to be late for a meeting with the next party planner."

"Would you like a ride? I am heading back to the estate."

"That would be awesome, thanks. You know you aren't nearly as mean and stuck up as I thought you were."

"Thanks? Well, you aren't as evil and vindictive as I thought you were. So—"

"Don't count me out just yet." She gives me a playful wink. I think she's flirting, so on a whim I do the thing I have been thinking about for the past hour.

I kiss her.

Her body freezes, but she doesn't pull away. It only takes her a second before she is kissing me back. Her lips are soft against mine. Her breath merging with my own. The others will hate me for this, but right now, I can't help it, and I don't want to.

CHAPTER TWELVE

Athena

I enter the mansion after having returned from a meeting with a florist for the garden party in a month, and of course, all the guys are in the living room. Perseus is sitting on my favorite couch with some skank on his lap.

Each day at this mansion, it gets harder and harder to deal with. It's ridiculous. Heph is still following me around, causing problems like a poltergeist that won't get off my ass. And Perseus does whatever he can to be a complete asshole.

Well, not all the boys are bad.

Paris and I go out for coffee almost daily and end up making out like teenagers in his car. He really is so sweet and makes me laugh when our lips aren't glued together. Then there is Eros. I might still think about the things we did after the masquerade party every time I get in the shower. He hasn't visited my room since, but we do text pretty much constantly. Well, we sext constantly. Not all of our conversations start like that, but that's how they end, with my pussy dripping wet and aching as I type out the filthiest things to him. He replies, taking my idea a step further, and usually with him in control.

It's adorable he thinks he would be the one on top.

The girl on Perseus's lap giggles and whispers as I walk past them. I ignore her. It's none of my business, but I know that in a matter of hours, or probably minutes, he is going to take that random girl to the bedroom right next to mine and fuck her against the wall of my room, making it as loud as possible. Telling her to scream his name. I have to wonder... does it really count if you have to *tell* the girl to scream for you?

"Ahh, look, Candy, it's my gold-digging whore of a stepsister," Perseus says.

"My name is Cindy," the girl says, but no one is listening to her.

"Not your stepsister or any kind of sister, really. Your bloodline wouldn't know the first thing of how to blend with mine." I smile, trying to head up to my room so I can put away my stuff and maybe run a bubble bath and text Eros.

I dart my gaze to him, and he is watching me

with a little smirk and his phone sitting next to him plugged in so he will have a full battery.

Good. Eros is on the same wavelength as me.

“So then, like, why are you in his house?” the girl asks.

“It’s my house,” I say, though why I’m speaking to this mouse of a girl, I don’t know.

“Not yet,” Perseus says. “It’s just a matter of time before you fuck up, and it’s all mine.”

“If you say so, *brother*,” I taunt him. I am ready to leave it at that and go take my bath when the little tramp whispers about gold-digging, thieving bitches, and I let my control snap, just a little. “Okay, Mindy, let me tell you how this is going to play out. You look like the kind of person that could use a head start to process everything.”

“Oh, shit,” Eros whispers, and Paris snickers.

“You are going to stay down here for a bit, and Perseus is going to tell you god only knows what and convince you to go to his room, so he can ‘make sweet love to you,’” I say with air quotes. “Or whatever bullshit line he gives you. But he won’t take you to his room. That is down the hallway. No, he will take you to the room next to mine, where he will fuck you against the wall not to please you, but in an attempt to annoy me. He will say things like ‘that’s right, baby. Scream for me louder,’ blah blah blah. He won’t call you again, and this cheap bastard probably won’t even pay for your Uber home. And trust me, Trudy, you will be gone by morning.”

The room is quiet for a moment. I'm content with that and about to head to my room when she has to say, "Sounds like a jealous bitch to me. Everyone knows Perseus and his friends are the best lovers out there, and tonight I get their king."

Oh, this poor dumb little bitch.

"Really? I mean, I don't know how good these men are firsthand, but I think you chose poorly."

"Excuse me," Perseus growls out.

"Well, I mean okay let's look at the options. Heph has some serious anger management issues that, if channeled into sex, would make him a fucking powerhouse. You wouldn't be able to walk for a week." I tap his chest, and he just glowers at me.

"Paris is sweet as fuck and would probably be the type of lover women swoon over for the rest of their lives, wondering why their husbands can't be as loving, gentle, and thorough as he is. Don't let the constant attachment to his laptop fool you. He would make sure his partner comes a few times before making love to them in a way that would be a soul-altering experience."

I smirk as Paris blushes at my praise.

"Then we have Eros." I stand behind him on the couch with my hands on his shoulders. "He is the dirtiest, kinkiest motherfucker you have ever met. He will find new ways to make you come that are so satisfying you don't even care that afterward you are going to wonder if you need therapy. Rumor has it, that he's not just pierced on his face." I give a wink.

"Damn straight," Eros says before taking a drink of his beer.

And just because I can, I add, "And he is on a personal mission to prove every woman can squirt. So you know it's going to be good."

Paris starts laughing as Eros chokes on his beer.

"So, yeah, as far as men go, I get the appeal for these three. But Perseus looks like he is a two-pump chump that thinks the female orgasm is a myth. And judging by how quickly his little escapades against my bedroom wall are over, I hope you are a talented actress. Because trust me, Barbie, you will be faking it tonight."

With that, I turn to leave. Eros and Paris are visibly trying hard not to laugh. Heph has his normal menacing stare, and without even looking, I know Perseus is staring daggers into my back as I calmly walk out of the room and head to my bedroom.

Just as I drop my purse and look over my collection of bath bombs, trying to pick out one for tonight, my phone pings.

Eros: You are a very bad girl.

I smirk as I type out my response.

Me: Are you going to punish me, Daddy?

Eros: I would take you over my knee right now if I wasn't sure you would like it.

Me: I know I'd like it.

Eros: Yes, you would.

Me: But was I wrong?

Eros: About me, nope. About the others? I think you nailed Paris. But Heph I don't know. And Perseus, I don't think so, but that wasn't what you were trying to do. Was it, bad girl?

Me: I don't know what you are talking about.

Eros: Yes, you do, but that's okay. He had it coming, and to be honest, it's kind of hot watching you stand up to him.

Me: Really?

Eros: Yeah, but it doesn't change the fact that you were an incredibly bad girl. Do you know how I punish bad girls?

Me: Tell me.

Eros: I punish them by making them beg for forgiveness. I make them crawl on their knees and beg me to take them back. And when they finally realize that they are mine, I make them scream my name until they can't think of anything else.

My breath hitches as I imagine what it would be like to have him punish me.

Eros: Do you want that, little one? Do you want to be punished?

The thought of him punishing me sends shivers down my spine. I bite my lip, trying to control the urge to beg him for it. But the truth is, I want it desperately. I want to feel his hands on me, his breath on my skin, and his power over me.

Me: Yes, Daddy. I want to be punished.

Eros: Good girl. Then get ready because you're in for a wild ride. I'm coming to your room.

Me: I'm still not going to fuck you... Daddy.

I'm lying. I'm so fucking turned on right now that I'd fuck Eros. No doubt about it. But I think he likes the chase. And one thing about me... I know how to run.

He doesn't even bother knocking at my door. "Strip," he commands as he enters my room all the way.

I obey without hesitation, peeling off my clothes one by one until I'm standing before him, completely naked. His eyes roam over my body, and I feel a rush of heat spread through me.

"Beautiful, but I'm afraid you still have to be punished."

I bite my lip, trying to hide my excitement, but I know he can see right through me. His eyes glint with a dark desire. He reaches down to undo his belt, slowly pulling it free from the loops of his pants. He folds it in half, letting it snap against his palm.

"You asked for this, baby girl. If you are going to act like a brat to one of us, just know that Daddy's coming at the end to make you pay for it."

I can feel my arousal building, and I know that Eros can see it, too. He stalks around me, the sound of his footsteps echoing in the room. The air moves as he swings the belt and strikes me across the ass.

I gasp. The pain is sharp, but it's in a different

universe compared to the pain of being punished when I was a child.

This is so different. So fucking different, and I love it.

My skin burns, and I close my eyes as I revel in the kinky passion flooding into my wet pussy.

Eros spanks me with the belt again. And again. I count three strikes before he replaces it with his hand.

His palm is warm and firm on my ass, and my skin burns under his touch. He pushes me down onto my knees, and I don't hesitate to obey.

He spanks me once, twice, and three times as I block out the fact that I'm literally burning up my feminist card as I submit to a man. Yet, I've never been more turned on in my life.

I close my eyes, focusing on the pain, trying to get lost in it. I don't want to think about anything but the fact that I'm kneeling naked in front of a man who demands it. A man who is not only earning my respect but is fucking taking it.

His hand comes down hard, a sharp sting spreading through me, but I don't cry out. He spanks me again, harder still. And then again. Each time, my ass is burning hotter and hotter, but I don't make a sound.

"Do you like that, baby girl?"

I say nothing, and he spanks me harder.

"Answer me."

"Yes."

"That's what I thought."

He lifts me off my knees and throws me onto the bed, pinning me underneath him. I gasp as the air is forced out of me.

"This is how bad girls get punished."

I can feel him hard against me, and I struggle to draw breath.

"Tell me to fuck you."

"Daddy, please fuck me."

"Tell me exactly what you want."

"Daddy, fuck me. I want your cock inside me. I want you to fuck me until I can't move."

"Good girls get rewarded, baby girl."

He flips me over so that my ass is up in the air. I shiver, the cool air on my overheated skin. His fingers are slipping inside me. He plays with me, teasing my clit, and I cry out.

"Please, Eros."

"Please what?"

"Fuck me."

He plunges his finger inside me, and I gasp, my hips grinding back against him. He gathers my hair, pulling it back so that he can bite the back of my neck. I gasp, my pussy quivering around his digit.

"You like that, don't you?"

"Yes."

"What do you want me to do to you?"

I swallow hard, unable to get the words out.

"Tell me what you want."

"I want you to fuck me, Daddy."

"Hard?"

"Hard. I want you to fuck me hard."

"That's right, baby girl. You tell Daddy what you want."

He spreads my ass cheeks, his fingers teasing me until I'm begging for it.

"Please, Daddy. Fuck me."

"You want me to take this virgin hole of yours?"

"Yes... yes." And I do. I desperately do.

"You've been a very bad girl, baby girl. You shouldn't just give your virginity to anyone."

He swats my ass hard, and I gasp, my fingers clawing at the sheets.

"There's a plan for this virginity. And right now... my baby girl is going to have to wait."

Without another word, or another touch, Eros leaves as quickly as he came.

My phone chimes and when I pick it up to read the text, it takes all my might not to throw my phone across the room.

Eros: That was your punishment, baby girl.

CHAPTER THIRTEEN

Athena

Eros got the upper hand on me... again. My body is making me weak, but I can't refuse it, either. I need to just have sex and get it over with. Maybe then I'll stop acting like some horny teenager who can't think of anything but getting laid. I consider masturbating to help ease the edge, but instead I close my eyes to let sleep take over. Tomorrow, I regain myself... and my body.

A loud bang pulls me from my sleep, and I sit up in my bed thinking someone is breaking in when it happens again, followed by a high-pitched feminine moan.

I roll over with my pillow on my head trying to block them out, but it doesn't work. Perseus is possibly trying to prove me wrong, so who knows how long this is going to last. I, of all people, know spite can be one hell of a motivator. And it sounds like I inspired this man to up his game by a few notches.

Unable to stay in my room and listen to the porn set next door, I grab my swimsuit and head down to the basement for a few laps in the hope that the other side of the house and a few floors will be enough to block out the moaning.

The water is cool and refreshing. As I glide through it, I lose myself in the laps, loving the burn in my arms and legs as I push myself harder. I've never been much of a swimmer—running being my exercise of choice—but there is something really soothing about it. Just me. Just my thoughts. I've never really given myself time to just... think. Never in my life have I not been consumed with Medusa, my father, my brothers, and my dark life. My mother's will is forcing me to take some time from all that. I'm not sure if it's a gift or a curse. Because when this break is over... Medusa is still there. The question is going to be how messed up will it be when I return.

Out of the corner of my eye, I catch movement in a dark shadow. My heart rate picks up, and I turn mid lap to swim to the other side of the pool. When I breach the water, the shape moves into the light, and I roll my eyes at myself.

It's just Perseus.

"What's wrong, princess? Did I scare you?" he asks with a sneer.

"Not scare so much as annoy. Why are you down here? Already done with the flavor of the night?" I try not to stare at his body. He is only wearing a pair of gray sweat pants that leave nothing to the imagination.

"Is that jealousy I hear?" He comes to the edge of the pool.

"Annoyance," I correct. "And pity for the girl."

"You and I need to have a little talk," he says before stripping down naked and diving in to the pool. His body makes a graceful arc as he slices into the water then comes up only inches from me.

"Talk about what?"

"About how you ran your mouth earlier today."

"Oh, that." I pretend to think about it for a moment. "Nope, I am pretty solid on everything I said."

"You don't know what you're talking about." He moves closer to me. "See, I don't think you believed a word you said."

"No, I am pretty sure Heph is a great lay, Paris is a romantic and a giver, and I am pretty positive Eros is incredibly kinky." My ass still stings from the spanking just to prove my point about Eros.

"About me." His voice drops. "I think you want me. And the women I bring back here make you jealous, and you hate yourself for it."

"I think you're delusional." My voice comes out shaky as I watch the drops of water from his hair drip onto his muscular shoulder, then run down his thick chest to his toned abs before disappearing in the pool.

"Am I?" He brings his hand out of the water to my shoulder. Perseus strokes his thumb across my clavicle, and I can't help the way my heart starts to race as little bolts of energy sizzle across my skin and heat builds in my core. "I think you want me to prove how wrong you are."

His gaze burns into me as he leans in closer. My mind is telling me to push him away, but my body betrays me as it responds to his touch. I feel myself getting wet with anticipation as he slides his hand down my arm and takes my hand.

He pulls me close to him, so I can feel his hardness against my thigh. And just like that, I'm lost in him. His lips crash onto mine, and his tongue sweeps into my mouth. I moan as he moves his lips down my neck, and I can feel him marking me as his.

Suddenly, I don't care about anything else. All I want is him. I know it's wrong, but the feeling of his strong arms around me and his lips on my skin make it seem so right.

But this is Perseus. My enemy.

I try to step back, but he moves closer. He snakes his other hand around my waist, holding me in place. My breaths come in short gasps as he leans in, his lips hovering just above mine.

"Don't deny it," he whispers, and I can feel his

hot breath on my skin. "I've seen the way you look at me when you think I'm not looking."

I shake my head, trying to dispel the lustful thoughts running through my mind. I shouldn't be feeling this way about him.

I try to push away from him again, but he tightens his grip.

"Go back to your flavor of the night," I say, hoping I sound more authoritative than I feel.

"I sent her away. I think I'd much rather taste you," he says.

I want to come back with something. Some sort of snappy retort. But nothing comes.

"Tell me you don't want this," he demands, his lips grazing my skin.

I swallow hard, my mind foggy with desire. "I can't." My voice is barely above a whisper.

I manage to put my back to him in the hope that not looking into his seductive eyes will help.

This is Eros's fault. He got my body so turned on, and without quenching my desires, I'm left defenseless to Perseus's attack.

He presses his body against mine, his chest firm against my back. He trails his hands down my arms, sending shivers through my body. I can feel his hard length pressing against me, and I can't help the moan that escapes my lips.

"Good," he growls, slipping his hands beneath my bikini top. He cups my breasts, teasing my already-hard nipples with his thumbs.

This is wrong, but I can't seem to stop. His hands are everywhere, trailing down my back and cupping my ass as he grinds against me. I'm lost in the sensations, the feel of his hard body pressed against mine, the sound of our breathing and the water sloshing around us.

I feel his erection against my ass, and I push myself harder against him. His teeth find my earlobe, and he tugs on it gently. Tingles course through my body, and I buck my hips against him.

I moan as he moves his fingers down between my legs, and he pushes my bikini bottoms to the side so that his fingers slide along my slit.

He steps back, and I turn to face him once again, waiting for him to remove my suit. He doesn't. He just looks at me, his lips parted and his breathing heavy. He reaches out to cup my breast as he leans in and takes my lips in a kiss that leaves me breathless. I moan into his mouth as I wrap my arms around his neck, clinging to him tightly as our tongues dance together.

He reaches down and picks me up. I tighten my arms around his neck as he carries me out of the pool and lays me on the floor's heated tiles. He kneels before me and kisses his way down my neck to my breasts. His mouth finds my nipple, and he teases it with his tongue before taking it between his teeth and biting down. I gasp as my core clenches.

"I won't stop until I'm inside you," he whispers, pulling my bikini bottoms off my hips.

I don't want him to stop. I want him to give me a night I won't forget, a night I can't remember without feeling weak in the knees.

He pulls my bikini top over my head and tosses it to the side.

Do I tell him? Do I confess a fact about me that I've never kept secret before? My virginity is a badge of honor. It's never been my shame before, and yet there is a part of me that doesn't want him to know. What if he stops like Eros did?

And is Perseus worthy of giving my virginity to?

"I'm a virgin," I blurt out, tired of overthinking it.

He takes my lips in a deep, searing kiss. "I know."

"Eros told you?"

"We tell each other everything, but we also dug into your past the minute you walked through the door."

My eyes widen in surprise. I don't know how to respond to that. I'm a little pissed, but I'm also flattered that these boys have done so much research on me, and I'm clearly a topic of their conversations.

Know thy opponent.

Impressive.

He pulls back, tracing my lips with his finger. "I've wanted to be your first since the first time I found out." His eyes lock with mine. "I've been recently tested and haven't had unprotected sex since. We all have."

My inexperience is clear right now. I'd never

think to stop and ask this question, and I should have.

"I'm on the pill," I admit. I prefer regular periods and—

"That's what I like to hear," he growls.

This is awkward. I try to turn away, but he grabs my chin and makes me look at him once again. His eyes are serious, and my stomach clenches.

He leans in to kiss me, and I relax, letting my arms loosen around him.

He pulls back and gives me that cheeky smile that I used to hate but suddenly find endearing. "Now, where were we?"

In an instant he's inside me, and I feel a sharp pain that quickly fades as he stills, his eyes taking on a look of concern.

"Did I hurt you?"

I shake my head. "No."

He pulls out, then slowly thrusts inside me again. The pain is still there, but as he thrusts deeper, it subsides. He continues to thrust in and out of me at a steady pace, and the pressure builds in my core.

"Then get ready. Because I plan to," he warns.

I wrap my legs around him, pulling him closer to me. He growls as he thrusts harder and deeper, his eyes locking on mine as he drives into me.

His eyes never leave mine, and I can tell he's watching me, waiting for me to tell him when to stop. It's the sexiest thing I've ever seen, and suddenly I want to see him lose control.

I lift my hips to meet his thrusts, urging him deeper. His lips curl up into a smile, and he picks up his pace, his thumb moving to my clit. I pant and moan, my nails digging into his back. The heat inside me intensifies, and I bite my lip, desperately trying to hold my orgasm.

I don't want him to stop. I moan as he slams into me, his teeth nipping at my neck. It's everything I ever imagined and more.

Perseus slows his pace but maintains a steady rhythm as he thrusts in and out of me. There's stretching and even a little pain—but I like it. I like it a lot.

The orgasm is building in my core even more, and I moan as I try to stave off the pressure. I've always heard virgins can't have orgasms, but I've been primed, and my body is ready. Overdue, in fact. My body disagrees with the rules of virginity.

"I'm close," I manage to say.

His thumb picks up the pace, his thrusts becoming faster and more urgent. "Me, too," he admits, his throaty voice rough with desire. His thumb strums my clit as he slams into me, his eyes holding mine.

"Oh, my God," I moan as heat explodes inside me, and I grip his shoulders tightly.

His thrusts come faster and harder, his groans mixing with my moans. His orgasm hits him, and he pulls out of me, his eyes focused on mine as he comes over the tile. He groans and thrusts back into me three times before stilling.

His eyes are closed, and his head drops to my shoulder as he tries to catch his breath. He collapses next to me, pulling me into his arms. My muscles are weak, and I can't help but curl into him as my body relaxes.

He kisses my forehead. "That was amazing."

I tilt my head to look at him. "Good."

He grins at me and kisses the tip of my nose.

I can already feel my body responding to him. The thought is slightly alarming.

"Are we still enemies?" he asks.

"Absolutely."

"Good. Because I'm digging this enemies-to-lovers thing."

CHAPTER FOURTEEN

Athena

Still reeling from last night and whatever the fuck that was, I go for my run, cutting it a little short, looking forward to spending some time with Paris. He is easy to be around. He makes me laugh, and he makes me feel wanted and cherished when he kisses me. He also respects that I'm not willing to give up my virginity quite yet... or at least wasn't willing before last night. Unlike Perseus, he doesn't push. But the way he kisses me, I know that if he does that when we are truly alone, it would go so much further.

Just because I fucked Perseus, doesn't mean some weird monogamous loyalty begins. Quite the opposite, in fact. I want to fuck someone else fast just so I can erase the feeling of his cock inside of me.

When I get to the coffee shop, the barista points to a table where Paris is sitting, looking all nerdy hot, typing away on his laptop with two cups of coffee and a few pastries sitting in front of him.

"Good morning," I say, taking the seat across from him.

"One second," he says, typing faster before he closes the laptop and puts it away. It makes me feel so important when he does that. All his attention is on me, not being divided between me and the code like it is when he hangs with the rest of his friends. "Good morning." His smile is bright and makes my knees a little weak. "Did you have a good run?"

"I did." I take my cup of coffee, enjoying the rich mocha flavor. "Though it looks like you are trying to negate all my hard work with carbs and sugar."

"The bakery had just dropped these off when I got here, and they were going fast. So I snagged us each one. I thought you would appreciate the hazelnuts and chocolate with your morning coffee-flavored hot chocolate," he teases.

"I'm sorry, those of us who aren't glued to a keyboard all day staring at code don't need straight black coffee. We get to enjoy our morning pick-me-up."

"Oh, I'll give you a morning pick-me-up you can enjoy," he says with a playful wink, making me giggle like the girls I used to detest.

"Uh huh, I bet this is part of your evil plan, isn't it?" I tease, and his brows furrow. "You're luring me into a false sense of security to make me fat. You'll claim it's a psychiatric break. That is the scandal you sell to the papers, letting your little buddy take everything."

He cracks up laughing. "We both know your body is perfect, and you don't run to stay in shape. I bet it's burning off frustration and helps you focus."

"It is helping me keep my competitive cut-throat edge while I wait to go back to work," I admit.

"So about last night," he starts, and my stomach flips. Does he know what happened at the pool last night?

"What about it?"

"You really threw poor Perseus for a fucking loop with your insults." He laughs.

Picking up my pastry, I give him a smile. "Good." I bite into the breakfast, and it's so good my eyes just about roll to the back of my head as I let out a moan that is a little too sexual for a morning coffee shop.

"Admit it, I did good at grabbing these." The smirk on Paris's face is the right amount of sexy and confident.

"Maybe."

"Well, now that I have you blissed out with chocolate, answer a question for me."

"Depends on the question," I say before taking another bite of the flaky heaven.

"Did you mean what you said?"

"You're going to have to be more specific," I

deadpan as I set the pastry down on the plate and pick up my coffee.

"About you thinking I would be the most gentle and thorough lover out of all of them."

"I was mostly saying that to point out how Perseus pales in comparison." God, how I wish that were true, but he is just as sexy as the rest of them. Physically, anyway. His personality still sucks. "But yes, I think that you would be the sweet, gentle one."

"What on earth gave you that idea?" He leans back in his chair, crossing his hands over his chest. I would think he was upset if he wasn't grinning at me with a mischievous sparkle in his eye.

"The way you kiss me," I answer. "You are sweet and attentive, and it's actually amazing. And not a hint of the brutality that I would expect from the others."

He nods like he is expecting that answer.

"You're not entirely wrong. When we kiss, I want to worship you and hide you from all the bad things in this world. But you should know that when I get you alone, I will do things to you that will make you wonder if I wasn't the monster that you should be protected from." He leans forward in his chair, his bright eyes holding mine even behind his glasses. "Trust me, angel. I will be the reason you fall from grace. And you will love very second of it and beg for more."

Heat rises to my cheeks and floods my panties.

Holy fuck, where has that come from? I am still looking for a response, any response.

Paris gives me that sexy, self-satisfied smile as he sits back in his chair with his coffee. "So, what are your plans today? More party planning?"

It takes me a moment to process the change in topic and to regain control over my hormones.

"Nope, the planner has some samples to get, and she and I will meet up tomorrow. Today I am going to do something far more important, and I was hoping to get your help." I lean back in the padded chair with my coffee in my hands.

"What's that?"

"I'm going to try to find out more about my mom. I was hoping you could tell me more about what she was like, especially toward the end."

Paris regards me for a moment, like he is deciding what to tell me. Then he gazes out the window. He could be watching the cars go by, or the clouds roll in, but I don't think he is. I think he is watching my reflection.

"How much do you want to know?" he finally says.

"Everything." My answer is immediate.

He nods and then looks at me again, making eye contact. "Okay, but not here. There are too many ears. And what I need to tell you isn't going to be easy to hear. So, eat your breakfast, then we will find somewhere quiet to talk."

"I can't eat anymore. Let's just go find that place

to talk now," I say, standing with my cup in my hands.

Hand in hand, he leads me out to his car. We get in, and he drives away from the coffee shop to a park overlooking a picturesque lake with ducks.

"In her last few months, Freya wasn't doing well. Perseus didn't want to see it, but she was sick. We took her to the best doctors, of course. They said it was a condition from the drinking, and she needed to stop. She said she would, but then I would find her in the kitchen, passed out on the table, and the stove on fire."

I gasp, but he keeps going.

"She could have gotten better. I think she chose not to. For as long as I have known her, Freya was never a cheerful person. She would laugh, of course, and I believe she loved all of us. She is the one who called us her protectors, but there was something inside her that was fractured, and that crack just kept growing. I think she got to the point where she gave up trying to fix it."

"What do you mean, gave up?"

"The doctors gave her meds she refused to take. She would just spend all day drinking and writing in her diaries. She wouldn't talk to us. And we all tried. A lot. I don't think she was trying to kill herself. I just think she fell into a depression so deep she didn't care if she could get out of it or not. Watching her fire slowly fade drove Perseus off the deep end, too, for a while."

We sit in the car in silence for a bit. Paris's eyes are glassy, like he is reliving all of it as I try to picture the woman he has been describing, and I just can't.

"You said she wrote in her dairies?" I say, making Paris snap back to reality.

"Yeah," he says after a moment. "She had a few. She never let any of us touch them. They should be in her room somewhere. You haven't found them?"

"I have, but I don't really like reading them. I keep trying and... I feel like I'm invading her privacy." My stomach twists in guilt. She is my mission, why I am here, and I have just forgotten about finding out her truth. Actually... I've been more focused on these guys and not letting them get the best of me, that I have lost touch with my original goal. "I guess I have my new mission for today."

"Do you want me to take you back now?"

"Please."

As we reach the mansion, and before we get out of the car, he stops me and pulls me into a heart-stopping kiss. This isn't the sweet Paris I know. His touch is heated and claiming, seeming to prove his words from earlier.

"What was that for?" I ask.

"Because I wanted to," he says before getting out of the car and leaving me there.

CHAPTER
FIFTEEN

Athena

Back in my room, I look through my mother's dresser and vanity again to find more of her diaries. The ones I've found have all had just ramblings of a bored woman. Nothing with any meat to them. But something tells me if I keep digging, I'll find more. Under her bed, nothing. Then I search the closets. Nothing but clothes in the first. I open the second to find it isn't a closet. It's another room entirely, with a desk and some bookshelves filled with beautiful leather-bound journals. I grab the first one. It is dated the day after she abandoned me. The day she left her entire family. The day we all believed she jumped off a cliff because she could no longer face life.

• • •

Dear Diary,

Today, I left my family. Forever.

I know that they'll be better off without me. I can't take the constant questions, the expectations, and the pressure of being the perfect wife and mother anymore. I've been suffocating for years, and I can't do it anymore.

I don't have what it takes to be a Godwin.

I know it's selfish, but I had to do it. And now here I am, alone in this new house... alone.

Someday my journals will be found. I think that's why I write them. Maybe someday my daughter or my sons will stumble upon them, and something in my words will ease the pain I caused them.

Or maybe not.

Maybe it will only hurt them more.

Troy got me set up in this house. It's large. Too large. It's outside of Seattle. I asked to be further away. So far that maybe I won't think about them. But he refused. He still wants his strangle on my neck.

I think I may have made a mistake. But it's too late. I'm dead. Troy told me he's going to make it look like I jumped off the cliff. Such a tragic way to die.

I don't want to read anymore. Something about it feels as if I'm invading her privacy. But at the same time... fuck her. And fuck her privacy.

Dear Diary,

I've been thinking a lot about Athena. I left her with a house full of men. Powerful, ruthless, and even dangerous men. Yes, she can hold her own. Maybe even more so than my sons. But that is what scares me. There's no one there to teach her how to be soft. To teach her how to be feminine. There's no one to teach her that she doesn't need a constant shield, ready for battle.

Or maybe she does. Maybe her life will be nothing but a war.

She is a Godwin after all.

When the butler fell down the stairs, I knew it was her that killed him. I could see the look of murder in her eyes. My daughter was now a killer. She wasn't the first Godwin to be one and wouldn't be the last.

But I should have been there for her.

Phoenix told me what happened. He revealed the butler had tried to molest Athena. She was just a child. A little girl! He got what was coming to him.

I should have been there for her.

I should have been the one to push the man to his death who dared to touch her.

It should have been me to have the courage. But I didn't.

It was Athena. The brave one. My brave daughter.

I didn't even have the courage to approach her and comfort her. To let her know that I knew, and she wasn't alone.

No. I allowed her to form a dark secret in her heart.

I allowed the Godwin curse to set in.

I knew it wouldn't be her only secret, and it wouldn't be the last darkness to enter her heart.

It's probably good that I left her with the ruthless men in her life. She'll learn from them rather than me.

She'll become the goddess of war, and that's a good thing.

She knew?

I thought only Phoenix knew what happened. My mother was right. I did form a dark secret at such a young age, but it wasn't a bad thing. It made me the woman I am today. I know that. Don't fuck with me. Don't fuck with Athena Godwin.

Did I kill a man?

I sure as fuck did, and I'd do it again. He touched me. He made me feel dirty. Wrong. And for that, he had to pay.

I didn't tell anyone besides Phoenix. Not because I was scared of going to jail or anything like that, but because I was embarrassed I let the man make me feel that way. I was ashamed of my momentary weakness. So, I regained my strength and pushed the fucker down the stairs, happy to hear his neck snap.

Can't touch me again, motherfucker. Can you?

I don't even try to stop the tears flowing down my face as I continue to read. Page after page of words all about how she was sorry she had to run. Apologies for how she failed us.

She spoke about me, Phoenix, Apollo, and Ares.

But she also spoke of her new boys—Perseus, Heph, Eros, and Paris. She found these boys, raised them, loved them as her own. They didn't have Godwin blood, and for that she was grateful. These boys would someday serve a purpose, however. With the kindness and support only a mother could give, she created an army meant for only one purpose. To protect her only daughter once she got me out of my father's clutches.

The sun has set before I leave the study for the night with a heavy weight on my heart. My head aches, and my soul has been torn to shreds, but I realize a few important things. I don't hate my mother. I don't resent her for leaving any longer. That wasn't what was fueling this mission. I missed her. When she left, there was a hole carved into my heart, and it had never scarred over.

I sit on my bed, and for the first time in a long while, I cry everything out.

I don't know how long it's been when the tears fade. All I know is my head is pounding, my throat feels thick, and I need to know more. She wrote that she sacrificed being my mother to keep me from a much darker life. What could have possibly been worse than believing that she chose to abandon me by killing herself?

I have all these questions in my head. They demand answers, but right now I just don't have the strength to find them.

CHAPTER SIXTEEN

Heph

Walking downstairs, I am psyching myself up for another day of giving the intruder hell. I'm thinking of all the things I can do when I find her sitting at the table staring at a piece of French toast. She isn't touching it. Her juice is also untouched. I'm kind of surprised to see her here at all.

"What the fuck are you doing here?" I ask.

"I live here. It's my house." Her words are right, but her tone is way off. There is no bite, no fight at all. She doesn't even lift her head to look at me.

"I have more right to be here than do you," I spit. Come on... let's rumble.

"If you say so." Again, no actual fire in her words.

"What's wrong with you?"

"Do you actually want to know?" She glances up

to meet my gaze, and she looks terrible. Her eyes are bloodshot and swollen, her hair is limp, and her skin is a little gray.

"No."

"Then please run along and go bother someone else. I'm not up for it today."

For a second, I'm almost worried about her. I almost miss the banter and the spirit of our normal encounters, and I have to stop myself from asking who hurt her so I can go hurt them. My goal is to hurt *her*. I should revel in her misery, but all I can feel in this odd pang of guilt and worry settles into my chest.

"Shouldn't you be out running?" I try.

"Not today." Her voice sounds different, lifeless.

"Oh, what's wrong? Did you break a nail, and your world came crashing down around you? Did Daddy yell at you for abandoning Medusa? Or maybe you didn't get to come this morning as you fingered yourself because no man will go near you," I taunt her, wanting her to lash out at me and show me she is all right.

Instead, she laughs – a high-pitched manic laugh that reminds me of the Joker.

"What the fuck is so funny?"

"You think I can't get a man?" she says between peals of crazy laughter.

"Well, you're here alone now, aren't you? You spend every night in bed alone. You don't go on dates. Clearly, no one wants you."

She laughs harder, and I am confused.

"I'm sorry, but you have no idea what your little buddies do all day, do you?"

"Of course I do." Now she is starting to piss me off. Good. Anger is easier to deal with then whatever unease I was feeling.

She laughs harder, and I cross my arms over my chest and hover over her, trying to intimidate her.

"Poor Heph, you are so fucking clueless. I go to bed early every night because I am sexting Eros. He's got a filthy mind and keeps me amused. He and I have also played around, and it was fucking hot. I also go on a date every morning with Paris. He and I meet for coffee and end up making out like teenagers in the back of his car."

"You're lying. They would never betray Perseus like that." I bang my fists on the table, and she starts laughing again.

"Perseus, your leader, the one who is supposed to hate me? Okay, he hates me, but he wants me just as badly. After I insinuated that he was a lousy lay, he felt the need to prove me wrong in the pool by showing me just how good he could fuck."

"You lie."

"Ask them." She rises from the table and pushes back her chair. "You seem to think that no man could possibly want me." Her hand is on my chest, and I hate how my heart hammers. "But you seem to the be only one who hasn't made a move. Tell me, Heph, is it because you're too loyal to Perseus? Or are you just not man enough to take what you want for yourself?"

"Lying little bitch! You think you can come between me and my friends?"

"Now there is a fun thought. Coming between a few of you all at once. I bet Paris, Perseus, and Eros would work so well together. They would make me *come between them* a few times." She winks at me, and I can feel my face flush with anger.

"Tell another lie and see what happens," I say between my clenched teeth.

"I'm not lying. Go ask them if you know them so well. You should be able to tell if they've touched me or not, right?" She pats my chest a few times, still chuckling before turning away from me. "Thanks for that. I really needed the laugh." She heads upstairs.

I hate how seeing a bit more life in her makes that unease unravel.

She is lying. She has to be lying.

I send a text to the others, demanding a meeting now, and it takes about fifteen minutes for each of them to reach the billiards room.

"What?" Eros whines. "Some of us need our fucking beauty sleep, man. Not all of us get up with the sun like you and Perseus."

"Why did I have to rush over here? I have plans in like an hour," Paris says as he enters into the room.

"Plans?" I can't believe the audacity of this man right now. "Plans, like your little date with the woman we are trying to destroy? And you..." I turn to

Eros who is lying on the couch half asleep. "What's wrong? Tired from spending all night sending dirty dick pics to that whore?"

"She isn't a whore," he yawns out. "She's a virgin, and I wish I could get her to send nudes. Trust me, I am trying."

"So, fucking what? How am I the only one not trying to tap that?" I ask.

"Because you know she won't want you?" Paris offers.

"Nah, it's because he just can't get the stones to try something," Eros says.

"You two know she has been messing around with all of you, and you don't care?" I can't believe what I am hearing.

"Well, she told me about sexting Eros," Paris says, taking a seat on the couch.

"And I knew she had coffee dates with Paris," Eros confirms. "I also know what she tastes like," he adds as he licks his fingertips with a devilish grin.

"Calm down, Heph." Perseus puts his hand on my shoulder.

"No." I knock away his hand. "Fuck those two disloyal bastards, but you, too? I'm trying to take this woman apart for you, and you are fucking her in the goddamn pool?"

"What?" Paris and Eros say together, finally both taking this seriously.

"Calm down. Nothing has changed," Perseus says calmly.

"How the fuck has nothing changed?" I snap. "You popped the girl's cherry, and act like it's no big deal?"

Perseus rolls his eyes, and I clench my fist. I would never hit him, however. Paris I might hit, Eros I will probably hit, but never Perseus. But that doesn't stop the anger and frustration burning through my veins.

"My plans haven't changed." He looks me dead in the eye. "Nothing has changed. If she thinks our little moment in the pool means something, then that will make our job easier."

I'm still not convinced, and he knows it.

"Paris," Perseus calls out, not looking away from me. "Has anything changed on your end?"

"No," he answers without hesitation.

"Is your plan still on track?"

"Yes."

"Eros," Perseus says.

"Yo," Eros replies.

"Are you still on board?"

"Yup."

"Has anything changed?"

"I'm jacking off a lot more and not sleeping around as much, but that's it," Eros answers. "Virgins aren't my cup of tea, but now that I know she's not one..."

I narrow my eyes at Eros. He has this goofy smile he gets whenever we talk about Athena. And now that I know he is texting her every night with jiz on his hands, I can't shake the feeling Eros can no longer be trusted.

"Fuck you guys. Seriously. Can we all stick to the damn plan? We aren't supposed to fall for the girl."

"Heph..." Perseus begins.

"She's a viper, and she needs to be forbidden," I say before storming out of the room.

CHAPTER SEVENTEEN

Perseus

My gut twists as I look Heph in the eye and lie to him. I've never lied to him before, but I have to. I can't admit that the night in the pool, having her in my arms moaning my name, watching her come apart beneath me, has done something to me. I didn't know about Paris and Eros, and part of me wants to rip them to shreds. Not because they betrayed me, but because they get to touch her, and to connect with her.

I tell myself over and over that it's nothing. It's only because she left me wanting more. Craving. So desirous that my mind can't focus on anything other than her. I should be plotting her demise, but what I really want to do is plunge my cock into her body again and again. Especially knowing that no man has had a taste of what I have.

She was a virgin.

But now that virginity is mine.

I simply took what I wanted.

I don't know why knowing she *was* a virgin makes me hard, but it does.

Since the pool, I have avoided her like she has the fucking plague. I stopped bringing women home. Though I haven't touched another woman since the pool, I haven't wanted to. I know they will never compare to how Athena's body squeezed my dick like a goddamn vise. I obsess over that woman like no one I have ever had before.

Sitting at a local bar with a beer in my hands, I am thinking about her again. Not playing pool, taking money off some of the regulars here, or flirting with the woman three stools down who is trying to eye fuck me.

Eros and Paris both sit down on either side of me.

"You wanted to talk to us out of the mansion?" Eros says.

"Yeah, I wanted to talk to you two about her." I can't even bring myself to say her name.

"Okay..." Paris says, waving down the bartender for a beer.

"She's getting in my head," I admit. "I didn't want to say that in front of Heph with him being so mad."

"Getting in your pants, too," Eros says with a

snicker. “Have to be honest. I’m a tad jealous. I may have to rectify that.”

Jealousy burns in my core. “See, that shouldn’t piss me off, and oddly... I think it does.”

Paris chuckles. “Suddenly stingy? Can’t share?”

“It’s not that. You know there isn’t anything of mine I wouldn’t share. I just have never felt this way about a chick before. Ever. Like I said. She’s fucking with my mind.”

“There’s something about her,” Paris agrees. “I’ll give you that.”

“How do you touch her and not crave her every single moment?” I don’t mean for those words to come out of my mouth, but they do.

“What makes you think we don’t crave her?” Eros asks. “That woman is sexy as fuck, kinky as hell, and she has this fire that is—”

“She is beautiful, smart, so fucking sweet, and responsive,” Paris cuts in. “Of course, we crave her. There is no one else like her, but at the end of the day, it doesn’t mean shit.”

“What?” I turn to look at him, confused.

“You need to get the fuck over yourself,” he says, “and figure out what you want.”

“I know what I want,” I say.

“Do you?” Eros asks. “You don’t get to pine after her like a teenager that saw his first tit and try to destroy her. You need to pick one. This emo shit has got to go.”

“It’s not that simple,” I argue.

"It is," Paris says. "If you want to fuck her, fine, go and get her. I'm looking forward to watching her knock you on your ass. If you want to destroy her, we have a plan. Work the plan. But if you want to love her, then you have some decisions to make."

"You can't cherish and protect her and still be the one who is trying to take her down," Eros adds.

"You two are." I'm definitely not pouting.

"No, we are enjoying her company, but that changes nothing. We have made our choice, and we are loyal to you first." Eros sounds offended.

"Right now, we can be loyal to our friendship and bond, or her. We both really like her, but the four of us are our family. We aren't willing to give that up for some girl, no matter how sweet her kiss is," Paris adds, before draining his beer.

They're right. I need to get my shit together. These guys are my family. Not this girl who just came in to take everything from me.

She is the enemy.

But then why don't I hate her the way I should?

All I have to do is avoid Athena and start acting like myself again. The weird feeling I have will fade. It has to. In the meantime, I'll just fake it until I make it.

I play pool, have a few more drinks, and even half-heartedly flirt with the girl at the bar then let her go down on me in the bar's back alley. I even lie and tell myself that I didn't wish the girl in front of me on her knees worshiping my cock was Athena.

Telling myself not to close my eyes and picture her rich-brown locks slipping between my fingers while her lush red lips wrap around me. When I pull this random chick up and push her against the cold brick wall, I don't think about what it would be like to push inside Athena's tight, innocent body again. And again. And then once again.

I fuck this nameless woman hard into the wall, punishing her with my cock for not being the woman I want.

The next few days go by in a blur. I avoid Athena the best I can, and I think it might be working. If I don't have to see her, I don't have to face her, then I can continue trying to destroy her. It's going well until I hear a loud explosion and a scream from outside. I run outside to see her standing next to her Porsche, shaking. The car has smoke streaming out from the back, and I run over and pull her away from the car in case it catches fire. She whirls around, and her hand slams into my face.

"Which one of you did it?" she screams.

"Did what?" Paris asks as he and the others come up beside me.

"Tampered with my car to try to kill me?"

Paris and Eros both go pale, eyes wide open.

Heph just stares, mouth slack.

"None of us," I say.

"Bullshit. I am calling a mechanic to figure out what the fuck happened, then I am going to make whoever did this pay!" Athena is so shaken, her face is bright red, and tears are streaming down her cheeks.

She swipes at her tears. "You assholes think you are the first to attack me?" She huffs. "Think again, motherfuckers. I've played nice up until now. But no more. You just unleashed the viper from her den."

Paris reaches out to comfort her, and she pushes him away and storms inside, making calls.

"Did one of you do this?" I ask.

They all shake their heads no.

"Fuck no," Eros says, his eyes darkening and his jaw locking, "but I'll kill anyone who did."

The mechanic arrives in a few hours, and I'm sitting in the living room on my phone, waiting to eavesdrop to find out what the fuck happened. He tells her there is something wrong with her car's mechanical controls. Athena asks if it looks like someone tampered with it. He says he honestly doesn't know but will have the car towed and let her know if they find anything.

The second the door closes, she turns on me again.

"Why?"

"Why what?" I cross my arms over my chest.

"I get you hate me, but is murder really the way you and your little band of psychopaths want to go? Do my mother's last wishes mean so little to you?"

"We didn't do this." I grit my teeth as she glares at me.

"I don't believe you. I think you did."

"Then you don't know shit about me or how I work."

"Really? Let's look at the facts, shall we?" She starts pacing in front of the couch I'm sitting on and lists her points with her fingers. "One, you want me gone. Two, the will says you can't hurt me, but if it's a freak accident with my car, the lawyer will give you everything. Three, it wasn't Paris or Eros."

"Oh, because you think your little flirtation is enough to turn them against me?" I sneer.

"No, because if Paris was going to do me harm, it would be through some sort of hacking. And an explosion in my car is too fast for Eros. He likes to take his time, and he would make it personal. And after the texts last night, I'm confident in saying he wouldn't kill me before he got his hands on me again. He'd make sure he at least gets to fuck me before he'd kill me."

I ignore the jealousy that burns through me and the idea of Eros touching her. She should be mine, and only mine. I laid claim.

"It's either Heph or you. And since Heph doesn't do anything without your approval, it was you."

"You don't know what the fuck you are talking about." I stand and tower over her, expecting her to cower, but she doesn't. "And if you ever fucking slap me again, I will make you wish you were in that fucking car."

"The second I have proof of what you did, I will have your balls in my fucking hands. The last man who truly fucked with me is dead. Just know I will make you pay for this. This violates the will, and you will be out on your ass!" she screams in my face, then marches away, slamming doors behind her.

I send out a text. "All of you, the billiards room now."

It takes less than five minutes to get all of us in a room.

"Who did it?" I ask.

Silence.

"Who fucked with her car?"

"No one," Heph says. "Wasn't part of the plan."

"Really?" I turn on him. "You would know how, and you are the only one who—"

"Who what?" Heph stands and squares off against me. "Who isn't trying to fuck her? Who remembers what the fuck we are supposed to be doing and how it had nothing to do with getting our dick wet? Yeah, I am. I am not a killer, and her car is a fucking German import. I don't know shit about German cars, I only work on American. So fuck you and your accusations."

He stomps out and I feel like an asshole. Eros and Paris are both looking at me, hostility pouring from them. They don't say anything; they just walk out.

Heph and I have fought before, but he has never

yelled at me like that. He has never gotten so defensive, and Eros and Paris... I don't know.

Sitting on the couch, I put my head in my hands and think. Is this my fault?

Are they telling me the truth? Did I make them think this was what we needed to do?

For the first time since the four of us came together, I'm not sure if I can trust the men I call my family.

CHAPTER EIGHTEEN

Athena

Pacing around my room, I am fuming. I don't know who I can trust, who just tried to kill me or if it was an accident. There is no way for me to know. My heart is racing with a mixture of rage and terror. Part of me thinks Heph sabotaged my car. He is the type, but he looked genuinely shocked. Maybe he was shocked that I was still alive? But if he did it, it's because Perseus told him to. But I don't think Perseus is the type to have someone else do his dirty work. I'll have my answers soon enough, once the mechanic gets back to me, and there will be hell to pay.

In the meantime, I have another mystery that needs to be solved. I sent my PI some information from my mother's diaries and asked him to keep looking into her death. Her later entries sound paranoid, saying things like her pills were poisoned. Someone was watching her, and she was afraid for her life. Could banishing her not have been enough for my father, or did he know I was looking for dirt on her *death* and took care of her before I found her?

I throw my phone across the room and let out a frustrated scream. It's too much. It's all too much, and I need to talk to someone about all of this. Someone I can trust. I trust my brothers, but no way can I get them involved in all this. They hated the idea of me staying here and getting involved, and I sure as hell don't want to admit that they may have been right. My father would just have everyone killed for daring to hurt his precious Godwin daughter and then order me back to Medusa as if nothing ever happened. No... my family is off the table.

Paris, he is the first name that pops in my head. He is sweet, kind, and chivalrous. I don't think Eros tried to kill me either, if I'm being honest, but it's Paris whom I need right now, so I find him.

He is sitting on the back patio with his laptop open on the table, typing away.

"Hey, you got a minute?" I run my fingers through his short hair.

"For you, of course." He closes his computer and pulls me down onto his lap. "How are you?"

"Scared," I answer honestly, leaning into him, letting his body heat soothe my nerves.

"I bet that was... intense."

I don't really reply to that. There is nothing to say.

"How do I make you feel better?" he asks, kissing my shoulder and holding me tighter.

"I don't know. I'm thinking about hiring a bodyguard." I'm not considering this. The words just fell from my lips, but it is a good idea. I have to stay here, but I don't know if I can if I don't feel safe.

"No one is going to hurt you while you are in this house. I don't think any of the guys messed with your car, but if it will make you feel better, whenever you go out, I'll be your bodyguard." He kisses my cheek then whispers in my ear, "I will keep you safe."

"Really? You would do that?" I move out of his arms so I can look him in the eye. "What if it means going against your friends?"

"Without hesitation." There isn't a hint of a lie on his face. He means every word.

"Why? What changed between the day you met me when you instantly hated me, to now?"

Paris rubs his jaw while he thinks about his answer. I wait patiently, wanting him to think about this. I want the truth, but I know it can take a moment to put such a sudden, complex shift into words.

"I got to know you," he eventually says. "When you came here, we all assumed you were just here to steal the money Freya left to Perseus. Now that we have really talked and gotten to know each other, I know that isn't you. I know you came looking for your mother because you needed answers. I also know you are stubborn as fuck, much like your mother. If Perseus hadn't challenged you when you first met, and instead talked to you like a person, I think you would have let him have it all. Except for maybe your mom's personal diaries and a few mementoes. Thankfully, Perseus is as stubborn as you are."

"Thankfully?"

Paris gives me a slow smile and nods. "I guess I am a little thankful for all this bullshit and drama. If civility had won out over hot heads, then you wouldn't be living here, and I might not have gotten the chance to know how amazing you are." He looks at me with his bright eyes shining through his glasses. "And I have enjoyed getting to know everything about you. So let me protect you. Let me keep you safe from the monsters under your bed."

He pulls me in for a slow feverish kiss that leaves me gasping for more. I don't know what happened with the others, but Paris doesn't seem worried about his friends walking in on us making out. Part of me wonders if this is his way of staking a claim on me in front of the others, or just showing that he doesn't see me as the enemy anymore.

After a while, Paris tells me he must go home to check on his mother. She's been sick lately. But he won't leave until I promise him I will stay inside the mansion for the rest of the night. There is another party tomorrow, so I swear to him I'm going to stay in to make sure everything is ready. He kisses me again at the front door before leaving for the night with his computer tucked under his arm.

"Well, that was a hot kiss. Where's mine?" Eros's voice comes from behind me, making me jump.

"You don't get one." I push past him and start heading for my room.

"Hey"—he grabs my arm to stop me from going upstairs—"stop for a second. I just want to talk to you."

I pull my arm from his hand. I don't think he's the one that messed with my car, but I can't be sure. "So, talk." My words come out harsher than I mean them, but with Paris leaving me here with the rest of the men who may all want me dead, I'm on edge.

"I just wanted to see if you're okay?"

"I'm fine. Is that it?"

"You're fine? Then you have bigger balls than I do. I would be terrified if I thought someone was trying to kill me."

"Are you?" I ask.

"Am I what?"

"Trying to kill me?"

Something almost like hurt flashes across his eyes.

"No, I'm not." His voice is hard now. "I wouldn't hurt you. I thought you knew that."

"I know nothing about you other than how you sext." I shrug. "To you, I'm nothing but a distraction while you bide your time for this shit show to be over."

He says nothing and clenches his jaw as he turns away.

Guilt twists in my stomach as I watch him walk away from me. But it's the truth. I don't really know him. Yeah, we stay up most nights sending each other dirty messages, but that's it. We haven't talked about our personal lives, where we come from, what we want. It's all sex. So how can I know if he cares about me or it's an act to let my guard down?

I go back to my room and think about it. Do I trust Eros? I want to. I really do, but all I know about him is he is dominant and sexy as sin. And, apparently, he has several fetishes he likes to explore mostly on the darker side. His words make my body ache for the things his texts promise. That is all surface level for him. I know so many men like that who hide their true motivations under charm and sex. I can't afford to let him do that to me.

The rest of the night, I spend going through more of my mother's journals. Once she says how she misses the lavish parties she used to throw for my father's business. For her, it was an escape from the dull, colorless drudgery of the day to day. You got to dress up, pretend to be a better version of yourself with people being the bright-shiny versions of themselves. For her, a party was an explosion of color and wonder, with people there to mingle, laugh, gossip, eat, and celebrate everything life is.

For me, the parties are nothing but a chore. A task. A means to the end.

I'm not sure if I agree with her sentiment, but from now on, I'm going to try to see these parties through her eyes. Maybe it will help me understand the woman who was taken from me.

CHAPTER NINETEEN

Eros

Athena has been locked away in her room all day. I can't even imagine how scared she is. I know she needs space, so I only sent her one text last night, not really expecting an answer. When she comes out of her room, I'll try to talk to her again. Until then, I help make sure the party tonight goes off without a hitch. Perseus and Heph keep looking at me funny, but fuck them. I may not have chosen her over them, but that was when it came to pushing her out of the house and keeping Perseus's money and home his. I did not sign on to kill her, or physically hurt her. The only physical pain I am willing to inflict is when she has a safe word, is lashed to my bed, and I can deliver the most exquisite pain with the most excruciating pleasure.

The guests arrive, and I am about to go get her when I see her at the top of the stairs. For the first time, I know what people mean when they say something takes their breath away. Her deep red dress has a narrow, plunging neckline that shows only a sliver of skin but is so tantalizing. It makes you think that if she moves in just the right way, you may just get a glimpse of her perfect breasts. The slit on the bottom is the same. It goes almost all the way to her hip, but only shows the tiniest hint of skin. That dress is made to torment me, and fuck is it working!

"Hello, gorgeous." I slide up to her side and offer my arm to escort her down the stairs.

"Good evening." Her tone is cold, but she takes my arm.

"I made sure everything was set up the way you like, and after those salmon puff things you had last time went so fast, I have the caterers staggering the trays so they last the whole night."

"Why?" She turns to face me directly. Her face is perfectly calm, but I can feel the annoyance radiating off of her.

"Because some people like to eat at parties," I answer, not knowing where the attitude is coming from. I thought she'd appreciate me picking up the slack for her.

"You know I'm not going to fuck you, right?" Her words come out in a hushed whisper, but the venom is still there. "If you want to keep helping out to get in my pants, you are welcome to, but it will never happen."

I lean in to whisper in her ear, letting my hand slide from the small of her back to her ass. "Oh no sweetheart, you are mistaken. When we fuck, it won't be because you 'allow' it. It will be because you are begging for my cock. And I will make you fucking beg for it." I squeeze her ass and feel her breath hitch before I move my hand back to the small of her back before we make a scene. "You think all we have is dirty words on a phone. That all you are to me is something pretty to play with while I bide my time. Well, you are wrong. But I believe actions speak louder than words. After your little tantrum yesterday, I could have let this entire event fall apart. You miss one party, and Perseus gets his home and money. Did I let that happen? Did I allow one scare to derail your chances in this little game? No. I didn't." My words must be registering with her. Her hands on my shoulder are shaking, and the skin under her ear down to the collar of her dress is pebbled.

"I—"

"No," I interrupt her. "You are going to be a good fucking girl, and you are going to play the part of hostess or else I'm going to spank that ass in front of every single guest in this room. Then you can find me later to apologize for accusing me of trying to kill you and assuming so much about me without getting to know me. Only then will I consider not taking my belt to your bare ass as you beg for mercy. Then you are going to remember that I am not the only one sending dirty texts, and *you* haven't tried once to get to know *me* outside of my sex drive, either." I let her go and turn her toward the party, giving her a little slap on the ass when she doesn't immediately go and join everyone else.

She glances over her shoulder at me, a sliver of submission. beneath her hooded eyes. A woman like Athena isn't used to a man standing up to her. I think she fucking liked it.

Following my order, she mingles and talks to almost everyone. Usually, she would be seen slinking off to somewhere to be alone. Tonight, she seems to be enjoying the party and getting to know her guests. Every time she gets too comfortable, I make a sly comment or pass her with my hand subtly grazing over her ass or pinching it. I'm having fun teasing her, and plan on doing it the rest of the night, when a skeevy-looking journalist manages to corner her. I don't like the way he is standing too close. Too fucking close. When his hand touches her shoulder and she tries to shy away but he presses forward, I see red.

The only thing that saves this asshole's life is how she brushes him off more firmly, and he doesn't touch her again. I'm considering backing off until I hear his questions.

"I'm just confused Ms. Godwin. First, we are told you lost your mother when you were fifteen. Now we find she only died a few months ago? Which is it?"

I march to Athena's side and stand between her and the reporter.

"This is not an angle you want to pursue," I tell him.

"The public deserves to know—"

"The public deserves a paper that reports newsworthy events, like corruption, crime, politics. Not the private family matters of those who have refrained from the public eye." I herd him toward the door.

"You don't think a woman faking her death is news?" he scoffs.

"There are three senators and a mayor here. If you want to harass someone, either pick someone who chose the public life or leave."

The threat in my voice is clear, and judging by how pale this man is becoming by the second, he has heard it. Without another word, he turns and scurries away, which is when I notice it is far quieter than it should be, and everyone is watching me.

"Fucking reporters, am I right?" I say, laughing it off. Several of the others also laugh, and the chatter starts again. Not wanting to make more of a scene, I leave the party and find a place I can go destress for a moment.

It takes less than fifteen minutes for Athena to

find me leaning against the railing of one of the balconies, smoking a joint.

"Thank you," she says, standing in front of me. Her words sound sincere, but I am still considering punishing her ass for thinking the worst of me.

"If you really want to thank me, you should be on your knees with my cock in your mouth showing me exactly how thank—" My words are cut off by her hand slamming into my chest hard enough to nearly throw me off the edge of the balcony.

I instantly have my hand around her throat and her body pressed against the brick wall.

"That is no way to treat a man who saved your ass twice."

"It's exactly how I should treat a man who ruins every nice thing he does by acting like my body is made to be used by him," she growls in my face. There is that fire that I adore.

"Your body was made for me to use, toy with, please and worship. You just keep assuming that's the only thing I want from you."

"It is the only thing men like you want from me," she fires back.

"For someone so smart, you are really fucking dumb, you know that?"

"Fuck you. Let me go."

"Is that what you want, baby girl?"

I lean into her, one hand still holding her by the throat, not hard enough that she can't breathe, but enough she can feel how much power I have in the situation. My other hand I run down the thin slit between her breasts when I find she isn't wearing a bra. I grin as I slip my entire hand in to cup her breasts. I pinch her nipple between two of my knuckles while I squeeze her breasts and revel in the low groan that escapes her lips.

"What was that?" I taunt. "You're going to be a good girl and let me eat this pussy on this balcony where anyone can find us? Then once I make you come on my tongue, you're going to get on your knees and show me how thankful you are for me saving you. Then you are going to let me protect you."

I expect her to press into my hand and tell me yes. Instead, she laughs. She fucking laughs at me, then takes my hand and bends my finger back, forcing me to let her go.

"I do like the idea of you on your knees telling me how sorry you are for causing a scene downstairs. I might even let you taste me if you beg. But I don't think you deserve to make me come. You haven't earned the privilege."

Fuck, her fire makes my cock rock hard. I want that. I want to make her come. I want to fight her for dominance. To have a woman under me who is strong enough to fight her urge to submit.

"Baby girl, you don't know what kind of man you are playing with." I grab both her wrists and pin them behind her back. "But if you want to find out, I can take you to my room right now."

She laughs again, and it is infuriatingly sexy.

"I will make you mine and ruin you," I promise.

"That's what I am afraid of. That I will spend one night in your bed, and I'll be so disappointed that it will just ruin sex for me forever."

"We both know that isn't what's going to happen. I have made you come almost every night since you got here with just my words on a screen. Imagine what I can do when I have you under me, begging."

"I think you are confused about who will be doing the begging."

I let her hands go and lace my fingers in her hair, pull it back tight, just a little rough like I know she will love.

"I bet if I reach under that dress right now, I will find your pussy dripping wet for me. Wouldn't I? I bet your body is already begging for my cock, and you are just too stubborn to give in to it."

She brings her hand around again, and I am braced for another slap when instead she palms my cock and starts rubbing it.

"Looks like it's not my body begging for release," she teases. "Aww baby, is this from feeling up one breast?"

"No, it's from that smart mouth and the way you fight me. I will make you give in to me," I say, trying to keep my focus as her hand strokes up and down my cock.

"What if I want to give in just a little?" Her hands

keep moving, and I will do anything for her. Anything.

"Name it," I say.

"Let me feel your tongue," she whispers.

And in a flash, I am on my knees moving her dress aside, so very thankful for that long slit. I don't have the patience to tease her right now. I will save that for when I have her in my bed and I can take my time. With her panties yanked to the side, I put my mouth on her perfectly bare pussy. Licking and sucking at her clit then sliding my tongue inside her.

I can feel her shaking and the soft moans and whines she can't hold in. I work her up hard and fast, knowing she needs this as much as I do. I wasn't planning on fucking her on a patio with a few hundred people in the house, but if this is what my girl wants, this is what she will get. I'm tonguing her clit again, and her thighs are shaking. She is going to come soon, and I need it.

"Stop," she gasps.

I keep going.

"I want to come on your cock. Please stop."

Those are the magic words. I'm back on my feet in a second, and she pulls my face down to hers, tasting her wetness on my lips. Her hands scramble to get my cock out, then slide up and down my shaft. I don't think I have ever been this hard.

She strokes me a few more times, and I growl, "Please baby, let me fuck you. Let me make you come on my cock. I'll make it so fucking good for you."

"Nah." She pushes me back and straightens her dress. "But I do like hearing you beg for me." She winks at me before sauntering back into the house, heading for the party, leaving me with painful blue balls and my jaw on the ground.

CHAPTER
TWENTY

Paris

I had hoped to see more of Athena at the party last night, but Eros was hovering around her all night. Then they both disappeared for a while. I ended up getting way too drunk and sleeping in one of the spare rooms here, then waking with the worst hangover ever. Mrs. Medea, being the godsend that she is, gave me all the hangover cures, which is where I am now. Sitting on the patio with sunglasses shading my eyes, soaking up the sunlight with a vitamin water, a cup of Irish coffee for the hair of the dog that bit me, and the biggest, greasiest, most amazing-looking bacon-and-egg sandwich I have ever seen.

God, it is nice to have a staff who looks after you.

Athena comes and sits next to me with her coffee.

"You're here early." She takes a sip of her coffee.

"Never left." I lean back in my chair, enjoying the warmth, but not the brightness of the sun.

"Get lucky?" she asks. I think that was meant to sound teasing, but it comes out a little harsh, and I have to bite back a smile. I think she's jealous.

"Nope, I was kind of hoping to, but the only woman I wanted seemed to disappear. So I somehow got into a drinking competition with a few politicians. Never do that, by the way, those men can hold their liquor."

"Aww, are you hung over?" There's that teasing tone, as she puts her hand on the side of my face, and I lean into her touch.

"Spend the day with me."

"I have things to do." She takes back her hand.

"No, you don't. The party for this month is done, the planner is taking the day off, and you deserve one, too."

She chews her bottom lip for a moment, considering it.

"Didn't your mom's will say she wanted you to discover who you are? What better way to do that than spend the day with the man you're totally smitten with?"

Her eyes light up as the beautiful laughter rings out. "Smitten? Who says smitten?"

"Well, I thought 'totally hot for' was a little presumptuous."

We both laugh, and I pull her out of her chair into

my lap and kiss her cheek. “Spend the day with me?” I ask.

“Sure.” She smiles. “What did you want to do?”

“For now, let’s just sit here and enjoy our coffee and each other.” I pull her closer to me, settling in so I have one arm draped around her, the other holding my coffee cup, with my chin resting on her shoulder.

“I like this.” She relaxes into my hold. “Tell me something.”

“Like what?”

“Something about you. I know how the others found my mom, or how she found them. But how did you get mixed up in all of this? You didn’t grow up on the streets.”

“When I was young, my father left, and it broke my mother. She has always been... eccentric. But when he left, it developed into mental instability then illness. Yeah, I had money, but having all those thrown at me so young made me a little bit bitter. Actually, a lot bitter. When Perseus, Heph, and Eros started at my school, I think they saw my pain and anger and saw how badly I needed a family that could support me. They pulled me in.”

“So you were a lost boy, too, just in a different way.”

The way she looks at me makes me feel like she can see right through me. I set my coffee on the table, then pull her face down to mine, kissing her gently. Her lips are so soft, I deepen the kiss, half expecting her to back off. It’s one thing kissing at the coffee shop or in my car where we really aren't alone, but here we aren't being watched.

She pulls back, but only to put her coffee on the table, then she turns to face me more directly, running her fingers through my hair. I let out a groan. Something so simple, but feels so good, sending shivers down my spine. Tightening her fingers in my hair, she pulls me toward her and kisses me. Her kiss is demanding, almost feverish, and I happily let her take the lead. When she turns to straddle me, her thighs on either side of mine, her skirt rises. I grab her tight ass and pull her down on my cock tenting my pants. She grinds against me, the only thing better than her heat and my cock is her thin panties and my jeans.

I can feel the warmth from her pussy through my jeans, and I need her, but I don't want to push her too hard, too fast. I move my hands under her skirt but just resting on her thighs, my thumbs stroking the delicate flesh on her inner thighs getting closer to her core with each pass.

She breaks the kiss and throws her head back with a moan as she grinds against me. As if by invitation, I kiss her cleavage.

Athena laces her fingers in my hair again, this time gripping tight and pulling my mouth away from her chest long enough for her to pull down her top a little more and stretch the neck over one of her breasts, pulling the bra aside to expose that perfect pink nipple to the air. The second she loosens her grip on my hair, my mouth is around that pale pink nipple, licking and sucking and even biting a little, loving the way it puckers between my lips as she gasps, and her hips start grinding into me harder.

I take back a little of the control and pull her shirt down more, needing to get my mouth on her other tit while I squeeze and pinch the first.

"Fuck, Paris," she gasps, and I love the sound of my name on her lips.

With one hand massaging her breast, I slide the other down her back, then between us, cupping her pussy. She has soaked through her panties, and I need to feel this hot, dripping cunt on me.

Staying on top of her underwear, for now, I palm her pussy, pressing hard, making her clit rub into the base of my palm with every single grind of her hips. Breath is coming out in pants and the skin on the tops of her breasts flush this beautiful rosy color.

"Oh god." The words come out in a broken cry from her lips.

"Yes, angel, show me how beautiful you are going to look when you come for me. Let me make you come on my hand and then in my bed on my cock. Come for me, beautiful."

She looks down at me, her eyes are a little glassy, her cheeks bright pink, and her lips kiss swollen and parted. I lean up and claim her lips with my own. The movement in her hips is becoming erratic.

"Let me show you how good it can be," I whisper

in her ear. "Let me show you how a lover can make his woman feel."

The word "yes" is on her lips. I can see the second she knows she is ready to give me everything when a yell comes from across the patio startling us both. I press Athena's head to my neck, hiding her exposed breasts with my body giving her a little privacy as she gathers herself and rights her shirt.

"What the fuck, Heph," I yell, pissed. I was so close, so close to claiming this woman as my own.

"Yeah, what the fuck, Paris?" Heph yells. "This is a public space. Why are you with *her*?"

"You sound a little jealous, man. Don't get all mad at me because you were too fucking stubborn to realize how amazing she is."

"Go home, Paris. You're clearly still drunk."

Athena stands, her shirt is now righted and other than her hair being a bit messed, and her lips swollen, you would have no idea what we were just doing. I, on the other hand, am a mess. My cock is still rock hard, pressing painfully against my jeans. And there is a wet spot from the pre cum soaking through the denim and another from her.

I keep arguing with Heph, trying to get him to fuck off, but it's no use. The moment is gone and while he and I are bickering back and forth, Athena leaves.

FUCK.

CHAPTER
TWENTY-ONE

Heph

What the fuck is happening with my family?

Does no one else remember the fucking plan?

We are supposed to be taking down Athena and securing Perseus's legacy. Eros follows her around like a lost puppy, and I caught Paris seconds away from fucking her on the patio. Hell, even Perseus has his dick buried in her and isn't going as hard as he should be with these plans.

I'm sitting in the library flipping through my phone when Athena comes downstairs. Doing my fucking job, I get up and follow her. I just can't bring myself to be an ass right now. I wouldn't say I'm losing my touch, but something has changed, and I need to check with Perseus before I push Athena further. After the past few months, I'm sure my presence is enough to rile her.

Truth be told, I have grown a soft spot for Athena, too. I really like her. She is quick-witted and sticks to her guns. She also doesn't fold under pressure, which is something to be admired. This morning, when I caught her with Paris, I may have watched a little longer than I should have before making myself known. She looked amazing with her shirt pulled down, her body flushed as she was about to come for Paris. Part of me wonders if I interrupted because he was being disloyal or because I wanted to be the one she was dry humping.

"Here to slut shame me?" she asks.

"Nah, not my style. If I was going to shame you, it would be for being a gold-digging thief, not because you're a woman who likes to feel good. Double standards aren't my thing."

She seems surprised. She looks like she is going to say something, then thinks better of it before deciding on a simple, "Thank you."

"Don't go all soft on me. You may have seduced the others, but I'm loyal to my family and not so easily swayed."

"I can respect that, though part of me wonders," she says, leaning against a counter, "if Perseus and I hadn't started with a vendetta, if you and I would be friends."

"The world will never know." I roll my eyes at her blatant attempt to turn me from Perseus. "But I'm going to say no. I don't like how you have changed my friends."

"I haven't changed any of them. Maybe you're just seeing sides to them you normally don't." She heads back upstairs, now with an apple and water bottle.

I think about what she said. She didn't change them, that I am seeing different sides, and the more I think about it, the less I believe her. Eros is always a flirt and a player, flitting from woman to woman after having them. Athena hasn't fucked Eros. He is working to get in her panties, so maybe... but Paris and Perseus?

No. Paris is always the calm one, even-tempered and refined. He is the gentleman out of all of us. His anger this morning, the way he yelled at me and the rage in his eyes. That isn't the Paris I know. Something is changing.

Perseus is nothing like the real him. He's avoiding Athena. He never avoids problems. He never ran from something, even when we were skinny homeless kids. He faced everything head on even when he should have run.

Right now, Perseus is in the basement gym working out in a place he knows he won't run into Athena.

I need to talk to him, find out if our plans are changing.

Downstairs in the basement, Perseus is on the bench press, and I try not to focus on the way his muscles flex under the strain of his workout that looks like it's been going on for a while.

"We need to talk," I say.

He pulls the earbuds from his ears and sits up while I toss him a bottle of water.

"Thanks, what's up?"

"Have our plans changed?" Leaning against the wall, I cross my arms over my chest.

"What are you talking about?"

"With Athena. Have you changed your mind about what we are going to do?"

"Absolutely not. I will get what is mine." He throws his towel off to the side. "Why? Are you saying you don't want to go against her now?"

"No, I am loyal to you, but you don't seem to be focused on taking her down anymore. Eros is being led by his dick, and I just caught Paris sucking her tits while she dry humped him on the fucking patio."

Perseus's face twists into rage. I stop for a moment and wonder if he is mad that the others like her, or mad Paris was touching what he covets. Dismissing that thought, I go back to riling him up.

"How much longer are we going to let her live in your house, our home? How much longer is she going to get to pretend this money is hers?"

"Not long." He jumps up and starts pacing. "Are Paris and Eros still on board?"

"I don't know," I answer honestly. "I hope so, but..."

He nods. “We will keep an eye on them. In the meantime, are we still on track?”

“My part is good to go. Yours?”

“Yeah. When Eros or Paris are with her, I want one of us close by at all times,” he says. “No more make-out sessions in coffee houses, and I want a copy of her texts with Eros. I want to make sure they are only sexting, and she isn’t seducing them to her side. We need this plan to go off without a hitch. So if they have jumped teams, we need to know.” He is pacing through the gym at this point, with his fingers running through his hair. Not for the first time, I wonder what his hair would feel like against my skin.

“I’m tired of hiding in my own home. We need that bitch out now!” Perseus roars. There he is. That is the man I would follow anywhere.

CHAPTER TWENTY-TWO

Athena

"I'm tired of hiding in my own home. We need that bitch out now!" Perseus's words keep ringing in my ears.

I went down to ask Perseus and Heph if they wanted to order Indian food, my treat. I was planning on making a peace offering after I heard from the mechanic saying he couldn't find any evidence of foul play, but then I heard Perseus and Heph talking, and I slipped away. I don't know what they are planning, and I don't really want to know.

Which is crazy. The old me—the woman who entered this house a couple of months ago—would be taking notes and preparing to go to battle. But now... I don't know what's happening.

I'm tired.

Maybe I'm growing soft.

Maybe I've lost my edge.

Maybe I'm simply done fighting.

Is all of this worth it? I have grown accustomed to this house, but it's not my penthouse apartment big enough for just me. The money really isn't that important.

The only thing I wanted when this all started was to get to know the woman my mother was. I think that through her diary I got that. I learned so much about the woman she was and the sacrifices she made. I learned how she loved me unconditionally and did what she felt would give me the best life.

Maybe I should just leave. I can pack up all her diaries, take a few dresses from her closet and the jewelry as my inheritance, and just move back home. It will void out the will. Perseus will get everything, and I won't have to wonder if Eros and Paris want me or want to destroy me. I'll find out one way or the other within days.

Giving up isn't in my nature, but neither is pouring time and effort into losing projects.

I'm considering what else I want to take with me when my phone rings. It's the P.I.

"This is Athena," I answer the phone.

"Ms. Godwin, I have been digging more into your mother's death as you asked, and I have something. I found these letters in a safety deposit box. I think your mother was killed, but not by your father. I'm not sure which, but I believe one of the men you're living with may have been the perpetrator. I need to do more digging, but I had to let you know. You may not be safe there. You may want to stay somewhere more secure."

I take a moment to digest his bomb of intel. One of the boys, my mother's boys, could be the snake that killed her.

"What makes you think that?" I ask. "From what I've seen, these men loved her."

"The letters I found are threatening her, demanding money. Few people knew she was alive, and your father paid her a handsome monthly stipend. Why would he need money? He would just stop the payments."

"I want to see pictures of the letters."

"I already sent them to you," he says, "but you'll see that whoever sent them, knew her closely. And since she lived the second part of her life as a hermit with those men in the house as her only associates. She remained hidden, as per your father's wishes."

I release a heavy sigh. "Okay, keep me posted on what else you find."

"Ms. Godwin... I really think you should consider leaving the mansion."

"I'm not going anywhere." I hang up the phone and look at the pictures the P.I. sent me.

They're everything he said... and more.

Threats on her life. Fucked up threats about exposing her as a fraud.

Who the fuck would threaten her? Is it truly possible that one of *her boys* is responsible?

Perseus. Eros. Paris. Heph.

I didn't have any of them pegged as a killer. Yet...

It can't be all of them. No way could it have been a group effort. That much I *know*. But then at the same time, do I know anything anymore? Have I allowed each of those men to get in my head? Was that their plan all along?

Have I misjudged each one of them?

My father always taught me to listen to my intuition. It's the most powerful tool I have. Instinct is a tool that the mighty can use to get ahead in business and in life. My instinct has always been good. Laser sharp, in fact. I just need to listen to it.

I close my eyes and focus. Who can I trust? Who out of those boys do I know without a doubt had nothing to do with Freya's death?

One name is clear...

Eros.

He didn't say he was on my side, or that I can trust him, but he has proven he is at least not a complete ass. And my instinct knows that he's not a killer.

I send him a text.

Me: I need you.

Eros: for...

Me: please.

Not even a full minute passes before a knock

sounds at my door. I open it to him standing in the doorway, his arms braced on the doorway.

"You called, baby girl?"

I step back, letting him into the room.

"So, is this a social visit or a booty call? Planning on leaving me with the world's worst blue balls again? Or is it my turn to leave you wanting again?" I know his words are meant as a tease, but I can't help the tears that spring to my eyes.

He turns to see the tracks rolling down my cheeks, and his entire demeanor changes. He isn't the cocky asshole anymore. His natural arrogance turns to concern as he pulls me into his arms and holds me.

"What happened, sweetheart?"

I can't talk about it. Not yet. I need to feel something other than overwhelming grief, so I lean up and place a questioning kiss on his lips. Eros returns this kiss. I pull him over to the bed and yank him down on top of me.

"Are you sure?" he asks.

I don't want to answer that. I don't want to make a decision about anything right now.

"Make me feel good," I say before kissing him again.

He takes over the kiss, running his hands down my side while lying over me.

"How good, sweetheart?"

"Eros, please," I whine.

He stops for a moment, and stares into my eyes,

clearly looking for the game or the angle I have. But instead, I think he can see how I am begging to turn my brain off and feel.

Eros begins to run his hands down my body, tracing every inch of skin with his fingertips. I shiver with anticipation, feeling my body come alive under his touch. He sips his hands beneath my shirt, his palms warm against my skin. His touch is fire, igniting a passion within.

He kisses me deeply, exploring my mouth with his tongue, and I moan softly. I wrap my arms around him, pulling him close, needing to feel his body against mine.

He breaks the connection and starts kissing his way down my neck, his lips leaving a trail of fire in their wake. I arch my back, offering him more access, and he takes advantage, nipping and sucking at my skin.

He slips his hand beneath my waistband, and I gasp as his fingers brush against my most sensitive spot. My body reacts instinctively, and I buck my hips against him.

He chuckles softly, knowing exactly what he's doing to me. He continues to tease me, his fingers tracing maddening circles around my clit. I'm so close to the edge.

He stops suddenly, and I groan in frustration.

"Not yet, baby girl" he says, a wicked grin on his face. "I want to make you feel so good that you forget everything else."

I nod, unable to speak, and he resumes his ministrations. He brings me to the brink of orgasm again and again, each time pulling back just before I can tip over the edge.

Eros smiles and begins to slowly undress me. Every touch of his fingers sends shivers down my spine, erasing all thoughts of the pain I was feeling moments before. He continues to kiss me, his tongue exploring every inch of my mouth as he skillfully removes my clothes. I become more and more aroused with every passing second, the heat between my legs almost unbearable.

Eros slides off my panties and moves his mouth to my core, expertly flicking his tongue over my clit. I grip the sheets, lost in the pleasure he's giving me.

But I want more. So much more.

As he reaches for the hem of his own shirt, I stop him.

"Let me," I say, sitting up and pushing him onto his back.

I take my time, savoring every moment as I undress him, tracing every line of his defined muscles with my fingers. Once he's naked, I straddle him, feeling his hard length pressing against me.

I nudge myself against him, teasing him, allowing him to feel my wetness against the tip of his cock. His eyes darken, and I have my answer to the question I'm about to ask.

"You want this, don't you?" I whisper as I let

myself sink onto him. I feel myself stretch to accommodate him, and I groan softly.

"Oh yeah," he answers, grabbing my hips and pulling me down all the way.

I begin to rock my hips, taking him in and out, in a slow and steady rhythm. He lets me set the pace, and I'm grateful for that. I want to feel every inch of him, to feel him fill me completely.

The piercing on his cock is everything I've heard rumors it can be.

My body is overwhelmed with sensation as I ride him, the vibrations of the piercing sending tingles throughout my body.

He leans forward to suck on my nipples, pinching them gently with his fingers, playing with them while I bob.

I lean back, resting on my hands, and watch Eros's face as he watches me.

His eyes are locked on mine, and I can see the same pleasure that I'm feeling reflected back at me. Heat suffuses my body, and I'm approaching the edge once more.

Eros's hips thrust forward in time with my movements. I look down to see his hand gripping my hip, nails digging into my skin.

"Do it, baby girl," he says. "Give it to me." His cock is twitching as he approaches his own orgasm, but he's holding on. It's clear he wants me to come first.

He moves his hands to my ass, and he begins to thrust in time with my movements. We move together, finding our rhythm, the pleasure building between us.

"Eros," I moan, the sensations coursing through my body too much to take.

"Come for me, baby," he demands.

He thrusts again, and so do I. I let go, my entire world narrowing to a single point of pleasure.

And then I'm falling.

I come back to myself slowly, Eros's strong arms holding me as I lie across his chest.

My entire body is covered in goose bumps, and my breathing is ragged. He kisses my forehead gently, running his fingers through my hair.

"Are you okay?" he asks.

"That," I say, "was...incredible."

"Good," he replies, "because I'm just getting started."

He sits up, pulling me with him. I straddle his lap, feeling his softening cock still inside me.

"Ride me, baby," Eros says, and I do.

I begin to move my hips, grinding against him, every nerve in my body still alive with pleasure. He hardens inside of me, and I ride him harder, giving him everything I have.

Hands on my ass, he helps me find the perfect angle, then begins to thrust in time with my movements.

He's hitting the spot inside me that makes the

pleasurable vibrations return, and I gasp as the sensation washes over me.

"That's it," Eros says, his voice hoarse with desire. "Let go, baby girl. Just like that."

I move harder, grinding against him, reveling in the way he grips my body, in the sounds he's making.

"You feel so good," he groans. "So fucking good."

He thrusts inside me, and I rock my hips down to meet him, needing every inch of him. "Fuck, that's it," he whispers, his hands on my hips, guiding me.

"Harder, Eros, please," I plead. He gives me what I want, and we fuck each other hard and fast, the intensity of what we feel exuding between us.

The harder I grip him, the harder he thrusts back. He begins to quiver, and I know he's getting close.

"Come for me again, baby girl." His voice is low and seductive. "I want to feel you coat my dick with your cream." His words are my undoing, and my body tighten as I come once more. He groans as he releases, his body shuddering against me.

He stays inside me as I collapse against his chest, both of us breathing hard. We lie there, wrapped in each other's arms, not talking, just savoring the moment.

His lips are at my neck, and I shiver. "Perfect. Just perfect."

He wraps the blankets around us, his arms tight around me. I feel safe and protected, like nothing could ever hurt me again.

"Are you ready to tell me what's wrong, Athena?"

I shake my head, but he grabs my chin and looks into my eyes.

"Baby, what just happened between you and me changes everything. You are mine now. Something primal, animalistic and raw surged through me. I have one goal from now on. You. I will keep you safe. I will take care of you. But to do that, I need to know who I need to make suffer."

In a moment of weakness I crack, the tears flow. I tell him how I don't give a fuck about the money anymore. I wasn't even planning on keeping it. I had planned to use it to honor my mother's memory. After reading her diary, I thought it was loneliness and neglect that killed her, but now there is evidence saying she could have been killed. I'm pacing the room like a caged tiger, blurting out everything, rarely taking the time to take a breath.

"Your father?" Eros asks, his voice shaking. I look into his eyes, and I can see his heart is breaking, too. He loved my mother.

"No, my P.I. thinks it was one of you."

"He's wrong." Eros pulls my head back down to his chest, sweeps me off my feet, and sits on the bed with me curled on his chest. "We would never hurt her."

"She got these letters threatening her, demanding money," I explain. "My father doesn't need money from her. He was the only one from her past that knew she was still alive."

"You don't know that. Maybe he made a bad

investment, or there was a revenge plot for everything the Godwin family has done to their enemies," he tries to explain.

I shake my head. "No. Absolutely no one knew she was alive. Everyone, including her children, thought she jumped off a cliff and died. Yes, many questioned if she really jumped or if, in fact, she was pushed off the cliff. But regardless, she was dead," I explained.

"So, it wasn't your father." He sighs. "But that doesn't mean—"

"Doesn't it?" I grab my phone and show him the picture the P.I. sent me of one of the letters. I can see the moment Eros realizes it's true.

"Fuck." His eyes are wide, and his face grows pale. "It can't be."

"It is. Who did this?"

He just shakes his head.

"Eros, who took my mother from us?"

"I don't know," he says, barely above a whisper. "But we will find out."

"How?" I ask.

"When do invites for the next event go out?" he asks.

"Tomorrow. Why?"

His face breaks into a smile that would be scary if it wasn't so fucking hot. "Don't send them. Only send them to Freya's boys. We are going to catch ourselves a rat."

CHAPTER TWENTY-THREE

Eros

Athena is asleep, still naked and cuddled in my arms, and I can't bring myself to move and risk waking her. Normally, I would be out the door with my pants still at my ankles minutes after my partner has come, but it's different with Athena. It's more than just sex. It's having her trust me enough to turn to me when her heart is broken and then give me something she has fiercely guarded her entire life. Athena giving me her body means something. Though I didn't take her virginity, I know she has given me her heart and soul. She *gave* it to me.

Who knows? Maybe I've earned it.

Which isn't something I ever cared to do before with another woman.

I am falling for Athena Godwin, and there is

nothing I won't do to keep her safe or make her happy. Nothing. I won't even stay loyal to my found brothers if it means hurting Athena.

Plus, there is a harsh truth that must be faced now. My gut tells me it's legit. One of them killed Freya. That alone is a betrayal of everything we are. She raised each of us out of the dirt and gave us everything we could need that we couldn't get on our own. Those of us who grew up on the street, yeah, she gave us food and clothing and the best education money could buy, but it was more than that. She made sure we all had a home and a family who loved and supported us. I don't understand how one of us could turn against that and destroy someone so good. And for something as dirty and common as money.

There is nothing she wouldn't have given us if we asked for it. Why would any of us need to steal from her?

I've been thinking. Stewing.

And as much as I don't want to admit it, I know which of us is the rat. Without a shadow of a doubt, I know.

But the others will never believe it. I have to show them. Soon. If he killed Freya to get his hands on her money, there is no telling what he is willing to do to Athena.

Athena is mine.

He will never lay a fucking finger on her.

If he touches her, I will kill him, slowly, painfully.

I will show him what is worth killing for, and it isn't fucking money.

There was already an attempt on Athena's life. I thought it could have been a freak accident at the time, but not now. It was a deliberate move to do to Athena that which was done to her mother. But it won't happen again. Not on my watch.

I don't leave her fucking side until the party. Heph keeps trying to cock block me, or get me away from her, but it isn't fucking happening, not until she is safe. She doesn't leave this house without me. She doesn't hang out in the common rooms without me. If Heph wants to sit across from us on the couch, fucking fine, but I am not leaving her unprotected.

I sneak in her room every night and sometimes we fuck like rabbits, and I show her all the ways I can take her apart and put her back together. And my little vixen likes to show me what the books on her e-reader have taught her. Other nights, we make love. It is slow and passionate and a new experience for me, but one I don't think I could have with any other woman than her. Some nights we just cuddle. I hold her and thank whatever god brought this woman into my life.

Time moves deliciously slow while we wait for the next event, but it also moves too fast. I don't know what the future brings, and for that, I'm fucking terrified.

One thing is for sure. Working with Athena on the plan for the party makes me respect her even more. This girl is devious. She's highly intelligent. And I love how ruthless she can be when she's backed into a corner. Though I've felt extremely protective of this woman, I have also seen that her bite could take down a room full of men without needing my assistance in the slightest. Not that I'm going to allow the opportunity to arise for her to have to prove she can decimate any opponent, simply knowing she could is a damn turn on.

Finally, it's time for the party, and we dismiss all the staff for the night, saying the caterer will bring their own people, so they get the night off, paid, of course. Part of me wants to warn the others who I know are innocent, but I don't. I won't risk this blowing up and Athena getting hurt. I can't.

"Are you ready?" I ask her, though I already know she is.

She smiles, stands up on her toes to kiss me, and flicks her tongue on my lip piercing. "We got this."

We wait for everyone in the library, dressed like the party is still happening. Heph is the first to arrive. He keeps staring at my arm on the small of Athena's back. I have no intention of moving it. Let him look. Everything will be out in the open soon enough, anyway.

We serve dinner before the 'party' that will never happen.

Athena tells them that she wanted dinner just the five of us, and surprisingly is able to chit chat as if nothing is out of the ordinary. Her acting skills are quite impressive. The woman truly can go in for the kill with a smile on her face. I'm glad she's on my side.

The drugs work quickly, and within moments they take effect. Paris is out first, his head falling back in his chair. Heph, a moment after landing in his soup. Perseus tries to fight the drugs, but he is under shortly after the others.

"Ready?" I ask Athena, and she pulls the zip ties out of her back pocket with a bright crazy smile like a little psychopath.

God, I really am falling in love with this girl.

They wake within the hour, all tied to chairs in the library.

"What the fuck?" Heph slurs. It makes sense he wakes first; he is the biggest, and we gave them all the same dose. Perseus after that. He and Paris both wake swearing and making threats.

I stand off to the side, out of sight. This is Athena's show. I will step in when I am needed. If I am needed.

"Hello, gentlemen. I have a few questions, then I will be happy to let you go." She speaks in a calm, almost professional tone. "Which one of you killed my mother?"

"Let us go, you stupid bitch," Perseus yells.

My fists tighten. I don't like him calling her names, but I stay where I am.

"Sure, I'll cut you free just as soon as you answer

my question. Which one of you switched my mother's medication to poison?"

"Nobody." Heph grunts, trying to pull the zip ties apart. It will never happen. There are eight ties on his arms alone. I may have gone a tad overboard. I just didn't trust him not to hurt Athena. Not after we drugged and tied up Perseus.

"Athena, angel, let me go. You know I didn't do this," Paris says, and I can't help the scoff that comes out of my mouth.

Paris turns as much as he is able in his chair, and I step into the light.

"What the fuck!" Perseus screams.

"Traitor," Heph roars, and I pull a gun out of the back of my pants. I won't use it. Probably.

"Tell her," I demand, looking at the gun. "Tell them all what you did to the woman who we all considered a mother."

CHAPTER TWENTY-FOUR

Athena

I freeze when Eros pulls the gun from the back of his pants and takes over. He is pacing around like a caged tiger with all tight lean muscles and determination. He is in complete control of the room, and it is the sexiest thing I have ever seen.

I should be pissed that he took over. This is supposed to be my interrogation. But the way he is moving, I decide to take a seat and see what is going to happen. Sometimes it's better to watch and learn, let someone else do the dirty work and jump in when it benefits me.

"Freya pulled all of us out of our own personal hell. We were each lost, abused, and unwanted. She gave us a home, a purpose, and a mother's love. Who did this?" Eros's voice rises with each word until he is practically screaming, his face is turning red and the thick vein in his forehead is pulsing in time with the tendons in his neck.

The room is silent. Each of them giving piercing glares at Eros as he paces like a general before his soldiers.

"Tell me which of you betrayed the only person who ever gave a shit about any of us." He lowers his voice to a deadly whisper as he cocks the gun.

I glance at each of the men, trying to read their expressions, looking for some sign of weakness or doubt. Some guilt, something. All I see are matching expressions of rage. I can't tell if they are angry they were drugged and tied up, angry because they think Eros betrayed them, or angry they have been caught.

"Put the gun down and untie us now," Perseus says between gritted teeth.

"I will happily let you all go as soon as I find out which one of you betrayed us," Eros snaps back. "I will have my confession."

"Oh, I don't know how about the one who drugged us and tied us all to fucking chairs," Heph booms. His face is turning flushed from trying to pull at the zip ties. If he breaks free, I think it's fair to say that Eros is a dead man.

"I need to hear the traitor say it. Admit what you did," Eros says, staring at the floor this time. His voice is still low, quiet, and somehow far more menacing than when he is shouting.

I grew up knowing about every part of my

father's business. How it runs, who runs it, and what tools are used both above board and far below. I have spent my fair share of time around violent men, and I have watched them work, with everything from curiosity, boredom and sometimes when I was much younger, fear.

My father raised me to know what these kinds of men are capable of, not only to keep myself safe, but so I know what was needed and what is expected of the next head of the family. I refuse to shy away from the less ladylike aspects of reality because of a weaker disposition. That being said, I have never seen a man quite like Eros in charge.

The way he moves, the way he commands attention, which I am pretty sure he could do without the gun in his hand. He looks like a vengeful angel, beautiful, graceful, and deadly. Watching him work like this is making heat build in my core. When all of this is over, I swear I am bringing this man home to make him an enforcer for Medusa just so I can watch him work. I want to see him work over someone trying to steal from me. I want to watch his muscles glisten with sweat as he takes out vengeance in my name. Then I want to take him home and reward him for doing such a good job.

"Eros, look at us," Perseus tries again. "We would never hurt Freya. We loved her. She was my fucking mother! She adopted me so that one of us would legally be hers. I was the chosen one. Do you really think I'd be the one to then kill her? You got it wrong.

She died after years of drinking herself to sleep every night. She abused her body, and it caught up with her far before her time."

"Yeah, why did she choose you?" Eros asks as Heph turns to look at Perseus. "Why not the rest of us? Did you convince her of that?"

"I don't know, man. We had a connection. But if you really want to know the truth, it's because she knew without a fucking doubt I'd never turn on any of you. She knew I'd protect and watch over." His eyes dart to me and then back to Eros. "She knew I'd share."

"Well if it wasn't you, then who?"

"No one!" A vein in Perseus's forehead appears as if it's going to pop.

"Lies. Someone was threatening her. Someone in this room was stealing from her and they wanted more. So they killed her," Eros spits before taking three long steps across the marble floor to grab Perseus by the back of the neck and press their foreheads together. "See, brother, I know. I know who did it. Just like I know that if I tried to talk to you or anyone about it, you wouldn't listen to me."

"I will, I am listening now."

"You are"—Eros nods—"but only because you don't have an option. I know you won't believe one of us is capable of this. I don't want to believe it, so you have to hear it from the traitor's lips."

"You're the only traitor here," Heph says. "You did this to us and for what? Some half-rate pussy?

You betrayed us all just so you could get your dick wet."

"Okay, first of all." Eros crosses over to face Heph. "It's first-rate pussy. Best I have ever had, in fact, but this isn't about me and Athena. It's about Freya. My loyalty was to her first, all of you second." He looks back at me and shoots me a wink. Fuck me this man is so hot. "Now I will admit lately my loyalty might be a little torn between my boys and Athena, but Freya came first."

"You are a traitor," Heph growls out.

"I'm not the one who murdered Freya," Eros says calmly. "The real traitor needs to confess now."

The room is dead silent again.

Eros lets out a breath and shakes his head like he is disappointed. "Confess now, and I will make sure you never feel a thing again." Eros moves to the center of the room. He keeps his eyes trained on Perseus as he slides the safety of the gun off with an audible click.

"Last chance."

The room is silent.

"So be it."

He extends his arm straight out with the gun pointed directly in Paris's face.

CHAPTER
TWENTY-FIVE

Athena

No. Not Paris, please, not sweet, caring Paris. My hands and feet are suddenly freezing and my head gets a little dizzy. It can't be Paris. I was so sure it was Heph. I figured Heph's loyalty didn't extend to my mother, only Perseus. There was even the passing thought that Perseus was sick of my mother and wanted it all for himself. But Paris? The thought didn't even crossed my mind.

"Tell them what you did." Eros holds the gun steadily pointed between Paris's eyes.

"Really, Eros." Paris's lips are pressed in a flat line, his eyes narrowing in on Eros as he glares. "Afraid that even after sleeping with you, she might still want me more?"

"Do you really think so little of Athena that she would still want you after you killed her mother?"

"She does want me. That is why you are trying to put this shit on me."

"I don't care if she wants you, too. I don't give a fuck how many of us she wants or has regularly. I'm cool with sharing." He shrugs like it's nothing. "What I'm not cool with is the lies, deception, and the murdering of family."

"I didn't do it!" He leans forward like he is trying to snap the ties binding him to the chair. "How could I? Why would I?"

"I don't believe you." Eros draws the hammer back on the gun.

Perseus starts screaming at him to put the gun down. He is swearing and promising pain and vengeance. Paris, however, is calm. Even with the gun pressed to his forehead, he looks bored.

"You have no proof," Paris says through clenched teeth, his voice full of rage and only a hint of fear.

"I will, once I have your confession," Eros replies just as calmly.

"I can't confess to something I didn't do. What are you going to do, Eros? If I don't confess, you are going to kill me. And if I do, you're going to kill me. So, what exactly are my options here?"

"Put the gun down, Eros. This has gone far enough." Perseus turns to me. "Stop this before someone gets killed."

"That's your problem. You know that you are all

action and no fucking reason. All brawn but no brains. Hell, even Heph thinks shit through more than you do," Paris adds.

"No one says you have to die quickly." Eros lowers the gun and points it at one of Paris's kneecaps.

"Eros, baby, don't. He didn't do it," I try to reason.

"Yeah, baby, I didn't fucking do it." The venom in Paris's voice is enough to make cold shivers run down my spine. I keep forgetting who this man really is.

I keep forgetting that Paris isn't just the sweet, nerdy loving one that gives tender kisses and makes me feel cherished. He isn't just the man who buys me coffee and calls me angel. He has another side to him. One that I don't see at the coffee shop when it is just the two of us.

He's just like the rest of them. He is capable of the same things Eros is. He may look more like a cute nerd, especially compared to the avenging fallen angel that is Eros, but he is so much more under the surface. To survive what life has thrown at him, to run with these men, he has to be cold, calculating, and ruthless. None of the men in this room is innocent. All of us have become the master of our own games. The question is, whose hands are dripping with my mother's blood?

My heart breaks a little for the man I thought

Paris was, what he could have been, what I thought he was.

"Put down the fucking gun," Perseus pleads. There is more fear in Perseus's eyes than in Paris's, but I guess that makes sense. Perseus has already lost a mother; losing a brother, too, might be enough to push him over the edge.

Heph lets out a roar as he manages to get to his feet, still tied to the chair, and rushes Eros, knocking them both to the ground. The chair shatters, and the men start to grapple. Heph is still bound, which limits his movement. Heph is trying to knock the gun out of Eros's hand by using his larger mass, but Eros won't let go. He won't give it up. Paris and Perseus are both yelling. I jump back, lifting my feet to avoid the shards of broken chair that are sliding across the wood floor.

My heart is pounding as I look at the two men brutally attacking each other on the floor. Heph is so much bigger, having at least forty pounds of muscle on Eros, but both are holding their own. Heph may have the bulk and strength, but his movements are being hindered by pieces of the chair still zip-tied to his arms and thighs. Even without the extra challenge, Eros is clearly a natural born brawler. He can take a hit and keep going. Heph has Eros's arm in his hands, and he is smashing it against the wood floor, trying to loosen the grip Eros has on the weapon.

This is the stupidest and most dangerous thing I

have ever seen. These assholes are going to shoot someone or each other.

Eros throws an elbow into Heph's neck and then swings the gun wide.

The gun goes off and a scream rips from my throat.

CHAPTER TWENTY-SIX

Perseus

The ringing in my ears finally subsides to my heart pounding in my head.

Heph is still on the floor with Eros fighting, but with the exception of a small cut on his brow, I don't see any blood. He hasn't been shot. He is fine.

Thank fuck. Tears of relief well in my eyes for a moment as much of the tension I didn't know I was holding slowly releases. I blink away the tears. Now is not the time. I will deal with why I was so scared at the idea that Heph was hurt later. I want to punch Eros in the fucking mouth and pull Heph into my arms just to reassure myself that he is unharmed.

I check on Athena next, she looks pale, and a bit shaken. A pit forms in my stomach until I see color starting to return to her cheeks. She isn't hit, just terrified. There is a small bullet hole in the couch next to her. She was almost shot. Another few centimeters, and she would have had a new hole in her shoulder.

Shame, all of my problems were almost solved.

The thought makes my gut twist. I didn't mean it. Why didn't I mean it? Why am I relieved she wasn't shot?

It doesn't matter. I will have to unpack those emotions later with a six-pack and a pretty little girl with golden-blonde hair sucking my cock.

That will all have to wait. The important thing right now is that Athena is fine.

Paris is still tied to his chair, looking pissed but not injured. With a deep breath, I try to calm my racing heart. Everyone is fine, no one has been shot. Yet.

"Let me go, now!" I yell again, trying to use the adrenaline still in my veins and redirect that energy into rage instead of fear. "Before you all kill each other."

No one even looks at me. I start pulling at the thick plastic holding my wrists and ankles in place, trying to break free, but it's no use.

"Athena." I call her name several times before she even looks at me. "Cut me free."

She looks like she is about to say something when Eros manages to roll Heph over, knocking into Paris and tipping his chair back. He makes a strangled yelping sound as he hits the floor, and I hear a massive crack.

"Are you okay?" I call to Paris.

"No, I am not fucking okay," he yells back in what is probably the only time I have heard Paris yell in anger or frustration. The situation definitely warrants it, but the malice in his tone still shocks the hell out of me. It's just out of character for the only even-tempered one in this group.

"Did you break something?" I ask.

"No, but I am about to."

Another loud banging starts up, and I take a moment to realize he is trying to break the chair. I start rocking in my chair, too. Maybe if I can twist enough to make it fall over on the back corner, I can get free. Another loud bang comes from Paris before a louder crack that sounds like wood being split.

These dining room chairs were clearly not meant to hold men our size, so with a little man handling and a little luck, I should be able to free myself. Then I have some serious ass to kick. Heph had better not maim Eros too badly before I get my hands on him. Tipping this chair is harder than it looks, my ankles are tied down as well as my hands. There is no ledge or step to try to push the chair off of. I can only shift my weight back and forth to tip and pray it will hit at the right angle.

That, and I really don't want to hurt myself while doing this.

I am still trying to knock my chair over when

another loud crack sounds and Paris stands up on the other side of the brawl, his face twisted in rage as he watches Eros and Heph fight. The malice in Paris's face makes me pause. It's understandable. I know why he is livid, but I have never seen Paris look like that. For half a second, it feels like I'm not looking at Paris, the man I call a brother, but a stranger.

"Paris, cut me free." He looks over at me, and the snarl on his face intensifies for a moment before it disappears completely. Still not sure what I am seeing, I ask again, "Help me."

He nods as he removes the last few pieces of wood still zip-tied to him, manages to cut the remaining zip tie off his wrists with the wood, and takes a step toward me. That's when Heph gets on top of Eros again, and the gun goes sliding across the wooden floor.

Paris and Athena see the gun at the same moment, and they both lunge for it. The two are on the ground fighting each other. For a moment, I can see how Paris is trying to restrain himself, and quickly losing patience. Athena has one hand on the gun, but so does he. She won't let go, and he rears back like he is going to backhand her, but before he gets the chance, she jerks her knee up between his legs hitting him square in the nuts. Even my balls ache just watching the hit. He falls to the side, and Athena stands with the gun in her hands. Her hair is all over the place, her eyes are wild, and her chest rising and lowering with each rapid breath.

Fuck she is beautiful, strong, powerful, and just a little crazy. My fingers flex. I want to own her. I want to pin her underneath me and tame her wild ways with my cock. Fuck her until she obeys, knowing she will never give in. Even if I am pleasuring her, even if she loves how I can make her feel. Just like in the pool, she will give in to the pleasure I can give her, and she will even thank me for it. But that is it. The second she has what she wants from me, she will go back to doing whatever she pleases. Why does that make my mouth water?

Why does the challenge of breaking Athena Godwin make my cock hard?

Athena raises the gun and fires three shots, one after the other.

CHAPTER
TWENTY-SEVEN

Athena

"Angel, give me the gun." Paris has his hand out to take the gun from me. I can't give it to him. My head is swimming, and a tightness around my ribs is making it hard to breathe. I don't know what to think or who to trust.

I fired three shots to make everyone stop. It worked. The yelling and fighting is over, and everyone is watching me, waiting to see what I'll do with the gun. I'm waiting to find out for myself. I have no idea what I'm doing. There is no plan here, and no time to make one.

"Why?" I ask Paris. Looking him in the eyes, I know he is keeping something from me.

"Hand me the gun so no one gets hurt," he says

slowly, approaching me with both hands out like he is trying to calm a wild animal.

"No. Did you kill my mother?" I ask.

He flinches back at my words. I can see the betrayal in his eyes before they harden.

"No, I didn't. I would never have hurt Freya," Paris says. "I could never hurt her. I loved her. She gave me a home when my mother wasn't there. She took care of me when my mother wasn't well enough to. Why would I hurt her?"

I don't know if I believe him. My hand is shaking so hard, I'm a little worried I will accidentally hurt someone, so I let my arm drop the gun now pointing at the ground, and the entire room seems to take a breath.

"Hand me the gun, baby girl." Eros comes to stand behind me. A small trail of blood runs from a cut on his temple, and bruises are already blooming on his jaw. I'm sure there will be plenty more soon. Even tied, Heph is a beast.

"No, I don't want..." I am not sure how I want to finish the sentence. Everything's happening so fast, and for the first time, I feel like I don't have control. I'm not the one dictating what happens here. I can only react to it, and I hate the feeling of being a pawn in someone else's game, especially when I am so uncertain who is controlling the board.

"It's okay, baby girl, I'm putting it away. No one is getting shot tonight," Eros says before taking the gun from my still-shaking fingers.

I clench my fist to stop the tremors. They make me feel weak. My father's voice is ringing in my head.

Never let them see your fear or worry. Never let them see you as anything less than steel. If they think you are weak, they will exploit it. You are a woman, so they will try to break you, never show them a single crack.

Sorry, Father.

"That's it, baby," Eros whispers, placing a kiss on my temple as my eyes slide closed and I try to compose myself. "It's over now."

A cold laugh comes from Paris that almost sounds a little manic. "You have got to be fucking kidding me. Him? You choose him to give yourself to?" He scoffs, his hands falling to his sides with his fist clenching.

"Stop talking now," Eros says in a low growl.

"No, fuck that," Paris says at Eros before looking at me. "You wait so fucking long to give yourself to someone claiming you want someone worthy of being your first, and then you give it up to the two of the biggest whores in the city. Perseus and then Eros! Why? Because Eros pretended to love you? Or did he just bat his eyes at you, and you fell over with your legs open like every other dumb slut he wants something from? Don't even get me started on why the fuck you'd allow Perseus to steal that flower of yours."

There isn't any hatred in his eyes or even backing his vile words, but they still cut deep. I feel my cheeks flush, my arms numb as my stomach tightens. He doesn't mean it. He is angry. Jealous. He can't mean the harshness.

"I thought you were so much fucking smarter than to be just another piece of ass that passes through his bed. I don't think any one of us killed your mother, but if it was anyone, it was him. He is incapable of love. He is too broken inside to love anyone, even himself." Paris motions to Eros.

He reaches up to touch my cheek, but Eros catches his hand before it even gets close to me, and Paris pulls out of his grip.

"Do not touch her."

"Please." Paris's top lip curls in disgust as he looks at Eros. "I'm the only man here worthy to touch her. At least if she had chosen me, she wouldn't have needed a penicillin bath and a therapist after."

"Paris..." I start but I don't know what to say.

Should I say: sorry, I didn't think Eros was going to accuse you of killing my mother. Sorry I thought you might have been the one to do it. Sorry I didn't fuck you?

"Don't." He saves me from having to say anything. "Perseus, I'm leaving. Get your house in order. I expect an apology once Eros gets his head out of his ass."

Paris doesn't wait for a response. He simply walks over to Heph with the sharp blade of wood in his hand, and cuts Heph free from what's left of his zip ties. He then just leaves and slams the front door behind him. Tears sting the back of my eyes, and I don't really understand why. I feel so betrayed, but by whom and for what?

Is Eros right? Did Paris kill my mother? Or have I made a mistake in trusting Eros? Has he blamed Paris to cover his crimes? Has he seduced me to get my money? It isn't out of the realm of possibility. My mind is racing, reliving everything, every conversation, every stolen moment of passion with both men, and I'm just so confused. The only thing I know for certain is I am far too sober for this.

I'm about to say we should cut Perseus loose and get a drink when Heph pulls out a blade from his back pocket. For a moment, I am worried he is going to attack Eros again. The way Eros stiffens behind me, I think he has the same thought.

Instead, Heph goes to Perseus and cuts him loose.

Perseus stands and straightens his suit before closing the distance between him and Eros in two large steps. His jaw is clenched, the cords in his neck standing out. There is no real warning before Perseus's fist slams into Eros's face hard enough that Eros falls to his knees, clenching his jaw.

CHAPTER
TWENTY-EIGHT

Eros

"That was for fucking drugging me and tying me to a goddamn chair," Perseus bellows, leaning over me, spittle flying in my face.

I may have had that one coming. The pain is instant followed by my mouth filling with the coppery taste of blood, and I spit most of it on the floor. I think he knocked a few of my back teeth loose.

Fuck, he has always had a killer right hook. Hits like a fucking sledge hammer.

"I thought Paris was the one..." I try to say, but my jaw is throbbing. There is a ringing in my ears, and a fresh wave of the metallic taste in my mouth.

"No!" he yells in my face again, his eyes so wide I can see the whites all the way around the blue. "You know one of us would never hurt Freya. And if you had evidence, you should have come to me."

"Would you have listened to me?" I shove him back far enough so I can get to my feet.

The room sways a little around me, and Athena reaches out to steady me. I look down at her and smile. Her brows furrow like she is worried, but I just pull her into my side where I can feel her warmth and know she's safe.

"Of course I would have listened," Perseus says, and I have to stop myself from rolling my eyes. Athena leads me out of the library, away from all the broken wood in the parlor, and helps me down to the couch.

"You all sit there." She points to the couch across from me. "And don't kill each other until I get back."

I don't know why, we listen to her. I tip my head to the back of the couch and allow my eyes to slide closed. I'm not falling asleep, but I have a headache starting. My ears are ringing, and the adrenaline is wearing off. I can feel every punch Heph landed. That motherfucker hits like a Mack truck. I am going to be sore as fuck in the morning, but with any luck, maybe I can get Athena to dress in one of those sexy little white costumes with the stethoscopes and plunging necklines, and she can nurse me back to health. It's going to take time, rest, aspirin, and blow jobs. Lots of blow jobs.

I don't know how long it is until I hear her return to the room with a silver tray from the bar with a bunch of different things on it, including the ice bucket, nice and full.

She comes over to me first and wipes something over the cut on my lip that stings like a bitch.

"What the fuck?" I grunt in a manly way, and not at all like a whining child.

"I am cleaning this so it doesn't get infected. Stop being a bitch, and I will give you a lollypop when I'm done."

"Really?" Maybe a nurse fantasy isn't too far off.

"No, now hold still."

I try not to make too many noises as she cleans the cut on my lip, putting some type of ointment on it as well as the gash on my temple. Guess she doesn't want my pretty face to scar. Which is fair. If she is going to use my face as a seat, she shouldn't have to deal with cracked upholstery. When she is done with that, she puts a bag of ice in one of my hands and moves it to the cut on my head, then puts a tumbler in the other with a healthy pour of something strong. It's perfect, but she really does need the stethoscope and tight plunging neckline.

Then she moves to Heph. She gives him the same treatment and the same scolding about being a bitch, hands him ice and bourbon. Perseus, she just hands the bourbon.

"What, no ice for me?" he asks.

"You weren't in a fight. You threw a single punch after a fight like a pussy. Be grateful you get the booze," she says before collapsing on the couch next to me.

It's silent for a moment while we all take a few drinks and let the alcohol dull the pain. Eventually, it's Heph that breaks the silence.

"Why do you think Paris killed Freya?"

"Freya got a letter from someone threatening her life if she didn't pay up," I answer.

"So it was probably her ex, Troy," Perseus says. "Still mad he paid out so much to her in the first place."

"But he didn't," Athena answers. "I had my P.I. do some digging. Yeah, she got a sizable payout when she left, and this house, but she also got a stipend of around $55,000 a quarter. Enough to keep this place running, but not much else. To put that into perspective, my father pulls a salary of twenty percent of the profits of Medusa Enterprises. To cut to the chase, the Godwins are wealthy as fuck. Every single one of us... especially my father. There was no reason to kill her. Troy Godwin will absolutely get his hands dirty if the situation calls for it, but killing Freya didn't get him a thing. He wouldn't have done it after all these years." She shrugs like that is just how it is. She knows her father better than I do, so I believe her.

"Okay, then one of your brothers," Perseus says.

"They think she died years ago. Just like me. When I told them she was alive until recently, they were just as surprised as I was. When Dad came clean, they didn't really care. My brothers detached a long time ago. And like my father, not one of them needs any more money."

"It had to be one of us," I say, looking at Perseus.

"No. I want you to go look. Find proof, actual proof of who did this. I'm sure the evidence will lead you outside one of us."

"I have proof." I throw my hands up in annoyance. "We are the only ones that knew she was alive. I know I didn't do it. I know you didn't do it. You loved her too much, and I know Heph didn't do it. He would never betray you."

"That doesn't prove shit," Heph yells.

"Why would Paris want her money?" Perseus asks. "He is the only one of us that grew up with money. He doesn't need it."

"I... I don't know," I admit. I haven't gotten that far in my investigation. I'm still sure it was him. I just know in my gut it was him.

"Okay stop, everyone." Athena pours us all another double. "Take a drink and calm down. Let's figure this shit out."

"Why the fuck would we need *you* to do that?" Heph holds out his glass for more. "Just because you fucked two of us does not make you part of us, and it certainly doesn't make you our boss."

Athena rolls her eyes before pouring more. "Really? Asshole? How many do I have to fuck for you to listen to me? Do I have to fuck you, too?"

I love the fire in this woman. It is sexy as fuck to

watch her stand up for herself and fight back. I can't wait to bring that fight out of her in the sack. It is going to be so amazing when I have her working through the anger of a bad day by riding my cock.

Heph grumbles something under his breath that I can't quite catch, but Athena does. She takes his glass from his hand and downs the contents before throwing it at the wall, where it shatters.

"No, fuck you, asshole. I am so sick of your shit. You want to have this fight? Let's go."

"Okay sit down, little girl, or leave," Heph snarls from his seat.

"Do not tell me what to fucking do, asshole. And don't ever think of calling me *little girl* again."

CHAPTER TWENTY-NINE

Athena

Really? With everything going on, even with me being nice and getting him ice and a drink and cleaning his cuts like a decent human being, he is still going to start shit. Well, fuck that. I am over his petty bullshit.

"Sit down and shut up. This is all your fucking fault."

"No, Heph, I am sick of your brutish temper tantrums. You seem to be under the impression that I am some evil seductress here to lure everyone into my magical vagina."

"Then why don't you fucking leave?" he yells.

"Because this is my house. You fucking leave!" I yell back like a mature adult. Ugh this man is throwing me off my game.

"Okay, can we not do this tonight?" Eros says behind me, then he stands up just long enough to pull me back to sitting next to him.

"Can we please fucking focus?" Perseus sighs, and he sounds as annoyed as I feel. He pours himself another drink and slams it back before refilling his glass.

"Fine, who else could have gotten to my mother? Who else knew about the money?"

"Only us." Perseus pushes the heels of his hands into his eyes.

"Any staff like the lawyer or anyone like that?" I ask.

"The lawyer is one Freya had forever. I think since she was with your father. The only time he was here that I can recall is after she died."

"Once before, about two years ago," Heph adds.

"That must have been when she set up the will. Did she have an accountant who had access to her accounts or bank statements?"

"Yes." Perseus lets out a sigh. "But Paris oversees all of her accounts." He takes a large swallow of his drink.

"Okay."

"That doesn't mean he—" Heph starts.

I say, "I know it doesn't mean anything. I am just trying to figure out who was in my mother's life that could have done this."

"Just us," Perseus says.

"So, Paris—" Eros says.

I turn on the couch to look directly at him. "How do we know it wasn't you? You would have had just as much opportunity as he would, and more motive."

Eros looks at me, swallows a few times, then bites his bottom lip and looks at the far wall before returning his gaze to mine. "Baby girl, after everything, do you really think so little of me?

"No, but—"

"All of what?" Heph barks out a laugh. "Let's not pretend you fucking someone is anything special. You have fucked half the women in this city. That's what you do, isn't it? If a woman has something you want, you fuck them and take it."

"Heph..." Perseus says in warning.

Eros's entire body goes still.

Heph continues, "No, that is who you are. Just a common whore that tricks women into wanting you. Promising them the world, then fucking them and getting whatever it is you were after, usually just some cash or jewelry. But maybe this time it was a little bit more. Wasn't it? Is that why you are all over Athena? Trying to get to the daughter and have her give you what her mother wouldn't."

Eros jumps off the couch and lunges at Heph, who is on his feet in an instant. "I haven't done that in years, and you fucking know it!" Eros screams in Heph's face.

The two men glare at each other, and the air is thick with tension. Any second, someone is going to throw another punch, and I am fucking over it.

"If you guys are going to keep staring into each other's eyes like that, either kiss or sit the fuck down," I say.

The tension fizzles out as Perseus huffs out a laugh, and Eros takes a half step back and turns to grin at me.

"Baby girl, you are the only person in this room I have any interest in kissing."

I roll my eyes and lean back into the couch, letting the alcohol work its magic and loosen the tension in my limbs. Heph still appears pissed, but I don't really care why anymore.

"Good, then come sit your ass back over here, and let's figure shit out."

He sits back down next to me, then pulls me into his lap and snuggles into my neck. "You don't think I—"

"No." I'm not sure why, but I don't think he had anything to do with Freya's death. And I don't think he fucked me to use me. In the beginning, that might have been his plan, but if one of us was using the other, it was me.

"I don't know if you are qualified to make that judgment," Perseus slurs. "You could have chosen any of us, and you picked Eros. Your judgment is off."

"What can I say?" I shrug. "Getting hate fucked in the pool was fun and all, but getting eaten out on the balcony, so much hotter." A part of me is saying to stop there, but I am a little too tipsy to listen to the voice of reason. "I mean, the whole broody grumpy thing might work for some people, but I just find it exhausting. Personally, I prefer when my men have a big dick, not men who are a big dick."

Eros throws his head back with laughter.

Perseus stands, stumbling only a little. "Keep talking, princess, and see what happens."

"Okay. I would bet the only women who are excited to fuck you are hookers that really need to make rent. You have the sex appeal of a dead... I don't know anything gross." My mind is a little fuzzy, so my insults aren't rolling off the tongue as fluently as I'd like.

"That's how it is?" he cocks his eyebrow at me.

"That is how it is," I confirm.

"Last chance to take it back." He kneels on the couch and leans over Eros to hover over me.

"Or what?"

"Or I will show you and everyone else in the room how full of shit you really are. Take it back."

"Nah, I said what I said."

His lips are on mine in a flash, in a devastatingly passionate kiss. I don't even have the brainpower to process what is happening before he pushes me back, so I am lying across Eros's lap with Perseus pressing to my front. His hard cock is digging into my thigh, while Eros's is hardening under my back.

I don't know if it's the way Perseus is devouring my mouth, the liquor warming my veins, the adrenaline from before or being sandwiched between two of the hottest men I have ever seen, but

I have never been more turned on in my life. My heart is racing, and I feel alive.

I need more.

I reach up with one hand and run it through Eros's hair, while I wrap my legs around Perseus, pressing my aching core against him. He rocks against me, just enough to feel the friction between our clothes. I'm so sensitive that even the little movement is enough for me to let out a whimper against his lips.

I still hate him, but I can't deny how my body responds to him.

When Perseus breaks the kiss, I tighten my legs so he can't go anywhere as I pull Eros's lips down to mine and kiss him with the same fervent intensity that Perseus kissed me.

Perseus leans up just enough to grab my throat and squeeze for a moment before trailing his hand down my body and under my shirt to pinch one of my nipples as my back arches for more.

"Do you like that, princess?" Perseus asks before pulling down my shirt to expose my breasts so he can start to lick and suck my nipples. Perseus's tongue is teasing while Eros is exploring my mouth. The combination is making my head swim, and my pussy is dripping. I am so turned on, I can feel my heartbeat in my clit, the subtle thrum making me ache with need.

I need more. Eros moves his hand to the waist of my pants and undoes the button. Breaking the kiss, he whispers against my lips. "Do you want us to make you feel good, baby girl?"

Another high-pitched whine escapes my lips as my hips buck into his touch.

"God, you are so fucking perfect," Perseus says before biting my nipple just hard enough it sends a sharp pain down my spine mixing with the pleasure, making it far more intense.

"I need more," I pant.

Eros slips his hand into my underwear, and his fingers immediately find my clit. He draws teasing little circles over it while Perseus focuses on my tits, licking one and pinching the other.

I look across the room, and Heph is still there, sitting on the couch, watching with a heated gaze. His jaw is clenched, and he looks mad, but the outline of his very large, very hard cock on his thigh pulls my attention.

Perseus is controlling.

Eros is demanding.

But I need to know what Heph is like.

Is his touch as hard and forceful as the others? Would he demand my pleasure like the others, or would he coax it from my body? I need to know.

I look at his face, and I reach out to him. "Join us."

CHAPTER THIRTY

Heph

Athena is waving me over, begging for me to join them.

I want to.

I want to feel her soft skin, to have her shudder under my touch like she does the others. My cock aches to have her lips around it, sucking while the others pet and pleasure her. I want to feel the vibrations from her moans traveling up my dick to my balls as I come inside that pretty little mouth.

But I don't move.

My stomach is in knots and my skin feels too tight, too hot. I don't know what this feeling is. It could be rage. These two just drugged us. They tied us up and pulled a gun on Paris, accusing him of being a traitor. One fight and a bottle of booze later, and Eros is forgiven, and we have the little gold-digger wet and begging for cock. Eros has admitted his loyalty is divided, so instead of getting rid of the problem, Perseus is going to fuck her?

Why her? Jealousy is definitely coloring everything. Perseus looks so fucking hot pinning this woman under him. The way his mouth is tasting her skin... why her?

I know why Eros wants her, but why Perseus? What is it about her that makes him lose all sense? And why do I want her this much, too? With another sip of my bourbon, I sit back and just watch all my fantasies, or a version of them, play out in front of me.

Eros stays focused on Athena, moving his hands in her panties. He is going to make her come soon. She has that glassy-eyed look, and her chest is rising rapidly.

Her eyes are on me. They are hungry, begging, but she isn't the only one looking at me. Perseus is still sucking on her tits, but he is watching me as he moves his palm to cup his cock that is straining against his zipper.

My mouth is watering, and I can't remember the last time my cock was this hard. I take another sip of my drink when I see Athena whisper to the others. I can't hear what she says. The others nod and take their hands off of her, leaving her pants open and her shirt pulled down, showing off her glorious tits.

I try to swallow my nerves as she approaches me, watching as her tits bounce a little with each step.

"Do you want me?" Her voice is deeper than usual, a little husky and sexy as fuck.

My mouth is suddenly dry. I can't speak, and I don't even know what I would say if I could. So I just nod. She bends at the waist, letting her breasts hang down, and places her palms on my thighs dangerously close to my cock, and leans in to kiss me.

She tastes like sweet smokey bourbon and something else, something more than just her. I can taste Perseus on her lips, and it makes something in me snap. I grab her hips and pull her onto my lap, grinding her down hard on my cock. When she gasps, I take control of the kiss, palming the back of her head and deepening it. I don't know if I want her or to taste more of Perseus, and I don't think it matters. Her body is melting into mine.

The only thing I can hear is my pulse thundering in my ears. My cock aches to plunge into her tight little body. I want to make her come over and over. I want to make her feel so good, then keep going until her pleasure turns against her and becomes too much. Then I want to use it to punish her.

She hurt Perseus; she kissed Perseus. Part of me wants her, but the rest of me still wants to make her pay.

The couch dips on either side of me, and the other two join us. I don't open my eyes. I just continue to bruise her lips with my kiss and grind her body down on mine, taking what I want from her. When she tries to lean back, I let her, moving my hands to her waist to hold her to me. She looks a little dazed as she sits back on my lap. Her lips are bright red, her cheeks flushed, and her eyes hazy as she tries to steady herself.

"Fuck, who knew Heph was the best kisser."

"What?" Eros says in mock outrage. "You must be drunk."

I'm about to say something witty or teasing back to him when Perseus says, "No, I can totally see that."

My heart stops. Has he just said that, or have I imagined it? And the way his breath caresses over my throat as he speaks in that low, seductive way that drips with sex, sends a shiver through me.

"Nope, I demand a recount." Eros grabs Athena by the hair, pulling her back just enough to meet his lips.

The way he kisses Athena is all fiery passion and battling tongues. I can't deny seeing her lost to him while sitting on my lap is kind of hot. It's like the best point-of-view porn a man can ask for, except this is happening now. I can touch her, feel her. I can make her moan my name while Eros tries to take control of her. Right now, I can not only fuck one of the sexiest women I have ever seen, but I can put Eros's smug ass to shame. Something about that gives me an odd sense of masculine pride. I'm going to show this cocky jackass he isn't the best lover in the group. Then long after Athena is gone, I still won't let him live it down.

I trail my hands up her body. I am about to show her what my mouth can do to those tits when Perseus leans in closer to my side.

"Eros might want a recount, but I need to find out for myself." His words are barely more than a slurred whisper in my ear before Perseus does the unthinkable.

His hand is on my jaw as he pulls me in for a soft kiss. The world around me melts away, and my plans of putting Eros in his place are instantly forgotten. The only things I can feel are the jack hammering of my heart, the dull needing pulse of my cock, and Perseus's lips finally on mine.

He tastes like everything I could ever want. The kiss starts off slow, gentle and unsure, then when he opens to me, I pour everything I am into that kiss. Every time I have wanted him, every time I have jacked off thinking about him or even hooked up with another man or woman pretending it was him. Without thought or hesitation, I pour all my hopes, all my dreams, and every filthy fantasy I have ever had about this man into our kiss.

And he is responding just as passionately.

For a moment, I forget where we are, I forget who is on my lap and who they are kissing. It is just me on this couch with Perseus's lips to mine, his fingers in my hair, and his heart hammering as hard as mine.

His kiss is better than anything I have ever dared

to imagine. I am lost to him when Athena rocks against my cock again, nearly taking me over the edge and pulling me back to the present.

Fuck.

My eyes meet Perseus's first. They are wide with shock. Fuck! I took it too far, and he is drunk and doesn't know what he is doing. What the fuck is wrong with me?

It's not me, it's her. This is all her fault.

Athena is still perched on my lap, her judging eyes looking down on me with a smirk and her eyebrows raised like she knows what she just did. What she discovered.

No, fuck her. She doesn't know shit.

"Heph." Perseus says, and I can't breathe. My throat gets tight, and it feels like I am suffocating. I can't do this. Not now, not with an audience, probably not ever.

I get to my feet, effectively dropping Athena in a pile at my feet. Eros is there to help her, and Perseus is still looking at me with those confused, accusatory eyes.

My fight or flight kicks in, and for the first time in my life, I choose flight. I step over Athena. Eros is calling me an asshole, and Perseus is calling my name. But I don't walk; I run out of that room like it's on fire.

I need out.

Now.

Fuck my life. That bitch has ruined everything.

CHAPTER THIRTY-ONE

Perseus

"Well, that killed the fucking mood," Athena says as Eros helps her to her feet.

My head is spinning, my chest tightens, and I have no idea what the fuck just happened.

"You okay, sweetheart?" Eros asks Athena, pulling my attention back to them.

She has already righted her clothes, tucking away those perfectly soft breasts, and I can't help but feel a little disappointed.

"Yeah, I'm okay." She lets out a disappointed sigh. "But I'm going to bed. It's been a really long day. Let's deal with all of this"—she waves her hand around the room—"in the morning."

"Sure." Eros places a kiss on her cheek. Part of me is jealous, but mostly I am still reeling from that kiss followed by Heph's abrupt departure. "I'll be up in a bit, if that's okay."

She must have said something because the next thing I know, Eros is handing me a glass of ice water and demanding I drink.

"Is it poisoned?" I still feel bitter about earlier.

"Not this time. That whole thing may have been an ill-advised clusterfuck," he admits.

"You fucking think?"

"Well, at least I'm not the only one who fucked up tonight." Eros shrugs, then plops down on the couch next to me.

"How do you figure that?"

"Dude, you and Heph have had this 'will they, won't they' vibe since I met you."

"I don't know what you are talking about." I sit back and drink water. The cold instantly clears away some of the fuzziness from my head, but I am still so confused.

"Bull shit." Eros rolls his eyes. "I know you have hooked up with men before."

"Yeah, and..." I have never gotten any shit from any of the guys for occasionally preferring a night with a hot guy instead of a pretty girl. Why the fuck would Eros bring it up now?

"So has Heph," Eros says.

I didn't know that, but it's not like I would judge him for it. I rarely see him hook up with anyone. So I guess it isn't surprising, though I am a little hurt he didn't tell me.

"What's your point?" I'm still not quite getting what he is trying to tell me.

"Jesus, you are thick." Eros leans his head against the back of the couch and closes his eyes. "You can't possibly need this spelled out for you."

"Look, just because I'm bi, and Heph has experimented a little, doesn't mean we should be fucking each other."

Eros opens his eyes and looks at me like I am the dumbest baby in preschool. "You're right, it doesn't. However, think about it. Who has always been the most loyal to you? Not Freya, not me..."

"Heph, but—"

"I'm not done. When you hit on a woman in the bars, where is Heph?"

"Around. Usually not too far." I still don't see what his point is.

"And where is he when you hit on men?"

"He usually leaves. Why?"

"Right, and why do you think that is?"

"I don't know." I shrug.

"Oh, Jesus fuck." Eros rolls his eyes before turning to face me directly. "Do you want Heph? Do you want him as more than a friend and an honorary brother?"

I think about that for a second, sipping my water, letting the coolness soothe my sudden cottonmouth.

Do I want Heph? The answer is an ecstatic YES.

I thought about him every time I was with a man. In fact, I only ever hit on men when I see Heph hitting on a woman, and I am jealous. Every time I am with another man, it is his name I am biting back when I came. There is no one I trust more, no one I care about more, and that second earlier when I thought he may have been shot was the most terrified I had ever been.

"It's not that simple," I finally answer.

"You want him. He clearly wants you. Where is the complication?"

"Athena," I answer honestly. "Well, women in general," I backtrack with a lie.

"What do you mean?"

"I don't want to give up being with women. I don't know if I can be faithful to just one person."

"Heph has been with women," Eros points out. "You saw how he responded to Athena on his lap. You saw how he kissed her. How he touched her. He clearly likes women, too."

"So..."

"So... maybe Heph doesn't want to be monogamous. Maybe he likes the idea of having more than one partner. Athena does."

"What?"

"Athena told me a while ago she doesn't think one man can ever be enough for her. She wants several lovers."

"And you're okay with that?"

"Am I okay with a woman self-aware enough to know what she will and won't be happy with and open enough to be honest about it. Yes. It actually takes the pressure off. And if I am being honest, group sex is hot as fuck. Monogamy isn't something I need, but open communication is." Eros shrugs, like he is talking about something as unimportant as picking paint colors. "Polyamory is not the end of the world."

"What if it is?" I ask, fear creeping up my spine. "What happens if I tell him I want him, but I want Athena, too? What if I tell him I can't give up women, and it breaks him? He thinks he isn't enough, and it breaks his confidence and his heart and he leaves?"

"What happens if he tires of waiting around and he finds someone willing to love him the way he deserves, and he leaves?" Eros's words rip through me like a blade to the gut.

Would he find someone better than me? Someone who isn't a coward?

"Fuck."

"Yeah, that about sums it up." Eros claps me on the back. "But those are your choices. Either way, it's a risk."

"How do I know which risk is right?" The icy feeling is running down my spine again, and my heart is racing.

"You don't. You just figure out which outcome you are willing to live with." Eros stands and stretches.

"How the fuck do I figure that out?"

"Well, would you rather lose him because you

were brave and took a chance, or because you were a coward and never told him how you feel?"

"Either way, he leaves, and I don't think I can live with that," I admit.

"Do you want him to leave because he thinks you don't want him, and he isn't good enough?"

That question makes my breath catch and my lungs burn. Can Heph think he isn't good enough? That he wasn't wanted or desired?

Eros leaves the room, probably going after Athena, abandoning me to my thoughts.

I make myself another drink for some liquid courage. There is no telling what is going to happen tonight, but fuck it. I can't not try.

CHAPTER THIRTY-TWO

Perseus

I find Heph in the gym, working through his frustration on free weights. A normal person would just go in and talk to their best friend. Instead, I stand just out of his view and watch him. The way he works through each muscle group with heavy weights and a punishing pace. I used to think it was just a hobby, but watching now, I wonder if it's a coping mechanism. He is frustrated with me or something else. He hits the gym until he is too tired to care.

God, with the size of this man, he must be in the gym constantly. I wonder when it started. I don't really remember a time before Heph. We were in the same group home dealing with the same asshole who was charming when the social worker came by but beat me when no one else was around. He called me stupid, said I was lazy because I had trouble reading. I wasn't stupid. I'm dyslexic. He never wanted to believe me. He said I was a white-trash loser and making things up.

Heph wasn't stupid. He could read and got good grades. He didn't get beaten.

When our foster father nearly killed me, I thought we were free. I thought they would see the bruises and fractures and finally take us away, but that man fooled everyone. He told them I fell, and they believed him. None of the other kids had visible bruises, so that must have been the case. It had to be my fault. I got three nights of peace in the hospital before they sent me back.

Heph was waiting for me. He had our bags packed, and we left. Traveling from Brooklyn to Seattle on a train, we managed to stow away on eating saltine crackers and peanut butter packets we stole from the food cart. Who assumes eight-year-old boys travel alone?

He has been at my side ever since. The only night I wasn't with him was the night I met Freya.

Tears fill my eyes, and my heart aches for Freya. I miss her. I miss her more than I ever thought I could miss anyone, except Heph. If he leaves, if he rejects me, I don't think I can survive it.

I can almost hear what Freya would have told me. *You boys are a family. Shit might piss you off, or make you mad, and something may try to split you up.*

But it will never work, not for a real family. You will always come back together. The blood of the covenant is thicker than the water of the womb. You boys are a family in the only way that matters. Don't make the same mistakes I did.

Then she would have given me a big hug and tell me to get my head out of my ass, grow some balls, and go after what I want.

"Yes, ma'am," I whisper under my breath as I push open the gym door.

Heph has his earbuds in, so he doesn't hear me. I wait for him to finish his set. Safety first in the gym, always. And I am enjoying the view.

Heph puts the weight on the ground with a solid *thunk,* and I go for what I want before I lose my nerve. My heart is racing as I approach Heph. I don't give him a chance to react. I just kiss him with everything I have. I push my tongue into his mouth to taste him. The sultry musky sweetness that is uniquely him, and I am rock hard in an instant. I push him back onto the bench, and it takes me a moment to realize he isn't kissing me back. I open my eyes and he pushes me off of him.

"What the fuck are you playing at?" he yells.

"I'm not playing at anything," I say. "I want you."

"So you think that just because you kissed me earlier, and I let you, you can just come and do it whenever the fuck you want with no regard to how I feel about it?" His cheeks are turning red at the top and his golden eyes swim with a mix of fury and pain. It would have been enough to tell me I fucked up and I need to leave, but he is also suddenly pitching a tent in his gym shorts. Just seeing it makes my mouth water.

"Then tell me how you feel about it. Tell me how you feel about me."

"I'm not playing this little fucking game with you. I am not some consolation prize you can pick up because Eros got the toy you want to play with."

"Who the fuck is playing?" I try to keep my voice calm and even. "I want you."

"You want Athena." He shoots before turning his back to me and picking up his next set of weights.

"You're right. I do want Athena. She is beautiful, smart, fiery, and she keeps constantly surprising me, which would be annoying as fuck if I didn't want her so badly. But what does that have to do with this?"

"I am not a consolation prize."

"No," I counter. "You are a hypocrite."

He drops the weights on the floor and turns towards me. "That is fucking rich coming from you."

"And why is that?" I say, deciding that I want to fight with him. If we are fighting, we are talking, and I can figure out where he is coming from.

"You tell us to destroy her. You tell us you want her gone. Then you're trying to get into her pants. Which is it? Revenge fuck isn't your style. What do you want?"

"I want you," I answer simply. "And I want her."

He rolls his eyes and turns his back on me again.

"And so do you," I add. "I see the way you look at her, how you kissed her, how your hands were gripping her waist like you were ready to impale her on your cock and help her ride you. I know you want her, like I want her. Like *we* want each other."

"You don't know what you're talking about," he says, but he doesn't turn around. He can't lie to my face.

I move to stand in front of him. "If that kiss meant nothing, if Eros was wrong, if you don't steal glances at me, if you aren't jealous as fuck when I hit on men, if you don't love me, the way I love you, then tell me now, and I will walk away. We will blame it on the booze, and I will never bring it up again. But if there is a chance that you think we could be together, in a relationship, then please don't turn away from me. I love you. Give us a chance." I'm begging, and I don't give a fuck.

"What? Just me, you and Athena?" Heph shakes his head and crosses his arms against his massive chest.

"I don't think Athena is going to give up Eros any time soon. If you are okay trying something poly, I would really like that. If you want to keep it just us, we can talk about it. Just..."

"Just what?" Heph asks. "Just let you take my heart and break it, killing not only my soul but taking my home from me, my family, all for one stupid drunken kiss. You don't think of me like that."

"You think I haven't wanted you for years?" I ask. "You think this is a spur-of-the-moment thing?"

Heph just nods.

"Let me show you what I have thought about doing almost every time I have been alone in the shower since we were sixteen." I kiss him again, and this time he kisses back. He brings his hands to my back, fisting my shirt as he pulls me closer and opens his lips to mine.

I want to get lost in this kiss, but when his body presses into me and I feel his hard cock against my thigh, my plans change. With my hands on his shoulders, I guide him to sitting on the weight bench. I drop to my knees in front of him and start kissing his neck, loving the slightly salty taste of his skin. I let my hands roam his thick abs and down to the cock that is pressed against the silky material of his gym shorts. It is begging for my undivided attention, with pre-cum already soaking the thin material.

I run my mouth over his cock, breathing hot damn air through the shorts while I untie the drawstring at his waist.

Finally, I get the knot free and pull the elastic waist down just enough to rescue his cock from the constraints. Fuck, I knew he was big, but Jesus I had no idea he was so thick. I am a little nervous for my gag reflex, but fuck it. I am already here, and I am going to swallow this cock like a man.

I start with just the head, swirling my tongue

around it before sucking it between my lips. He tastes perfect, a little salty and just so damn good. I let out a small groan of satisfaction before drawing more of his cock into my mouth and sucking.

"Oh god yes." The words escape Heph's mouth like a prayer, and if that doesn't do amazing things to my ego.

I take more of him, sliding to the back of my throat and holding him there, trying not to gag myself before slowly sliding back to the tip and swirling my tongue around it.

"Don't fucking tease me," Heph growls out, the sound going straight to my own balls.

I reach under me and grip my cock through my pants, trying to get much-needed friction. I suck harder and start moving faster up and down his shaft, trying to take as much as I can. Heph's hips thrust up with each pass I make, and soon his hands are in my hair, holding me still while he can fuck my mouth.

I love it so much, my cock leaks pre-cum into my pants. The only thing that could have made this moment better was if Athena was licking the cum from my cock while Heph fucked my throat. Just the mental picture of that makes my cock twitch so a fresh wave of pre-cum gets absorbed into my jeans.

"Fuck-fuck-fuck." Heph pulls me off his cock, and I immediately try to get it back in my mouth until he says, "Stop."

"What, what's wrong? What did I do? Why did you stop me?"

"Nothing, I was just about to come," he pants.

"And..."

"And what? I was about to come." He grips the base of his cock as he speaks, trying to stave off the orgasm I was working so hard for.

"I get that. I don't get why you stopped me."

"Because, if you meant all that, I don't want our first time to be in the gym room and rushed. I want a bed, your bed. And I want to make you feel good before you take every single drop of my cum that I give you."

I smile so hard my cheeks hurt. "Then why the fuck are we still in this gym?"

He laughs as he helps me to my feet, then kisses me again. "Your bed or mine?"

"Whichever one is closer," I answer before kissing his neck.

He makes a sound low in his throat like he is purring, and fuck, I want him to make that sound again.

"My room." I grab his hand.

We don't even pretend we aren't running for my bedroom. When we get there, the air grows thick with tension. This is suddenly very real, and I want it. I just... I don't know what he wants, how he wants it.

"Have you ever..." I start.

"Fucked a man?" he finishes for me. "Yes. Been

fucked by a man? No." Then he looks over and meets my eyes. "But I want to..."

I nod and pull him towards me for another kiss while I push his shorts to the ground then run my hands under his shirt before pushing it off him. "Lie back on the bed. I want to keep sucking your cock while I get you ready for me."

He bites his bottom lip, color appearing on the tops of his cheeks as he sits on the bed, then scoots back so he can lie back against the headboard. I go over to my side table and grab some lube. It is a thick, silky viscous liquid that will feel so good when I slide into him. I hold out a condom and raise my eyebrow, asking if he wants me to use it.

"All of us just went and got our regular testing."

I nod, thanking god—and Eros since he insisted we all go—that we all decided to be more diligent about testing now that Athena was in the house, and our sexual chemistry told me that it was likely we'd fuck again. Never in a million years would I have thought the testing could benefit me now.

"I haven't been with anyone since," I say.

"I trust you, and I want to feel you," he says.

Fuck, that is the right answer.

Ignoring my aching cock, I move to position myself between his thighs, and this time I start a little slower. I look up at him, staring into those golden eyes while I drag my tongue over his balls and up his shaft.

His eyes are heavy lidded, but he doesn't close

them. He watches me with his lips parted, and he is so fucking hot like that. I lick again while I pour lube into my fingers, letting it warm on my skin for a moment. I start to gently suck on one of his balls while I slowly circle his asshole with my slippery fingers. His entire body jolts the first time I touch him, and I let out a little chuckle.

"I need you to relax for me, baby. I'll never fit it all in if you are so tense."

I'm teasing him, and he knows it. He just flips me the bird before redirecting my mouth where he wants it. So needy. I massage his asshole, coaxing it to relax and open for me while I suck on the head of his cock. He starts to melt into the bed and his body relaxes as I push just one finger inside him. I am slow, careful, and using a ton of lube to make sure I don't hurt him. Eventually, I work in a second finger while I am back to tonguing his balls, and he is a leaking moaning mess. I love licking up the pre-cum he gives me. I love that I can make him feel this good, and I can't wait to make it better.

When I have two fingers almost all the way, I spread my fingers as I work them in and out. He is practically shaking for me and it is beautiful. His skin is glowing with a thin sheen of sweat and his teeth keep catching on his bottom lip. This is the most beautiful man I have ever seen. And a small part of me can't wait to do this while Athena is sitting on his cock, keeping it warm and wet while I go between licking his balls and her clit while opening Heph up for me. Hell, maybe I will be doing this while her mouth is on my cock and Eros is opening her ass for him.

So many possibilities, but right now my focus is Heph. Just Heph.

I go back to licking his balls, not wanting him too close to the edge as I curl my fingers in just the right spot. I know I hit it when he sucks in a breath, and his back arches off the bed.

"Fuck," he breathes.

"You okay, baby?" I tease.

"I'm ready." Is the only thing he can get out, and I think he is right. Standing up, I grab his ankles and pull him closer to the edge of the bed, then I rip off my shirt and step out of my pants. My cock is hard and an angry red. Heph stares at it and licks his lips.

Next time.

I grab the lube and work some on my cock, liking the way he watches as I stroke myself, coating my cock, getting it ready for him.

He moves to roll over, and I stop him.

"No, I want to see your face as you take every inch of me. Put your thighs on my shoulders."

He does as I ask. It's so much different having his thick powerful thighs on my chest instead of the thin feminine ones that are usually there.

I grip my cock and press into him slowly. Stopping every inch giving him time to adjust.

"How does it feel?"

"It feels so big. So fucking good. It feels fantastic," Heph shudders out.

I slide out slowly, almost all the way, and pour some fresh lube on my cock before sliding back in. This time he moans, and it's a sound of pure pleasure.

I keep my pace slow, making sure to hit a little deeper with every thrust. By the time I start slowly increasing my speed, he is gripping the headboard so hard his knuckles are white, and a stream of pre-cum is running down the length of his cock. I wonder briefly if I could make him cum like this. Completely untouched, just by fucking him.

I'm planning on having a lot of fun finding out, but not right now. My cock is sliding back and forth easily now, and I can really start fucking him. As I grab his cock with my lubed-up hand and hold my fingers still, letting my thrusts push him through my fist.

"Fuck, right there. Fuck," Heph chants as I push him a little harder.

He is squeezing my cock hard, taking me so well. I grit my teeth to stop myself from coming too soon. I will be damned if I come before he does. It will not happen. I will not leave my lover unsatisfied. Ever.

I angle my hips to hit his prostate more directly while tightening my fist around Heph's cock. His thighs are quivering on my shoulders as his chest is rapidly rising and falling with his labored breaths.

He is almost there. Just a little more and I will fill him up.

"Oh, god," Heph cries out as stream after stream of thick cum shoots out of his cock, covering his chest and abs.

I tighten my fist and keep going, fucking him through his orgasm, and as soon as his cock is lying spent on his stomach, I refocus my attention on my own cock that is so close to exploding. Grabbing Heph's thighs for leverage, I fuck into him hard, pushing him higher in his bliss and bringing me to mine.

When I come, it's with a yell, and my vision whites out for a moment. It's the strongest one I have ever had. I take a few moments to come down enough to pull out of Heph and lie next to him to catch my breath.

"Wow," Heph says, and I can't help the goofy satisfied grin on my face.

"Yeah?" I ask, pulling him into my arms, just needing to feel his skin against mine.

"You sure you want to do that? I'm a mess." He laughs.

"I'm sure, and as soon as we can stand again, we are going in that shower together to clean up. And I hope you plan on staying in my bed tonight."

"Honestly, I don't think I could make it back to my bed," he says on a yawn. "My thighs feel like I just did a three-hour leg day. How is that possible?"

"I don't know. Maybe next time you can fuck me, and we will compare notes. How does that sound?"

"Like a plan."

"Good, but for right now, let me just hold you."

"Hey, Perseus?"

I answer with a hmm, my eyes already closed, just enjoying the high of having Heph in my arms and in my bed.

"Do you think Paris could have killed Freya?"

CHAPTER THIRTY-THREE

Athena

The next morning, I wake thankfully not hungover. Eros came in last night, rousing me to drink a glass of water and take some aspirin. Then he ate me out before letting me go back to sleep, swearing it was part of his magic hangover prevention method. It was probably the water and aspirin, but if he wants to eat me out like that every night I have a few too many, then I am not opposed to developing a drinking problem.

When I open my eyes, I feel rested, rejuvenated, and ready to start the day. I try to get out of bed, but two muscular arms drag me back under the covers.

"Morning, baby girl." Eros pulls me into his chest.

"Good morning. How did you sleep?"

"It's not a good morning yet, but it can be." He pushes his hard cock into my thigh.

Eros rolls me onto my back and straddles me. He darts his tongue out and licks my neck.

"You taste so good," he says.

He leans down and kisses me. Our tongues dance and our lips lock. My nipples stiffen, and my pussy aches to be touched.

"I want you," he pants. "I want your virginity."

I freeze. He knows that Perseus… "Uh?"

Smirking, he adds. "I want this virgin *ass.* I allowed Perseus to pop that cherry of yours, but this time"—he reaches down to touch my anus—"it's my turn."

I've never seen Eros so determined, so primal.

"Kiss me," he orders.

I lean up, and our lips meet. Then he attacks my neck. My nipples, my pussy, my belly—he attacks every inch of my body. I moan as my body reacts to his touch.

He rakes his teeth over my nipples and bites them gently, pushing them together as he sucks them into his mouth, hard. I cry out as he quickly gets off me, reaches for his discarded pants on the floor and pulls out a bottle of lubrication.

Clearly, this is a planned event.

Returning to the bed with a wicked gleam in his eyes, he says, "This ass is mine."

He reaches between my legs and his fingers glide through my wetness. I close my eyes and mewl in erotic need. The feel of his fingers on me is delicious.

"Please don't cry, baby," he whispers.

"I'm not going to cry," I tell him, and I kiss him, although the idea of having his large cock in my ass is terrifying. But the last thing I'll ever do is cry. Athena Godwin doesn't cry.

"We'll see about that." His eyes darken, and his upper lip raises into a devilish smirk.

He gently helps me turn onto my stomach and parts my legs, and I feel his body move up the bed. He kneels on the bed, and I hear the bottle of lube open. I shiver, and my body trembles. Eros runs his hands over my back and ass.

"Relax, baby girl," he whispers, and he kisses my neck. "It's the only way you're going to be able to take my cock."

I feel his fingers on my ass again. His fingers slide into me—just a tip. It doesn't hurt, but it feels... foreign.

Oh Jesus Christ. Am I really going to allow this?

He rubs the lubrication over my anus and pokes a finger inside again. This time, it's all the way in. I wince but try to relax. He then squirts more lubrication and starts massaging it into my tight hole.

I consider telling him to stop, but the curiosity is too much. I want to know what this feels like. I also want to give this part of me to Eros first.

He wants it, and I'm going to let him take it.

"Are you ready?" he asks.

"Yes," I answer.

He moves into position behind me. I feel the head of his cock rub the outer lips of my pussy before pushing in.

I cry out. Fuuuuuuuuck, he's too big.

"Shhh, baby," he says as he kisses my back. "You'll get used to it. I'm going to go really slow. The head of my cock is the only thing inside you right now. You can take it. I know you can."

He kisses my back and neck, and I start to relax. With that, he pushes the head of his cock into me a little further.

"Oh my God," I moan.

He slowly pushes his cock all the way into me. I cry out, but I don't tell him to stop. I clench my teeth, and I try to focus on relaxing like he told me to do.

"You're so fucking hot, baby, and tight," he groans. "I'm gonna open your ass wide, and you're going to take every inch of my cock. Yes, baby. That's it. Fuck, you feel so good."

I'm closed in all around him and it... hurts. But then it doesn't. I feel so full, so complete.

He pushes in deeper. I squeal, and he stops.

"Stay still, baby girl." He kisses my back and waits for me to calm down. "Good girl. Get used to my size. Are you okay?"

"Yes," I pant. I nod as I start to believe what I say.

Satisfied, he begins slowly pushing in again.

I feel like I'm going to split in two, but all of my pain is soon replaced by... pleasure.

Eros reaches around to play with my clit. His fingers are magical. I feel my pussy start to lubricate again. The pain is gone. Only warmth remains.

The feeling of his cock in my ass is beyond anything I could've ever imagined. It's as if Eros is reaching deep within me, connecting to my very soul. I'm never letting him go.

"Oh, God. You feel so fucking good, baby. You are so fucking tight."

Eros starts slowly thrusting again, going deeper and deeper with every thrust. It hurts, but it's not really pain. It's so much more. He's fucking me deep, and I feel his balls against my ass. He pulls almost all the way out, and then thrusts back into me, balls deep.

I cry out, and I push back against him. He's not going to dominate me completely. I'm going to have my say, and I start to fuck him back. He grunts and growls, and it turns me on even more.

"Yes, Athena, yes," he gasps. "Ride my cock. You are so fucking sexy and beautiful."

I lean back and push my ass into him. He grabs my breasts, and I feel him kiss the side of my neck.

I grab the sheets and pull them off the bed. I'm trying to hold onto something, anything. I have no idea why my body is reacting this way.

It hurts and feels good at the same time.

"That's it, baby. Take it. Take every fucking inch

of my cock. I'm going to take it all in your tight little ass."

He grabs my hair and pulls back my head. His cock goes deep into me, and I can't help but moan.

My body starts to shake. He pulls my hair again and thrusts into me faster.

Then it happens.

I can't control myself. I orgasm around the mass in my asshole, and I love every second of it.

He yanks my hair back and growls. His cock is pulsing inside me as he fills my ass with his warm cum.

"Oh my God, baby," he says as he collapses on top of me.

Eros kisses my neck, and I could get used to this.

After a few moments, he pulls out his cock.

"I'm sorry. I should've fucked you slower. I know it was your first time having anal sex."

I turn over and look him in the eyes. "I didn't cry." I give him a smile and a wink.

"Well, the challenge is on for next time."

After another round in the shower, Eros and I make it downstairs. The staff has all come back, and thankfully, no one is asking about the broken chairs or the bullet holes. Mrs. Medea is busy in the kitchen, making pancakes, and shoos Eros and me into the dining room, saying Perseus and Heph are on their way up, so she is just making one big breakfast.

When Eros and I sit down, I ask him, "How sure are you that it's Paris?"

He draws a deep breath and sets down his coffee cup. "Last night I was positive, but this morning, after seeing how he reacted and how pissed he was and hurt, I just"—he takes another deep breath—"I don't know anymore."

"Don't know what?" Perseus comes around to sit at the table. Heph, looking unusually happy, follows behind him.

"About Paris," he answers. "I was so sure, but his reaction, and I still can't place a motive..."

"Where does he live?" I ask as Mrs. Medea brings in breakfast and everyone fills their plate.

"His family has an estate not too far from here," Perseus says. "Why don't we all go? We all need to talk this shit out and make sure he doesn't just shoot Eros."

He isn't wrong.

CHAPTER
THIRTY-FOUR

Athena

After breakfast, we all pile into Perseus's car. I figured his is the safest. No one is fucking with his mechanics. And we head to Paris's family estate. It's only about a five-minute drive, and from the outside, it looks beautiful. But the second we pass the gate, you can tell something is off. The lawn hasn't been tended. The house has a few windows boarded up, and paint is flaking off the Roman columns on the porch.

This estate is in worse shape than my mother's was. There is an excuse for that. They were waiting for the funds to be unfrozen to pay staff. But what is the excuse here? This is clearly years of neglect.

Perseus is the first on the porch, and he rings the

doorbell. There is nothing. I don't mean that no one answers. No bell sounds.

He tries again and nothing, so he knocks, and the front door just opens. It isn't locked. It isn't even closed all the way.

"This isn't terrifying at all," Eros says under his breath before wrapping his arm around me and pulling me into his body.

I'm not sure if he is trying to keep me close because he wants to protect me or use me as a human shield. Either way, I'm not having it. I shrug him off and enter the house, calling out for Paris.

There is nothing. No staff, no Paris, no furniture, nothing.

"What the fuck is with this place?" Eros says behind me.

"When was the last time you guys were here?" I ask.

The fixtures all have a thick layer of dust, and when I try a light switch, nothing happens. Thankfully, all the window dressings have been removed, so there is enough light.

"It's been a while. Paris usually comes to us. His mother doesn't like company," Heph says, taking a few more steps in.

A creaking comes from above us, and the hair on my arms rises, sending shivers down my spine. "Which one of you strong sexy men are brave enough to go see what that was?"

"Not it." All three of them say at the same time.

"Pussies," I say under my breath, rolling my eyes as I make my way up the stairs.

The upstairs hallway is in the same dusty, barren condition. Dust motes float in the few beams of sunlight intruding from outside. All the doors are open, the rooms all empty except for the last one at the end of the hallway. That door is closed, with light peeking out from underneath and a constant creaking coming from the other side of the door. All kinds of gruesome images flash through my mind as I think of what could be in there.

Decaying animals and a crazy person chained to a radiator.

Pet demon pacing in a trap.

Serial killer having already taken care of Paris, just waiting for us to look for him.

The ghost of my dead mother coming to haunt us for what happened last night.

Paris's body hanging from the light fixture with a note saying this was my fault.

When I reach for the door, my hand is shaking. I grip it and pull, it swings open and inside is a woman in her mid to late fifties smoking a cigarette wearing a satin housecoat that is so old it has lost its luster and is threadbare in many places. Her silver hair is in curlers, and she is sitting in a rocking chair watching reruns of *Dark Shadows* on a TV that looks old enough to have aired the black-and-white show when it premiered.

"Oh, hello. You must be a friend of my son," she

says, smiling at me. She looks a little off, her skin a slight graying hue, and her eyes don't quite focus.

"Yes, ma'am. I'm Athena Godwin. It's a pleasure to meet you. I'm actually looking for Paris. Have you seen him?"

"Oh, him." She waves her hand in the air, the long ash on the cigarette falling in a pile of ash on the floor. "He came home all in a tizzy last night. Something about the goddess of war all up on her throne casting down hellfire."

This woman is bat-shit crazy.

"But goddesses are known for their tempers. He went away to the cabin in the woods. It's important for men to do that, you know. Have a place to go to think. There is so much pressure to be a god that they must work and work and work, and it's so much stress. Sometimes, they need to go back to the old ways. Back to the cabin in the woods, back to living off the land. Like his father taught him before he left. Left for his new life, for his new family. My husband was supposed to be loyal. He was not. He lied."

The woman is rambling, and I am having a really hard time following what she is saying.

"That boy of mine. I love him, I do, but sometimes he is too much like his father," she rattles more, rocking in her chair. "He forgot about me. Like his father. He brings my breakfast every morning, but not this morning. My breakfast and my medication. It makes me strong, it makes me clear. Clear as water, clear as air. It makes the world clear."

Looking around, I can see several orange pill bottles, some empty on the floor, knocked over on the counter, and one that appears as if it has a few in it.

Okay, we need to get this woman some food and then get her medicated. Maybe then I can get some answers. I peek back out the door. The three men are all standing there staring wide-eyed.

"I'm going to stay here and try to figure out what is happening. Can you please run and grab some food for Paris's mom?"

Heph nods, and he and Eros head out.

Perseus enters the room. "Hello, ma'am."

She ignores him.

"Is there anything particular you would like for breakfast?" I ask, thinking I can text Eros and Heph.

"Who are you? Why are you in my house?" she shrieks, gripping her housecoat to her chest. Note to self: keep her engaged.

"I'm Athena, a friend of—"

"Oh! Athena, the woman who is marrying my son. Yes, of course he has told me all about the golden angel who will bring this family back to its rightful status. Yes, yes, yes, sit dear. I am Ellen, but you may call me Mother. Now, where is my son?"

Okay then. I exchange a look with Perseus. He is as lost as I am.

"I am actually looking for him. Do you know where he is?"

"Oh, yes, how silly of me, the cabin in the woods.

So very, very far. But he must, you see, he must go into the cabin in the woods to plan his revenge. He must get revenge on the evil hag who has so much when he now has so little. She took it, you see. She did not come from power. She should not have power. Power is for those who are born to power." Ellen is rocking faster now, her arms waving in the air and her voice becoming louder and higher pitched. "Yes, yes, yes, he will kill the witch and take her power, and her snakes. This Medusa has so many snakes, all slithering and striking. She took my son with her power and made him a snake. She ensnared him, but he broke free when he saw the truth. He broke from her spell. She must suffer. He must save the others and take the power back."

"How do we reach Paris?" I ask.

She calms down, and her rocking slows again.

"As long as the witch is dead and the snakes are set free, he will marry the angel, and he will return to me. Return to me whole again. Make our family whole again. We will get it all back, you'll see. My son, the hero, he will save me, and return what was taken from me."

She is speaking in circles. She is clearly very ill and requires round-the-clock care. I can't leave her like this. And I can't shake the terrible sinking suspicion I know who the hag is in this story, and it breaks my heart.

It isn't Ellen's fault, though, whatever her son did. Ellen needs help, and I need to find Paris.

Eros was right about Paris. I hate to admit it, but there is no telling what Paris is going to do next.

Ellen sits in her rocker, her eyes glazing over as she stares at her TV. I'm pretty sure she isn't paying attention to the old soap opera, but if it comforts her, who am I to stop it?

"Text Heph and tell them to bring something simple, like chicken soup and fresh bread. She needs some protein, but I don't know what her body can handle," I whisper to Perseus, who just stares at Ellen. He doesn't move, doesn't even blink. Waving my hand in front of his face doesn't get his attention, so I punch him in the arm.

That does it.

"Ow." He rubs his arm, and I smirk.

"Text the others, tell them chicken soup and fresh bread. Now."

He steps out of the room, and I look around. The curtains are tightly drawn, and a rickety bed stands in the corner. Calling it a bed is generous. It's really more of a metal frame with rusted springs holding up a thin mattress pad with a flat pillow. Ellen is one bad night away from tetanus. I pick up the pill bottles that are strewn all over the floor. They are all for Clozapine. A quick google search on my phone tells me it's an antipsychotic and a very high dosage.

That explains a lot.

I tidy up her room as best I can. When I go downstairs in search of a broom, dustpan, and something to dust with, I find Perseus sitting on the floor in what I assume used to be a living room.

"Are you okay?" I ask, sitting next to him.

"How did I not know?" He is staring at a knot in the wood floor. "How did I not know he needed help? He was drowning and sold off everything. How could I not have seen it?"

"Because he didn't want you to." This is the only plausible explanation I can give him. "You know Paris better than I do. So, I'm not going to sit here and guess what his motives are, but I know that whatever he did or didn't do, his mother needs help."

"Why should I help her if he took Freya from me? I know she was your mother by blood, but she was mine by choice."

I wince as his words cut into me, but he is right. Whether she chose to leave me, she chose to raise Perseus, and her love for him was laced throughout her journals.

"Sorry, I didn't mean it like—"

"It's okay," I interrupt him. "You aren't wrong, but Ellen isn't the one who may or may not have betrayed all of you. And she is clearly unwell. We don't know how much of what she is saying is true." I take a deep breath. "In her diary, my mother said she and her boys were a family. Is that true?"

"Yes." He doesn't even hesitate.

"Then Paris is family."

"But he betrayed us."

"He might have. We still don't know that for a

fact," I reason, not really believing my own words, but we don't have solid proof yet. "Does he deserve the benefit of a doubt?"

"He does," Perseus says with a sigh.

"So, is he still family?"

"Yes."

"Good." I stand. "Then that makes Ellen family, and right now she needs our help." I offer Perseus a hand and pull him to his feet.

"What do you need me to do?"

"Find out why her room is the only one with electricity. See if you can find any sign of Paris, and I need some cleaning supplies."

Twenty minutes later, Perseus comes back upstairs with the supplies I asked for. He says the breakers were flipped to intentionally turn off the electricity to the rest of the house, probably to limit the electric bill. I get to work on cleaning Ellen's living space while she chatters about the snakes and the hag and hidden families. It's another twenty minutes before the others return with food. I help Ellen eat and take her meds. She then insists on taking a nap. While she does that, I go downstairs to see what the others are doing.

"I figured out which room he was sleeping in," Perseus says when he sees me. "But there is no sign of him now."

"I figured he left last night." I sit down, leaning against the wall. "Do we have any idea where he could have gone?"

The boys keep brainstorming, talking everything out while my eyes slide shut, and I try to process everything. Seeing Ellen like that after hearing Paris tell me stories about his mother, the strong woman who raised him, who would take on the world for him. He clearly loves her, and yet look at what she has become, a shell of her former self talking nonsense, living in between reality and an old black-and-white TV show.

My eyes are still closed when I hear Perseus's phone chirp, and he says, "What the actual fuck."

"What?" Heph asks, and I pry open my eyes.

"An automatic payment on my card was declined for insufficient funds."

"Okay... and?" I ask.

"There should be a few hundred thousand in that account." He taps off his phone screen for a few moments, his brows drawn down over his eyes in confusion.

"Is it a banking error?" Heph asks.

"I don't think so. It looks like this account has had several smaller transfers in the last few months, then a massive one of almost seventy grand last night."

I am about to say something about calling the bank and seeing if his card info was stolen when the creaking of the rocking chair starts again above us.

"Do any of you have access to my mother's bank accounts?" I ask.

"I can get it. Why?" Perseus asks.

"Because I have a hunch, and I am praying I am wrong. Can you look through my mom's account to see if there are any transfers to that same account?"

"Yeah... Why?"

"Something Ellen said. I want to see if it's true. Just look into all of that, and if you can follow the money and see where it goes."

"What are you going to be doing?" Eros asks, taking my hand in his and lacing our fingers together.

"I'm going to stay here with Ellen. I don't want to leave her alone. I'm hoping her meds have cleared her head a little, and I can get some real info from her. Either way, I am also going to look into getting her into a care facility. She needs round-the-clock care."

"I'm staying here." Eros places a kiss on the back of my hand. "I don't want you alone in case Paris comes back, and he isn't right in the head or something."

"I need your help with the bank stuff, man." Perseus shakes his head. "Aside from Paris, you are the best with the computer."

"I'll stay with her," Heph volunteers, making all of us stop and stare at him for a moment.

"Are you sure?" Eros narrows his eyes like he is trying to look through Heph to see his real motives.

"I'm sure. Aside from our security system, I am completely useless on the computer." He shrugs.

"But I can help Athena with Ellen and keep both women safe, if I have to."

"Then it's settled." I stand up and brush the dust and dirt from my jeans. "You two head out. Call us if you find anything, and we will do the same." I head back to Helen's room to see if she is more lucid.

CHAPTER THIRTY-FIVE

Perseus

"I hate this so much." Eros leans back in his chair, his hands pressed to his eyes. We have been sitting at the breakfast table for the past four hours staring at these screens trying to trace payments and coming up empty.

"The good news is, this hacker didn't touch all of my accounts." I sit back in my chair and slam my computer closed.

"That helps us, how exactly?" Eros asks. I know he is tired and frustrated like I am, but the attitude is still not appreciated.

"It means I can make sure the staff here keep getting paid and we can hire someone else to figure this shit out. Someone far more versed in forensic accounting than we are. Our guy Max should have been on this, and we're going to get his ass out here to fix this shit."

"Thank fuck!" Eros shouts, closing his computer, too.

He is silent for a moment, but the way he is chewing his bottom lip tells me he wants to say something. He is just looking for the words. So I sit and wait for it.

"Do you think Paris..."

"You were pretty sure of it last night," I point out, and he slams his hand on the table a few times.

"I was positive. I just knew it was him, but after seeing his eyes when I accused him of that... and after talking to Athena about all of it... I wasn't so sure. But this..."

"I know." I do.

I know exactly how that conflicting emotion in your gut feels. I have it every single time I look at Athena. I want her. I want to trust her, and I want to bring her in. And so does Heph. He even admitted last night as we kissed in the shower that he wasn't sure if he was willing to give up women completely either. He, like me, doesn't want to choose, and I see no reason we should. I just don't know if I can let her in fully, no matter how much a part of me wants to.

Hopefully, spending time with her this afternoon has helped them get a little closer. There is still the whole matter of the inheritance between us, but that is a problem for later.

"Do you know someone we can hire?" Eros asks

as he gets up to grab a drink from the fridge. He holds up a bottle of water, asking if I want one, too.

"Yeah," I answer both questions at once. I catch the bottle in midair and take a long drink. "The lawyer that Freya used mentioned having an accountant brother-in-law. I figured I would reach out to him first."

"Good deal. Make the call, then come out and join me on the patio."

"Okay." He walks off, and I make the calls.

I leave a message for Max to get his ass out here. I want to know where my fucking money has gone. Heads are going to roll, and I'll start with my accountant who dropped the ball if I have to.

Before heading out to sit on the patio with Eros, I send Heph a message.

Perseus: Everything good there?

Heph: Yeah, we are good. The meds really help, but we don't have a location for Paris yet. Athena is making calls to find an available place for Ellen to stay. It's a good thing she thinks Athena is her to be daughter-in-law. Which is weird as fuck, but coming in handy at the moment.

Perseus: That is weird.

Heph: How about you guys, any luck?

What he means is if there is any proof. Heph, like me, does not want this to be all on Paris. Even the thought of that level of betrayal guts us both.

Perseus: Nothing yet either way. I have a professional looking at the accounts now. I'll keep you updated.

Heph: Okay. Keep me posted.

Perseus: You too. I'll see you tonight. My bed again or yours?

I can feel the heat rising to my cheeks.

Heph: My bed, but your ass.

I bite back a laugh as I type.

Perseus: Deal, but only after I get your mouth.

I put away my phone, grab two beers from the fridge, and go to meet Eros on the porch.

"So are we going to talk about it?" he asks, looking out over the back gardens.

"Talk about what?" I sit next to him and hand him one beer. We twist off the tops and flick them into the nearby garbage can before settling to look over the backyard. I hate to admit it, but since Athena took over the house and instructing the staff, this place looks stunning. It looks like something out of a fairy tale.

"How you're going to make me pay for last night. How we both love the same girl, or how you and Heph finally fucked last night? Your pick."

"How do you know Heph and I fucked?"

"I didn't until just now." He looks over at me with a huge grin. Cocky bastard. I answered the only one I knew wasn't a minefield.

"I'm not in love with Athena."

He glances over at me and gives me a bored expression. "If you are not already in love with her, then you are well on your way. It's hard not to fall for a woman like that. I did try..."

This time I give him the bored look.

"Okay," he adds. "I didn't try very hard, but I tried a little bit."

"I don't know her well enough to love her, but I want her. I don't think I have ever wanted to fight with a woman just to have her end up under me so I can take my frustrations out on her pussy more in my life."

"Yeah, she is good at inspiring hate fucking." Eros nods, taking a sip of his beer. "You know, when I asked her why she was still a virgin, I expected her to tell me it was none of my business, something sarcastic or even a non-answer. Do you know what she said?"

"She slapped you across the face and told you it's because all men are disappointments," I say, watching a butterfly land on some of the red flowers she had planted.

"No, well, kind of, but without the hit." Eros takes a deep breath. "She told me she heard all the stories from women about not having their needs met, and how every woman wished that sometimes their lovers were different. That if they had a man who was kind and tender, they just wanted to be railed into next week, making them feel like they are desired and their man can't control themselves around her. If they had a man who fucked them hard, they wanted one who could make soft, gentle love to them and make them feel cherished and loved. She said that she never wanted to choose. She has no interest in picking one man to fuck for the rest of her life. She said the men she has dated would never be okay with the idea of sharing her. Instead, they treated her like they owned her or had some exclusive rights to her body. Athena would never settle for one man, so she decided she wouldn't have any."

"Okay, then she had sex with you because..."

"She was dealing with intense emotions and decided to self-medicate with my dick."

I spit out the beer that was in my mouth and started choking.

"You okay there buddy?" Eros pats my back while I try to regain my composure and the ability to breathe.

"Really?" I ask after I take a full breath. "That's how you phrase that?"

"No, that is how she phrased that. At first, I felt a little used, but then I figured that just means I have a medical-grade dick."

"Jesus Christ." I laugh. "What the fuck am I going to do with you?"

"I'm hoping that you and I and the others are going to sort this shit with Paris out, whatever that means. Then we will pull Athena into our family and let her use all of us for our FDA-certified dicks and cuddles. I really enjoy cuddling her. It's weird. I never liked that before. It always felt all gross and clingy, but now I am like fuck yes, give me the soft fuzzy blankets and all the pillows and my girl and I will cuddle her so hard."

"I can't with you right now, man." The laughter makes me feel lighter than I have in a long time. It's kind of nice, if I am being honest, but it doesn't change the fact that some really awful shit had gone down, and I have this hollow feeling in the pit of my stomach that it is going to get a lot worse before it gets better.

CHAPTER
THIRTY-SIX

Heph

The second the others leave, Athena gets to work, and puts me to work, too. Ellen is back on her rocker, and Athena kneels at her feet. "Hey Ellen, when was the last time you had a proper bath with warm water and bubbles?"

"It has been some time," the old lady answers and smiles wistfully. "I used to adore baths, but our hot water doesn't work, so I'm afraid it is a luxury I can't afford at the moment."

"I can restore power to the hot water heater," I offer. "See if I can get it working."

"Thank you, young man," the old woman says.

I leave them to go fix it, and as I thought, the heater is a little old, a little rusty, but works okay as soon as I turn the power on. I go back up to tell them to give it a little bit of time and it should be fine. But when I get to the door, I hear the two women talking.

"How long have you been up here all by yourself?" Athena asks.

"Oh, not long," Ellen answers. "My son was here yesterday, I think. He brought my new prescription and said the bills were paid for a while, but he had to go back to the cabin in the woods. He said he would be home in a week. As long as I didn't have another episode, I would be good."

"What is it like when you have an episode?"

"The world turns, and I can't think right. I get confused. I haven't had one in such a long time, though." Athena must give her a look or something. The next thing the old woman is saying, "Oh dear, I had another, didn't I?"

"I think so." Athena's voice is soft, soothing, without being condescending. "Ellen, do you remember who I am?"

"Yes, you are Athena, the woman my Paris has told me about. He says he will marry you, and you will help me. Where is my son? Why isn't he here?" Her voice rises, and she sounds a little frantic. Athena must be doing something to soothe her because Ellen's next words come out barely more than a whisper. "He has done something terrible, hasn't he?"

"I don't know." Athena doesn't lie to her, and I admire that about her. She is stubborn and has a mouth that will not fucking stop. Sometimes, she is worse than Eros, but she is never unkind unless provoked, and she is always honest. Even when a lie would make things so much easier. She takes truth over convenience. I hate how much I admire her for that.

"It's not his fault, not really. When he found out about you, it brought up so much of his past, so much ugliness. For weeks, he was all rage and spite. Then he met you, and I think he fell in love."

"What do you mean? Why would finding out about me trigger him?" That is a good question. I didn't notice anything off about Paris until I caught him and Athena on the patio seconds from fucking.

"His father had a mistress, you see. Well, over the years, I think he had several. I knew, of course, but I chose not to say anything. I figured it would be an office romance, a way to leave the stress of his job at work, then come home ready to be a proper father at least, if not a good husband. They never lasted long, and he put Paris above everything, so I pretended I didn't know. What is it you kids say? I let it slide." She laughs at her own joke.

"Yeah, that's what we say. Then what happened?"

"Oh well, when Paris was about twelve, one of my husband's women got pregnant. She had a boy, and he tried to keep it quiet, but I knew, of course. It was fine until she got pregnant again with twins. Then my husband decided that his whore having three children was more important than his wife and first son. He spouted on about the needs of the many outweighing the needs of the few or some such nonsense twisted to somehow justify leaving his legitimate family for the false one."

"That is terrible." Athena's voice is calming to the old woman again.

The rocking of her chair has slowed. I press forward a bit, and the wood under my foot creaks. I freeze, hoping the women haven't heard me. I didn't know any of this about Paris. It makes me feel terrible. Paris knows all of our damage. How do I not know the extent of his? Did he choose to keep it from us, or did we never give him the opportunity to share?

Fuck.

"But I'm still confused. What any of this had to do with me," Athena asks.

"Well, dear," Ellen continues. "Paris saw that other woman, Freya, as another parent. When he found out she also had another secret family, he was so angry. For days, he raged. I urged him to go talk to Freya, find out what happened. Why weren't you in her life anymore? Why did she keep all of this from him?"

"Wait, he found out about me before she died?" Athena sounds shocked, and frankly, so am I.

I thought none of us had any idea she had children, a family. We knew she was running from something, but we thought it was just her ex. Never a family. How could Paris not have told us? Did we know him at all?

"Oh yes, dear, but not long before. I am afraid, as he was working up the nerve to ask her about you. That is when she passed. So tragic. That was also when Paris's father stopped sending alimony. It all happened at once, and he said that it will all be over soon. He has a plan, and I know he will get us out of this."

Fuck. It might have been him. For the first time, I really think Eros is right. I don't know if Paris killed Freya, but I bet he was the one taking the money.

I can't hear anymore. I just can't. So, I knock on the door and peek in. Tears are running down Athena's face, and she quickly wipes them away.

"Hot water should be good now," I say, then I head downstairs to find something to do.

Athena finds me in the kitchen, sweeping.

"Hey, can I get you to do that in her room? There is so much dust I didn't want to kick it all up in the air while she was in there."

"Yeah, did you leave her in the bath?"

"She is sitting on the toilet while the tub fills. She seems more with it now that she took her pill, and it pulled her out of whatever episode she was having when we got here. But just in case, I don't want to leave her alone in there."

"Probably a good call. I'll go take care of it now."

She moves to go back upstairs but stops and turns back around to face me, her arms wrapped around her middle. I can't see her fire, her fight. She looks sad, and for the first time I have seen her, small.

"Heph, did Paris kill my mother because I was looking for her? Was this my fault?"

"No." I don't know why, but I can't lie to her, not about this. "If Paris did this, it's on him. Not you. Maybe Freya should have told us. I don't know why she didn't. Her reasons were her own, but it doesn't justify her death. I promise we will find out what happened."

She nods and goes upstairs. While I resist the urge to follow her and pull her into a hug. I have been a complete ass to her while she was grieving the loss of a mother she never got to know. I haven't earned the right to comfort her. Yet.

CHAPTER THIRTY-SEVEN

Athena

Ellen and I keep chatting about this and that. I don't want to upset her further. It seems when I upset her, she slowly slips back into madness. I need her to be calm and happy. She is telling me about Paris when he was a child, so full of life and so smart. Always the picture of a well-behaved young man in public, saving his emotional outbursts for home.

I help her out of the tub and into a nice clean dressing gown made of soft cotton. I then get her back to her chair and comfortable before I approach what we are going to do from here.

"Ellen," I start.

"Mother," she corrects.

"Mother," I say, ignoring the lump forming in my throat. "I'm afraid Paris may not be back for a while."

"Oh, is he on a trip?"

"Yes." I give her a smile. "Something like that. It all happened so suddenly, and we aren't sure when he will be back. I don't feel right leaving you here alone."

"Oh, you're a sweet thing, but I am sure my Paris wouldn't leave me for too long."

"I'm sure you are right." I place my hand on her shoulder. "But for my peace of mind, would you be open to letting me put you up somewhere nice, where the staff can see to your needs? Just until Paris comes back."

"Oh, that sounds lovely, dear." She smiles at me, and I feel sick to my stomach. I hate not telling her the full truth, but she isn't well, and I don't want something to happen that I can't safely handle.

"Okay. I am going to make a few calls. Why don't you watch your show?" I turn the TV back on and step out of the room. Heph is waiting for me.

"She okay?" he asks.

"Yeah, and she is good with going to a facility until Paris is back."

"Shady Pines?" he asks.

"No, I was thinking Elysian Fields. My dad's mom was there the last year of her life, and it was really nice. She liked it, even if she ran the staff ragged," I say while typing on my phone, looking for the number. "Wait." I look up at Heph with wide eyes. "Was that a *The Golden Girls* reference?"

"I don't know what you are talking about." He turns and heads down the hallway.

Oh My God. Heph likes *The Golden Girls*. He would, he is such a Dorothy. I smile to myself as I find the number and make the call, arranging for them to prepare the nicest suite for Ellen and get her medical records. I give them the name of her doctor on her pill bottle and my credit card to prepay for the next three months. If we are all wrong, it will take at least that long to refurbish the house as an apology. It is the least we can do. And if we are right, then three months should give us enough time to make a plan.

I help Ellen pack a few things, mostly worn slippers, threadbare dressing gowns, and her rollers that are older than I am. She makes me call down to the facility a few times to make sure they have a rocker and TV, even after I assure her each room will. The room I am moving her to is more like her own apartment. She will have a bedroom, dining room, living room, and a kitchenette with an electric kettle, a microwave, refrigerator and things of that nature. Though I have also paid for a meal package that will have her food brought in from the main kitchens for each meal. It takes less than two hours for the front desk to call me back saying her suite is ready. Her doctor's office is sending over files, and her doctor will be in to do a checkup in the morning. All that is left is to arrange transport. They do offer to come pick her up, but I decline, saying she needs to arrive in style. Once again, the Godwin name does me well, and this process wasn't anywhere as difficult as it could have been.

I call my father's Town Car service and have them take both of us so I can make sure she is settled. I don't know why, but I think about my mother, and how if she was in this position I would want someone to help her.

I suppose she was in a similar position, and *her boys* took care of her for a time, even Paris. I will repay that debt by taking care of his mother.

If I was worried that getting Ellen settled would be difficult, I shouldn't have been. She is sweet, and the longer her medication has to work, the more coherent she becomes. The fog in her eyes seems to clear to reveal a sharp woman with a quick wit and a kind heart.

"Athena, dear. Can I ask you something?"

"Anything," I say, sliding into the Town Car next to her while Heph gets into the front to give the driver directions.

"My son, is he a good man? Or is he like his father?"

I don't expect such a blunt question. I take a moment, struggling to find the right words. "I don't know. Paris and I have only known each other a short time."

Ellen's lips purse, and she looks down at her hands folded on her lap.

She knows something is wrong, but not what,

and I can't bring myself to leave her like this, worried for her son and what kind of man he is. I still don't know if he is as calculating and cold as Eros seems to think...

"But," I add, "in the short time we have known each other, Paris has shown himself to be a kind gentleman. He is charming and sweet, and the portrait of modern chivalry."

Ellen's eyes light up at my words, and it makes me feel all warm and fuzzy inside. Like the pride she feels for her son is somehow reflected in me.

Heph helps me get her settled, and by the time we are back in the car, it's getting dark, and I am starving.

"Hey, should we grab dinner before heading back?" I ask.

"They already ate," he answers, "but why don't we go have dinner?" He rubs the back of his neck. "I feel like I owe you an apology, and I want to do it right."

"Okay." I'm a little hesitant and looking for the trap, but I can't see one. We are in my father's car, with one of his drivers, and we will be in public. What's the worst he can do? And more importantly, I really am hungry. "What kind of food are you thinking?"

"There is a steakhouse not too far from here. Is that okay?"

"It is." I grab my phone and send Eros a text.

Athena: Heph is taking me to dinner. Should I steal his knife?

Eros: Only if you want him eating half a cow with his bare hands.

Athena: Seriously, how worried should I be?

Eros: It will be fine. We know who is behind everything. Enjoy your dinner and when you get back, I'll explain everything.

Athena: Or you could tell me now.

Eros: Enjoy your dinner, baby girl. Perseus and I are still gathering information. We should be done by the time you two are back.

CHAPTER THIRTY-EIGHT

Heph

"Why?" I ask Athena as we pull up to the restaurant.

"Why what?"

"Why are you helping Ellen? She is nobody to you. She's worse than nobody, she is the mother of the man who may have killed your mother. Who lied to you?"

"None of that was her doing. Even if it was, I don't think she is in the right headspace to be making evil plots." She shrugs. I'm ready to drop it when she adds, "Paris told me something, and I don't know if it's true. I don't know who to trust."

"You can ask me. I won't lie."

She looks at me for a few moments, like she is trying to figure me out. It makes my skin crawl.

"I don't think you would lie to me, or anyone.

Why lie when you can use the truth like a war-hammer." She laughs, making this cute little sound.

"That is fair." I open the car door and step out, holding it open for her. It's a popular restaurant, and I haven't realized there would be a line around the building.

"Maybe we should try somewhere else," I offer.

"No, it's okay. I know the owner, and the Godwin family has a standing table here."

"The Godwins have a table?" I'm a little confused.

She smiles at me and leads the way into the restaurant. Sure enough, the hostess sees her, greets her by name, and guides us straight to one of the best tables in the place.

The second the hostess is gone, a waiter is there to take our drink order.

"Do you eat red meat?" Athena asks me.

"Absolutely."

"Allergic to anything?"

"No."

"Good." She takes both of our menus and hands them to the waiter. "We will take two of your largest ribeyes and one of all the sides, and a bottle of Macallan. Put it all on my family's tab."

"Yes, Ms. Godwin." The waiter shuffles away, and I can't help feeling a little emasculated.

"I can pay for my own meal."

"Oh, I'm sure you can, but a few years ago my father and I had a bet going, he lost badly, and now I get to come here whenever I want, with whomever I want, and he foots the bill. Trust me, this will be one of the smallest he has seen from me." She gives a devilish grin. "You're actually doing me a favor. I like to jab at my father whenever I can."

That does make me feel a little better.

We sit in silence for a bit. Not awkward silence, however, and I'm finding myself getting more and more comfortable.

"So what was your question?" I prompt.

"Right! You asked why I am looking after Ellen. Paris told me how she and Perseus met, and that for a while she put you and him up at a little apartment when you were young."

"Yes." I'm not sure where she is going with this, but I am treading carefully.

"Right, well. He then told me that you guys were brought to the estate when she needed someone. It would have been right after she left my father, and he banished her."

"Yes."

"He said that you, Perseus, and Eros took care of my mother in a way I couldn't. I've read a little of her journal and letters she wrote during that time, and I know that she was depressed and you three helped her get out of bed and eventually became the reason she started living again."

"A lot of good it did in the end."

Athena reaches across the table to take my hand. "It did a lot of good. You helped her in a way I wasn't given the opportunity to, and I am forever grateful to you for that. Showing Ellen the same generosity is my way of paying that back. Maybe not for Paris, but for the universe. I am putting more of that kind of energy into the world. Maybe I am paying it forward."

"Don't tell anyone this," I say leaning forward, "but I fucking love that movie."

Her eyes light up with laughter. "I won't tell a soul."

"I may have misjudged you," I say once the waitress drops off our steaks and ton of little bowls piled high with all kinds of side dishes.

"No, you got it right. I'm a bitch. I'm proud of that fact. I was there to take what should have been mine. Granted, if Perseus just talked to me, and had given me what I was after, then maybe I would have let him have it, but probably not." She takes a sip of her whiskey. "I have made it my life's mission to be the one person you do not want to put against in this city. We were on opposite sides of a problem, and if you hadn't come at me the way you did, I wouldn't respect you."

Her words take me by surprise. Apparently, I'm not the only one who can use the truth like a warhammer. I don't know what to say, so I take a bite of my steak, which of course is the best steak I have ever had.

"But, in light of everything, I hope we can be on the same team."

"You mean with Paris."

"I mean with Perseus." She sets her fork down, so I do the same, preparing for this to go very bad very fast.

"What about him?"

"I am calling the lawyer and seeing what options are available with my mother's estate. After reading her journals, I can see that he was just as much a son to her as I was her daughter. So, I am looking at options where we can split it all. Equal distribution without selling the estate. I know it's your home, and I'm not taking it. The lawyer is to come up with several options that he can present to Perseus and me. Then I intend to come up with a solution that we are both amenable if not content with."

"Why would you do that? As of right now, everything would be yours."

"Because it shouldn't be. I may be a badass bitch, and trust me I am, but that doesn't mean I am unreasonable, some of the time. That, and I like you. All of you. I envy the family you have built. The bond."

"Don't you have brothers? Don't you have a real family to go home to?"

"Let's just say there are reasons my mother left." She gives me a tight smile. "But yes, I have two brothers and my father. It's complicated. I'd die for them. I'd also kill for them. But that doesn't mean we have the same bond that you have with Perseus, Heph, and even Paris. I have an extended family that is a nightmare, and my family owns an island where it's fair to say the occupants of Heathens Hollow hate every single Godwin. So, I've never really felt... at home."

I nearly choke on my steak. "Your family owns Heathens Hollow? The island in Puget Sound? Are you kidding me?"

"We have a family estate on it. Olympus Manor. It's where Freya used to live. It's where she died... or where we believed she died."

I know Athena Godwin runs Medusa. I know Medusa is a huge company. But owning an island. That is next-level billionaire type of stuff.

"So why have you been fighting so hard for Freya's house? It sounds like you have more money and assets than you know what to do with."

She looks down at her lap and then back at me. "I'm stubborn. I don't like to lose. And I despise being underestimated. You all thought you could scare me away. My goal was to show you that nothing can break me. Nothing."

"You've proven that," I admit. "Nothing we did could."

"You can thank my upbringing for that. Life was not easy at Olympus Manor."

"So you grew up on the island?" I ask. "I've never been, but I can imagine it's beautiful."

"It's creepy as fuck," she says with a scowl. "It's wet, it's foggy, it's full of cliffs and jagged rocks. It's a fishing town, so it always has a stench. Basically, it's the backdrop to a gothic novel. So no, I'm not a fan of Heathens Hollow. I know you all think I'm a princess and lived this fairy tale life. But trust me, it wasn't. Like the island, it was cold, dark, and often times gloomy. I couldn't wait to move to Seattle. And the minute I could, I did. And for the most part, I'll stay here. Yes, I visit Olympus Manor to see my family. But I will never see that place as home. I haven't felt a true sense of home since... well, my mother's house is starting to. I know Perseus has tried to get me out of there. All of you have but—"

"I think he might be falling in love with you," I say.

"Eros?"

"Perseus," I correct.

She nods. "I know, but you know if he loves me, that doesn't mean he doesn't love you."

"I know." I take another bite of my steak. "So, Paris gave you all our secrets. Tell me one of yours."

"Then it wouldn't be a secret," she says, stabbing a piece of scalloped potato.

"Consider it a peace offering."

"Are we discussing peace?" She blinks back at me. "Are we going to have a truce?"

"I'm not Perseus. I don't hate fuck. So a truce would make it a lot more fun when I finally have you riding my cock."

"Okay then." She gives me a sultry smile that makes my dick start to swell. "I have had more fun fighting with you and the others than I have had in a long time. I can't remember the last time I was really challenged, and I love it."

I smile and shake my head. "That's not a secret. I watch how your eyes light up when you are in the heat of battle. You have to give me something better than that. Something darker."

She pauses, studies my face, and then licks her lips. "Fine." She leans forward and in a low voice says, "I killed a man when I was a teenager."

I can't tell if she's joking. It doesn't appear that she is, but surely she must be.

"It was our butler. I pushed him down the stairs, and his neck snapped."

"An accident?" I ask.

She shakes her head. "The fucker came into my room and tried to have sex with me. If it weren't for Phoenix stopping him... Well, let's just say I wouldn't have been a virgin in my twenties."

"So you killed him?"

She nods. "I'd do it again. Over and over again." She takes a drink of her whiskey. "Is that a dark enough secret for you?"

Fuck...

This woman truly is something. Fascinating.

"I think I'm falling in love with you." I raise my glass to cheers her. "At the very least, in awe of you. Here's to wiping out assholes from the face of the earth." We clink glasses, and I ask, "Did you get into trouble?"

She smiles. "I'm a Godwin."

CHAPTER THIRTY-NINE

Eros

"Okay, Heph is taking Athena out to dinner. We have maybe another hour before they are back," I tell Perseus as I come up next to him and stand over the forensic accountant who is sweating bullets as he is frantically typing at his computer. "What's wrong, Max? You seem a little nervous." Yeah, I'm being an asshole, but I don't really care.

"You would be too if you were trying to work with a gun in your back." The weaselly little accountant's voice is trembling. God, I hope he doesn't piss himself. He probably will, but I really don't want him to piss himself. Then I might just have to rub his face in it like a dog, and then I am going to need a shower before my girl gets home.

"You wouldn't have a gun in your back if you

would just do the job we paid you for," Perseus grinds out, and judging by the whimper the weasel lets out, I will bet Perseus just pressed the gun in a bit further.

"I can't trace these funds," he whines. God I hate the fucking sound. What self-respecting grown man whines like a puppy? "It's not that I don't want to. Trust me, I do. I really, really do, but I can't. I can tell there has been a total of almost four million dollars being siphoned from these accounts over the last five years. The amounts were always percentages that were small enough to go unnoticed but as the account grew, so did the transfers until they were several thousand dollars. When the owner died, the accounts were frozen, so the money stopped. That is when the transfers started coming out of your account. I tried tracing the money, but it goes to banks in the Cayman Islands and there is no way for me to get that account information. You don't need an accountant, you need a hacker," Max blubbers, a disgusting mix of snot and tears running down his face.

"Ugh gross." I take a step away from him, still looking over his shoulder at the screen.

"Do you believe him?" Perseus asks me.

"I do. But where are we going to find a hacker for hire?"

"I know one," Max says. "I can call him now. I can get him here in ten minutes."

"No. I can call him. What's his name and number?"

"Harry." Max rattles off his number, and I call.

"How did you get this number?" a male asks.

"Is this Harry?"

"Yes, who is this?"

"I'm a friend of Max, and I need a hacker. You up for a job?"

"Depends on the job, depends on the pay," Harry says.

"Fifty thousand dollars to hack some money trails in the Caymans, and if you do it quick, we might not kill Max."

"Kill him. I don't give a fuck, but I will take the fifty large. Let me grab my rig, and I will come to you."

"Okay, you need the address?"

"Are you there now?" he asks.

"Yeah..." I say, a little uncertain.

"Then nah. I got it. See you in a few." He disconnects the line.

"Weird little dude, but he will take the job. He is on his way now."

Max sags in his seat with relief, so just for shits and giggles, I add, "He says he will do it for the cash. We can kill Max."

Perseus raises an eyebrow at me while Max cries out.

"Calm your tits, dude. He said we *can*. I didn't say we would. As long as your little buddy comes through, there is no reason you won't be able to walk out of here. Now pull yourself together. But next time we hire you to do a job—overseeing our fucking money—you better do your fucking job."

Harry is tall and wiry, with hipster glasses, and looks like he might be fourteen. It is not helped by the Capri Sun he is sucking down.

"Are you lost, little boy?" Perseus asks.

"Nah, I'm here to find your cash and collect my payment." He marches past Perseus like he is a butler, not a heavily armed man who could bench press this kid and snap him in half like a toothpick.

"Hey, right in here. Max can give you the account information." I look him up and down again. "Anything you need, milk, some Teddy Grahams?"

"You joke, but Teddy Grahams are the shit, and yeah, I need the Wi-Fi password."

He tells Max what he needs, and to be fair, Max tries to get it to him, but he is shaking so hard Harry just pulls out the wheeled chair Max is sitting on and shoves it out of the way sending poor Max caterwauling down the basement steps.

"Fucking useless piece of shit," Harry mutters as he gets the information straight from Max's screen.

"So, you and Max are not as close as he would make it seem. According to him, you two are great friends."

"That waste of flesh is less a friend. He screwed me out of some money and thought I was just too dumb of a kid to notice. But my bullshit is not why we are here. Let me work."

Max emerges from the basement and scurries to the door to leave. I nod my approval. We scared the man enough for one day.

"Kind of mouthy for a kid," I whisper to Perseus, who just nods as he watches the kid work, his fingers flying over keys and lines and lines of code fly over the screen.

"So how did you let someone steal from you for so fucking long before you found out? So fucking rich a missing million or four isn't a big deal?" he asks. "It must be rough when your card gets declined when you try to buy gold-leaf toilet paper."

"It didn't start in my account," Perseus says, grinding his teeth.

"I can see that. It started in some dead chick's account. Freya Godwin. Oh older woman... Had a bit of a mommy kink going on? Nice."

Perseus starts to clench his fists, and I move to stand between him and the kid. We need answers, not charges for assaulting a minor.

"Older women are the best, aren't they? Not shy, they know what they want, and have no problem teaching a young pup a few new tricks. Am I right?"

"You're about to die a brutal death," Perseus growls out as I try to hold him back.

"Damn, you guys don't play."

"No they don't." Athena's voice comes from

behind me, and I turn to see my girl come through the door holding a plastic bag.

"Hey, baby girl. I thought you were going out to dinner."

"We did. We were seated and served immediately."

"I changed my mind. She can stay," Heph says as he comes in after her looking strangely happy and satisfied.

"What did you two do, fuck in the car?"

"No, I just told the waitress we wanted two of the biggest steaks and all the sides." Athena shrugs, and that explains it. Heph is in a happy food coma.

This woman really was made to be the center of our little club. There is a saying that the quickest way to a man's heart is his stomach. Which is absolutely true in Heph's case. Feeding him a huge steak and carbs is the way to break down his walls.

Perseus isn't that easy. For him it is his mind, challenging him, and he loves the fight. Athena met each of his attacks and countered.

And for me it's about the chase. The game and okay, mostly about my dick.

"What's in the bag?" Perseus asks, pulling me from my thoughts.

"I brought back a few more steaks and some fresh rolls in case you guys got hungry," she answers as she peers around me to see the kid. "Who's this?"

"I'm the guy who is going to find your money..." his voice trails off when he takes in Athena, and his jaw practically hits the floor as he looks her up and down. "Hello, beautiful. I'm the man who can give you everything you need."

"Down boy. She is spoken for," I growl out. Athena pushes the bags to my chest and steps around me.

"And what is it that you think I need?"

"A real man." He looks her up and down and licks his lips.

"So what? You're going to call one for me... or...?"

"Oh, Mommy got jokes."

"Call me Mommy again and see what happens."

"Sure, but my safe word is pineapple." Harry just grins at Athena.

I hold back a red-faced Perseus who looks like he is going to murder this kid. Thank fuck Heph is still in his happy food coma and is lying on the couch not paying attention.

"Are we really going to let him talk to her like that?" Perseus bites out.

"Yup, Athena can handle him. If she needs us, she will let us know." I grit my teeth, still trying to hold him back.

"Damn, Mommy, you got those good boys house broken, don't you?" Harry laughs.

"Don't make any mistake, kid. You touch her, and I'll kill you," I say over my shoulder.

"You mean touch her like this?" He reaches out a hand to touch her arm. In a blink, Athena has Harry face down on the desk with the offending arm twisted around his back.

"Who the fuck is this kid?" she asks.

When it's clear she has the kid under control and in his place, I let Perseus go.

"He is supposed to be figuring out who has been taking the money and where it is going."

"I'm finished," the kid coughs out, and Athena loosens her grip. Harry rubs his arm as he turns back to the screen. He is all business again, apparently having learned his lesson.

"Then spill," Perseus says.

"The money was routed through a few shell corporations, including a Brothers LLC, which has a lot of money in it. Then the same amount that was funneled in through back channels was funneled out and put into an account here under the name Ellen Trust. I went ahead and did a little digging into that account. It was set up by a man when he left his wife and kid. He was paying into it until about seven-ish years ago."

"When Paris turned eighteen," I say. This was the proof. Paris was a traitor.

"You got to all of that really fast," Perseus says, a bit of mistrust coloring his voice.

"Yeah, I am kind of known for my speed. I get in and out fast," he says with a cocky grin.

I'm about to make a joke when Athena beats me to it.

"Aw, it's okay, sweetie. Endurance comes with practice. I'm sure you will get there."

"That isn't what I..." Harry crosses his arms over his chest and sits back, giving up on his retort. "Is there anything else you need me to do, or can I get paid and go nurse what's left of my fragile male ego?"

"Can you reverse the transfers from my account, putting my money back?" Perseus asks.

"No, but I can make a transfer from this account into yours, minus my fee of course."

"Do it, add twenty percent to your fee."

"Oh a tip, nice."

"Not a tip, a retainer. I want you to be on call for the next few months while we get this sorted. And can you stop the hacker from accessing my accounts again?"

"Kinda, I can't rewrite the bank security, but I can make it send you an alert anytime money goes out of this account. Though I would suggest just getting a new account, with new numbers."

"Set the alert, move the money and we'll be in touch." Perseus pauses, looks the kid up and down. "And, good job."

CHAPTER FORTY

Athena

Since the kid left last night, a melancholy cloud has descended on the entire house. I hoped it would only last the night, but even I must admit, sitting here with my cup of coffee in the morning seems oppressively sad. We know without a shadow of a doubt Paris betrayed us all. Not just the girl he was flirting with the past several weeks, but his honorary brothers, and my mother.

For the life of me, I can't figure out why.

Yes, his mother is ill, and his father cut them off, but that isn't where the money was going. Maybe if his mother was being taken care of better, if she had a nurse and a whole house that was furnished and heated, but she wasn't. Well, she is now, but that wasn't what Paris was using the money for.

He fooled me. He isn't the man I thought he was, and I'm not the only one taking it hard. Eros is resigned. Not a single 'I told you so,' has fallen from his lips. Heph is angry, and Perseus is beating himself up, like it is somehow his fault.

I want to be in my feelings about this. I want to lock myself away and cry out the hurt and the anger brewing inside me. Anger at him for his lies, his betrayal of me and my mother, but mostly anger at myself for falling for his sweet nerdy bullshit.

I'm better than this. I'm Athena motherfucking Godwin.

Though currently, I feel anything but.

I am lost in thought when Mrs. Medea puts the mail in front of me with a huge manilla envelope addressed to me on top.

I pick it up and notice it simply has my name on it. No address or postage, so it was hand delivered... weird.

"What's that?" Eros takes a seat at the kitchen table in front of me.

"Only one way to find out." I open the envelope and slide its contents out on the table in front of me and stare, not really believing what I am seeing.

It's page after page of tabloid headlines:

Godwin Princess Fallen from Grace.

Who Says Three is a Crowd?

Lost Son of Freya Godwin Getting Close to His Baby Sister.

The pages go on and on, each one with a picture

of me in a compromising position with one of the guys. Making out with Paris in his car. Eros going down on me at the party. Perseus lying me on top of Eros while he kisses me. Even one where I am kissing Eros while straddling Heph. It looks like I am fucking him while kissing Eros, and Perseus is watching, waiting for his turn.

"Fuck!" I scream, pushing the photos across the table. "When did these run? I need to call my lawyer. I need to call my father. I can't believe—"

"They are fake," Eros interrupts my melt down.

"Uh, no all those things happened, kind of. The pictures are real."

"No, the headlines are fake."

"I know they are, but it doesn't matter. The scandal will—"

"Athena," Eros barks out, getting my attention. "The headlines are fake." His voice is much calmer now that he has my full attention. He hands me his cell phone that has the front page of one of the tabloids. There's nothing about me on it. "These are a threat. Nothing has been released to the press *yet*. Is there a note with the pictures?"

"I don't know." I sit back down on the chair, my heart racing and tears stinging the backs of my eyes.

"Let's look, but first I am keeping this picture for my wallet." He takes the one of him on his knees with my dress pulled up and his face is buried in my cunt.

I roll my eyes and start sifting through the pages,

ignoring the misogynist headlines about me being a whore. God forbid a woman likes sex.

Finally, I find a note handwritten in red.

"Call the estate lawyer. Give up everything. Leave, go back to work, back to your life. Leave the men you've manipulated and their inheritance behind, and no one will ever find out what you really are. If you stay, I will release these photos to every website and news outlet in this country. Your reputation as an untouchable ruthless ice queen will be shattered. Everyone will know you are nothing but a cock hungry slut who belongs on her knees serving men, not in a boardroom giving orders. You will still lose everything."

Hot tears spill over my cheeks as I draw deep breaths, trying not to throw up all over the table.

"Baby girl, don't be sad. We will figure this out."

"Sad?" I laugh. My heart is thundering in my ears, my face and neck getting hot. "I am not sad. These are not tears of sadness. These are tears of rage. This is an act of fucking war. I don't want to be comforted. I want to wage a battle, and I will rip this lying piece of shit apart limb by fucking limb. So help me god, I will have blood on my hands after this." My palms sting from slapping them on the table hard enough that some of the papers go sliding off.

"What happened?" Heph asks as he and Perseus enter the room. One of the papers lands at Perseus's feet. He picks it up, and the blood drains from his face.

I can't hear the men talking for a few moments. The ringing in my ears is too loud. I need to focus, but my thoughts are racing, and I can't make any of it stop. It's getting harder to breathe, and a sharp pain is stabbing through my chest. I close my eyes and try to slow my breathing. I can't kill Paris with my bare hands if I give myself a heart attack or let my emotions dictate my actions. My response needs to be carefully crafted, meticulously executed, perfectly targeted, and devastating.

If I act from a place of raw emotion, I can burn myself in the process.

I count to five in my head, inhaling then holding my breath for a few beats before I slowly exhale. I do this a few more times, letting my heart calm and the fog in my mind clear so I can focus. When I open my eyes, the others look as mad as I feel. Good.

"He wouldn't do this," Perseus says. "It's an empty threat."

"Is it worth the risk?" Heph asks. "Is the money and this house really worth the damage this could do to Athena? If this is let out, she loses all that anyway."

"I don't do ultimatums." My voice is calm and in control. My emotions are raging just under the surface, but I have a lock on them. I won't let rage control my decisions, but I have no problems with harnessing it to fuel my actions.

"What do you suggest?" Heph asks.

"We come up with a third option," I say. "I am

not giving up this house." I look Perseus in the eye when I say that. Just because our feud has cooled doesn't mean I am giving up, and he needs to be reminded of that.

He answers with a single nod.

"We need to figure out how to take the power from him," I add.

"Like what, hacking his computer? The only one who could do that is Paris," Eros says.

"We could call the kid back. He is a mouthy little fucker, but he is talented," Heph suggests.

"No, it's too risky. What if he has hard copies, or a backup drive, or the kid uses the photos. We need to make the photos worthless."

"How the fuck do we do that?" Perseus asks.

A slow smile spreads over my face. "We change the narrative."

CHAPTER
FORTY-ONE

Perseus

Watching Athena on the warpath is the hottest thing I have ever seen. The initial shock wears off fast, and she becomes very still and focused. Like a snake about to strike. She refuses to play by Paris's rules. It isn't about inheritance anymore. It is about not letting other people make her choices for her.

"Do any of you know any reporters?" she asks. "I need someone with enough juice to get a story everywhere. My usual contacts are too risky for me. I don't want my father getting involved, and he has ears everywhere."

"Yes, but releasing this first won't make it any less of a scandal," Eros said. "You will still lose everything."

"No, I wont. This trash"—she gestures towards

the pile of papers—"is all slut-shaming nonsense. It may still be okay to trash women in the tabloids if it's something dirty and secret. But if I own it, then it's not shameful. It's empowering. If we launch the story first, but frame it as a woman being the center of a consensual alternative relationship, then the tabloids won't touch those pictures. It's an invasion of privacy that is no longer salacious. There is no secret. Plus, I'll throw a lot of money at it, the fear of the Godwin name, and get the reporters on my side." She pauses for a moment. "That is, if you guys are okay with it." She looks at me and Heph. "I don't know if either of you are out or—"

"We are both openly bisexual." Heph nudges me in the back. "I don't mind if you don't."

"So you want to come out and say what exactly?" I have to admit her idea sounds like it has merit. I just don't know if it could work.

"I would say the four of us are in a relationship. That my mother's passing brought us together, and polyamory is becoming more popular. I know it isn't exactly true, but since all of you are in the photos I can't really—"

"I don't know," I interrupt. "I mean I'm good with it, and Heph's good with it, but Eros, man are you really ready to tell every single woman in the area that your dick is now owned by one of the scariest bitches on the western seaboard?"

"Absolutely." He wraps his arms around Athena, and she smiles back up at him.

I wait for the pang of jealousy to rip through me, and it doesn't. Seeing them together doesn't hurt. I still want her, but I like seeing her with Eros, too. That is something I am going to have to look at more some other time.

"Okay, I'll make the call," Eros says before kissing Athena on the cheek and leaving the room.

Heph and I look at each other. The spark of mischief is visible in his eyes as he glances back at Athena, and I instantly know what he wants.

"So since apparently we are a thing now, Heph and I have a little wager going, and we wanted to know if you could be the judge for us."

"Oh, what's that?" Athena asks, mostly distracted by the papers on the table. I stand behind her putting my hands flat on the tabletop, caging her in and waiting for her to put down the paper and look at me.

"Well, we wanted to know which of us has the more talented tongue," I whisper in her ear before dragging my nose up the column of her neck. Her pulse quickens against my touch. "Heph and I haven't had breakfast yet, and I think the best thing to do is to put your sweet ass on this table and let us have our little contest.

Athena turns her head to look at me, her eyes darkening with desire. A hint of a smile is tugging at the corners of her lips. She reaches up to tuck a strand of hair behind her ear before turning to look at Heph.

I cup Athena's face between my hands and tilt her head to meet my gaze. I capture her lips in a searing kiss, my tongue trailing along the seam of her mouth until she opens up for me.

Heph groans behind me, and I can feel his eyes on us as I deepen the kiss. I allow my hands to roam over Athena's body, gripping her waist and pulling her closer to me. She moans into my mouth, her fingers tangling in my hair.

I sense her need to take over, be in control, but it's not going to happen. It's time to tame this vixen.

But just as I'm about to pull away, Heph steps forward, grabbing Athena by the waist and pressing his lips to hers in a fierce kiss. I watch as their tongues dance, my jealousy and arousal both spiking at the sight.

As the kiss breaks, Athena looks at us, a wicked gleam in her eye. "Well then, let the games begin." Her voice is practically dripping with desire. "Let's see what those tongues can do."

Heph and I both grin at each other, eager to prove who has the more talented tongue. The three of us lock in a passionate embrace, our bodies entwined as we explore each other's mouths with wild abandon. The sounds of our moans and gasps echo off the walls, as the game continues, each of us trying to outdo the other. Athena proves to be an equal match, her tongue working wonders as she moves between us, driving us both to the brink of ecstasy.

I can feel the heat rising between us, the tension

thickening as we each try to outdo the other. Athena's body writhes beneath us, her fingers digging into our hair as she moans in pleasure. The two of us continue our relentless onslaught, our tongues dueling for dominance.

It's impossible to tell who's winning, as each of us alternates between being the aggressor and the submissive. Athena's body trembles with every touch. We take turns exploring her neck, her collarbone, and her breasts, eliciting more moans and gasps from her.

I bite. Hard. I want to mark her as mine.

Not to be outdone, Heph does the same, and though a small cry escapes Athena's lips, she doesn't pull away.

Our dirty girl likes the pain.

Athena's body writhes under our touch, with her clutching at our hair and pulling us closer to her. Heph's tongue brushes against mine, and it's time to up the ante.

I pull away from Athena, turning my attention to Heph. I grab him roughly by the collar and pull him towards me, crashing our lips together in a fierce kiss. But as we kiss, I feel Athena's hands on my back, pulling me closer to her. She's not content to just watch us, she wants to be a part of the action.

I break the kiss with Heph, turning to look at Athena. She grins at me, her eyes full of devilment. Not pausing for a second, I remove every inch of Athena's clothing, watching from the corner of my eye as Heph removes his and then helps me with my own.

Athena gasps as we both take in the sight of her naked body. Her breasts are full and round, her nipples already puckered with desire. Wetness glistens between her thighs, and I know that she's ready for us.

We each take one of her hands and lift her to the table, laying her down on her back, her legs spread wide. I hover over her, while Heph positions himself at her head, his fingers trailing down her body as he makes his way towards her breasts.

I watch as Heph takes one of Athena's nipples into his mouth, flicking his tongue back and forth over the sensitive bud. Her body arches toward him, begging for more.

Not hesitating, I kiss my way up Athena's thighs, running my hands up and down her legs. Athena moans as we both work our way toward her center, both of us intent on claiming victory.

Heph's breath is on my neck, his tongue flicking against my earlobe. It's all I can do to keep my focus on Athena as I bring her closer and closer to the edge.

As I work my tongue over Athena's clit, Heph slides two fingers inside of her, setting a frenzied pace that has Athena writhing on the table.

"That's it, princess. Come for us. We want to watch what we do to your body," Heph says as he scissors his fingers, spreading her pussy as I lap up the juices.

I bite her inner thigh, causing her to buck against Heph's hand.

"That hurts," she says, not much louder than a whisper.

"Good," I say.

"Kiss it better," Heph tells me, which I gladly do.

Finger fucking, and devouring her cunt, we both continue to pleasure her. Her moans grow loud as Athena reaches her peak, her body shaking with pleasure. We both pull away, grinning at each other with satisfaction. Athena lies there, panting and sated, a satisfied smile on her face.

Heph pulls his soaked fingers out of Athena then grabs me by the waist. In one swift movement, he pulls me up and spins me around, pressing me against the table.

He then uses his wet fingers full of Athena's arousal and rubs them over, and in, my anus. Without pause, he slides inside of me, the sensation of him filling me up driving me wild. My eyes connect with Athena's as Heph fucks my ass in front of her.

Athena watches with rapt attention, tracing circles around her clit with her fingers as she watches us. I'm so turned on that it only takes a few thrusts before I'm on the brink. I let out a groan, waves of pleasure crashing over me as my vision goes white. But with one more thrust, Heph drives me over the edge so that I'm left shaking and riding my high as my cum shoots onto the table.

Heph pushes my face towards Athena's wet center, and I don't hesitate, knowing exactly what he wants me to do. I push my tongue inside of her pussy and swirl it around, causing Athena to mewl and grab a hold of my hair. I can feel Heph's hands on my ass, spreading me open for his access and viewing as he continues to fuck me relentlessly. The rocking motion is aiding in my task to continue giving Athena pleasure.

"More," she gasps, never being one to not make her demands known. Demands I'm more than willing to accommodate.

I moan against Athena's pussy, still lapping at her clit while Heph's cock drives in and out of me. Athena's body is trembling, her fingers tangled in my hair as she pulls me deeper into her pussy. I'm about to come again, and I move my tongue faster, eager to bring Athena to her second orgasm.

Heph thrusts one last time inside of me and comes with a primal grunt. "Fuck yeah."

Athena's eyes are on me, watching as I'm taken by Heph. She waits until his orgasm is over before she joins in, her fingers once again delving between her own thighs.

Heph pulls away, leaving me shaking on top of the table. He runs his finger over my cum on the table and brings it to my mouth, while Athena takes the same action and runs her fingers along her wet pussy, collecting her own arousal. They both slide their fingers into my mouth, and I suck greedily, savoring the sweetness of desire on my tongue.

Athena brings her head down to mine, and we all share a kiss, our hands entwined around each other. The three of us lie on the table, gasping but content. Heph runs his hands over my body, tracing patterns over my skin with his fingers.

"So who has the best tongue?" I finally ask as the buzz of the most erotic sex of my life wears off.

"I can't decide," Athena says. "I call for a redo. Just to be sure."

CHAPTER
FORTY-TWO

Perseus

The interview with the reporter is going smoothly. I like to think Heph and I have a little something to do with that. We have worked hard to distract Athena before the interview and fill her head with some feel-good hormones so she is nice and relaxed. At least until the reporter starts making suggestive comments and flirting with Eros, who is just dumb enough to flirt back.

Then she shifts from charming to passive aggressive so fluidly it takes the reporter about ten minutes to even realize she is being insulted. When the reporter puts her hand on my thigh, I see the fire in Athena's eyes, and I think she is ready to stab the reporter in the throat with a pencil. Heph is getting just as irritated, and if that doesn't make me feel all kinds of warm and fuzzy, I don't know what will. Until I realize that both Heph and Athena are perfectly capable of killing this reporter and getting rid of the body.

I interrupt the last question and make up a bullshit excuse about having a reservation soon and see the reporter out.

Putting this plan in motion, setting up the sales of the interview to all types of publications has taken all day, and I am on edge. When I return to the library, I expect to see them each with a tumbler of whiskey in their hands as they talk about the next steps. What I find is Athena sitting on the couch with the top of her dress pulled under her tits and Heph licking her breasts while Eros is fingering her while watching the way Heph tongues Athene's tight pink nipples.

"Fuck me," I say.

Athena just opens one eye and says, "Me first."

I grab my own glass and take a seat on the couch across from them and watch my best friend and my lover take apart our girl. My cock is aching within minutes, and I don't even bother being shy. I take it out and start stroking it, watching the way Eros and Heph bring Athena to new levels.

Heph pulls up her skirt and slides off her panties to show off her dripping wet pussy that is hot and swollen with need. Then Heph helps her to her feet before lowering her back down on Eros's cock. She is still facing me, so I have the perfect view to see how his cock stretches her. I can watch her tits bounce as she rides him, and I can even see the ecstasy on her face as she moves up and down.

Heph leans in to lick her clit a few times before crawling like a jungle cat on the floor to me.

"Keep your eyes on them," he tells me before replacing my hand with his hot sucking mouth.

Fuck. Heph's lips feel so good around my cock I have to stop myself from coming down his throat in a minute, when I look back up to see Athena's heated gaze as she watches Heph's head bob. I grit my teeth to hold on.

Eventually, I calm down enough to tell her she should come get a closer look. She nods and gets off of Eros and comes over to my couch. She watches Heph for a moment until he grabs her and puts her on my lap, sliding my cock inside her. I can't help thrusting up into her, and when Heph moves to licking my balls as I drive deep into Athena, I am sure this is the most pleasure a man can stand without dying.

Next, Eros comes and kneels next to me on the couch, sticking his cock in Athena's face and she immediately takes to it and starts to suck.

It dawns on me that this is our new normal. This is our life. Our family.

Athena has always been the missing piece. I've been resistant to admit that fact, but it's true. For the first time in my life, I know without a doubt this is right. It's what was meant to be.

Athena.

Our fucking goes on for hours in what feels like an erotic dream.

We all switch positions, we fuck her hard, we make her come over and over, and she doesn't stop moaning and screaming till the late hours of the night.

Is this love? Maybe. But I don't care what it is as long as it always feels this amazing.

After cleaning up, we all go back to Athena's room to crash on her bed, since she has the biggest. And after everything with Paris and the incredible sex, I think we all just needed to feel close to each other.

Athena and Eros fall asleep almost immediately, but my mind is racing with conflicting thoughts and emotions. I get out of the crammed bed and go to the window, glancing down at the grounds below.

Did I ever hate Athena? How could I hate her and want her so fiercely at the same time? Is this lust? Is this love? Is this—

"I can hear your brain on overdrive. What's wrong?" Heph whispers, pulling me tighter in his arms from behind.

"I just... I don't know..."

"What do you know?"

"I know I love you." I place a kiss on his chest. "I know I want Athena. And I know what we all just did was one of the most erotic things I have ever experienced, and I want to do it again."

"I love you, too. So what's got your mind spinning?"

"I'm supposed to hate her. We are fighting over this house and the inheritance and everything, and I just... How can I fight for what should be mine when every instinct I have tells me to love her, protect her, help her? How do I know that once all this is over, she won't just pack up Eros and leave?"

Heph draws a deep breath. "Honestly, you can't. You won't know what is real between you two until this inheritance is no longer an issue between you. We are all in the middle of a war with Paris, and we need to figure out when this fight is over, where our loyalties lie and what that is going to look like."

"You're right."

"I know," he says, nuzzling into my neck, "but can we figure this out in the morning. Sleep first."

"Okay." I give him another kiss on the head and close my eyes. "Let's go to my bed. There's more room."

Tomorrow, I will start my own cold war, and by the time Paris is handled, there will be nothing in the way between Athena and me.

CHAPTER FORTY-THREE

Athena

All day I have been running around trying to get the last details for this party handled. Thankfully, my party planner can handle most of everything after I change the original date. The theme is the roaring twenties, and I am throwing a ball so extravagant Gatsby himself would be proud. I guess the theme of excess is fitting, considering the responses I have received from the article. Most have praised me as a strong woman taking what I want, while others call me a greedy whore. I don't think I have ever had a theme so accidentally on point.

The best part is the way it has come out as a women's interest story, meaning most people don't care, which has made all those photos worthless. Except maybe that one of Eros on his knees on the balcony. I look good in that one. I am thinking of having it framed.

The only thing I am nervous about is my father's, and even my brothers', reactions. It turns out he doesn't really care who I am seeing, and my brothers are so busy with their women, that they barely even notice. My father has even made a crack about me needing that many men to keep me in line. I roll my eyes when he says that, but we now have a standing invitation to dinner at my family home—Olympus—when he gets back in town next week. I'm not sure if the guys will be ready to meet my dad and brothers quite that soon. I'm not even sure if *I* want to bring them home.

I think back to the conversation I heard between Perseus and Heph last night. I got maybe the tail end of it, and Heph is right. I can't know what Perseus and I have, what we all can be, while that inheritance is sitting between us. But the idea of giving it up for a man makes my stomach twist.

If I am going to give it up, it will be on my terms, but it's a huge sacrifice to make for a man. Plus, there's a bigger fear. One I don't want to face...

I am not sure they will want me without it.

What if it's the game, and the fight, keeping them interested? Not me.

I slip on my silver-and-black beaded flapper dress and the string of pearls that hit my waist. I twist my body in the mirror a few times, loving the way the beads shake and catch the light.

"Hey, baby girl." Eros enters my room without knocking. "Awe you're dressed. I was hoping to catch you naked and fuck you over the vanity before the party."

"Sorry." I shrug, but stand on tip toe and kiss his piercing, dancing my tongue on the metal.

"It's okay. We don't have time anyway, but I wanted to show you something before the guests start arriving."

He leads me down stairs to the large hallway off the entryway. The lights are all off, and it is pitch black.

"Eros, what did you do?" I ask.

"Well, I know how much you miss your mom and how you have been learning about her through her journals. I thought it would be nice for you to learn about her through our eyes, too. This is what we saw the last several years."

The lights come on, and the hallway is lined with easels, each one holding a picture of my mother. Some are posed, others candid, and they all talk about the charity donations she made, the causes she supported still even while under threat from my father. Several of the photos have one or more of the guys in it. They are all so wholesome and sweet.

"I thought we should have these up for the party. Allow the guests to meet Freya," Eros says.

"These pictures," I begin as I take in each one, paying attention to every little detail about the woman I missed out on for so many years. "Wow. To see her smile. To see her happy."

"She wasn't always smiling. She was also a vicious woman who refused to take anyone's shit. She was stubborn and swore like a sailor, but when she loved, she loved hard and fiercely. And god help the person who tried to hurt something or someone she loved," Eros speaks next to my ear. "There was always something missing with Freya. Someone she was missing. We always thought maybe she was a widow and lost the love of her life, but now we know. She lost you and her other children. She was never quite whole without her only daughter but she was still a formidable woman, and the world deserves to know how much she did for it."

I can't say anything. I simply study the pictures of the woman who was in all my dreams. Tears spill down my cheeks.

"Tears of rage?" Eros asks with a wince.

"No. Joy." I wrap my arms around him. "Thank you. This was a really special gift. It means a lot."

"I told you, baby girl. Actions speak louder than words."

"And what is this action saying, Eros?"

He leans down and kisses me. It's soft and chaste and makes my heart ache in a way I have never felt before.

"It's saying I know all that stuff we said yesterday was for the article, and we haven't actually talked about what the four of us are and how everything fits, but I don't care." He cups the side of my face with his warm hand and tilts my face up so I meet his eyes. "It's saying that I like what the four of us have going on, but more importantly, I love you. This is all about you. You. My perfect goddess of war."

"I love you," I whisper, and he pulls me into another kiss. "I've never said those words before you all. I've never... Love didn't fit the woman I was brought up to be. But it fits now. I truly do love you."

"Good, now go upstairs and fix all that makeup I just ruined so I can ruin it again tonight doing something really dirty."

"You better keep that promise." I laugh as I head back upstairs, feeling lighter somehow, hearing his words echo in my ears. He likes what the *four* of us have. The *four* of us.

It only takes me a few minutes to fix my makeup and add a few other accessories to my dress for the night. I can't wait for Eros and the others to see the silk stockings with the seams up the back and the black lace and pearl garters I have on under this dress. The entire look makes me feel sexy, powerful and untouchable.

"You are quite lovely, you know that?" A familiar voice comes from behind me, startling me. I look up in the mirror, and it takes me a second to recognize Paris.

The sweet man I knew is gone. In his place is a man with wild, crazed, and blood-shot eyes. His usual neat hair is sticking up all over the place, and his clothes are dirty and torn.

"Sadly, Cinderella, this ball is going to be missing its princess," he snarls as he takes a white cloth out of his pocket and holds it over my face. I try to fight him off. I try to kick and claw and scream. But my limbs get heavy, and harder to move before the world fades into nothingness.

CHAPTER FORTY-FOUR

Perseus

"Hey, have you seen Athena?" I grab two champagne flutes from a waiter and hand one to Eros. "I haven't seen her yet, and most of the guests are here and asking for her."

"I haven't seen her since before the party when I showed her that surprise."

"I still cannot believe you showed her that before the party then took all the credit for it," I grumble.

Actually... I can believe it. That is definitely something Eros would do.

Fucker.

The monument isn't even for Athena, not really. It is for Freya—a way for us to say goodbye since I was working with the lawyer to find a way around the crazy-ass rules of the will. If I can find a way to bypass them, I will forfeit everything to Athena. She gets the house and the money, all of it. Then once I give her what should be hers, I'll leave, unless she wants me and the others to stay.

I want to give Athena a choice. *Her* choice.

Also, deep down, I know this is what Freya would have wanted.

That memorial is my goodbye to the life I have dedicated to Freya. Not a way for Eros to drop the "L" word. Though I will admit, that is the first time I know of that Eros has used that word that it isn't followed by 'pussy, tacos, or whiskey.'

I'm still ratting his ass out.

"I'll go upstairs and find her," he says, and I grab him by the back of his tux.

"I will go get her before you take credit for something else. Like oxygen or the stars." I throw back my champagne and head upstairs.

It's quieter up here. The jazz band can still be heard, but not the laughter and chatter of the rest of the party.

"Athena, are you okay?" I say, knocking on her door. There is no answer. So I try again. Still nothing.

I crack open the door, and my heart stops.

A lamp is lying on the floor, shattered. The standing mirror is broken, and loose pearls are scattered all over the floor.

Red lipstick is smeared on the vanity mirror.

This will all be over soon.

I stare at the words written in the deep red shade

of lipstick Athena favors for these parties, and my blood runs cold.

He has taken her.

That crazy treasonous son of a bitch has taken Athena.

I grab my phone and send a message to Eros and Heph to come to Athena's room immediately.

I don't know how long they take to get here, but I am sitting on my ass still staring at those fucking words when Heph struts through the door—a smile on his lips—as he laughs with Eros about something. The smile fades from his face the second he sees me.

"What happened?" Heph rushes to my side.

At the same time, Eros asks, "Where is Athena?"

I can't speak. The words are caught in my throat, so I point.

"Fuck," Eros bites out as he starts to pace the room.

Heph takes a seat next to me and laces his fingers in mine. I don't know if he is offering me support or taking it for himself, but either way, it's appreciated.

"Okay, where could he have taken her?" Eros asks.

"Anywhere."

"When did he take her?"

"I don't know." I lean my head against the wall and close my eyes, internally begging to God, any God, to keep her safe.

"Fuck! I saw her about an hour ago," Eros says. "I showed her the memorial wall. She cried, and it fucked up her makeup, so she came up here to fix it. It had to have been in the last sixty minutes. So, he couldn't have gotten far." Eros is pacing the room, running his hands through his previously slicked-back hair. He shrugs off his pinstripe jacket and undoes the buttons at the top of his shirt. He is looking more and more like a 1920s gangster. All he needs is a Tommy gun.

"Paris probably doesn't expect us to realize she is gone so quickly," Heph says, pulling my attention on him. "I don't want to tip him off that we already know. Let's sneak downstairs to the basement. I don't want anyone at the party knowing something is off."

"Sneak downstairs and do what?" Eros asks.

"Check the security feed. We can at least make sure that it was Paris who took her. Maybe, at the very least, see what car he is driving and what direction he went."

"Then what," Eros snaps. "Go roaming around the city looking for a car?"

"No, asshole, think." Heph is suddenly on his feet, and I miss his body heat. "Who is her father? Her brothers? We call them. The Godwins have connections with the police. If we can give them a make and model and a license plate, they can have everyone in the city looking for her."

"And we show we aren't good enough to protect her," Eros adds.

"We show her family the truth. That her safety is

more important than our ego." Heph is yelling at this point, and although it's sexy as fuck, I want it to end.

"Stop," I say but Heph and Eros keep yelling at each other. That's when I notice an earring by my hand. A single pearl on a dangling silver chain. It is simple, elegant and bold all at once. It's exactly how Athena is, and she needs to get it back. I need to have her back. "Stop!"

They both stop yelling and turn to look at me, faces red and twisted in rage and panic. I know how they feel.

"Let's go see what we can find on the security systems. Then we will go from there." I get up and start making my way down, taking the back stairs to avoid as many guests as possible.

I run into a few familiar faces, and I make what I hope are appropriate excuses as to why Athena hasn't made an appearance yet, and where I am off to. Honestly, I can't tell who I talk to or what I say, I simply reach the basement as quickly as possible, Heph and Eros on my heels. They both sit down at the bar with their computers in hand and start typing. I grab the tablet that controls the security and see that it was disabled this morning. Probably to let the planner come in and out as she pleased with the caters and other staff working the party.

"The cameras were tampered with," Eros says.

"What do you mean?" I put the tablet back and move to look over his shoulder.

"I mean, I can't find any trace of anyone going upstairs or coming down that isn't supposed to."

"What are you saying? Paris got a magic carpet and went to her window Aladdin style?"

"No," Heph interrupts. "He tampered with the cameras. Look at the time stamp. He erased fifteen minutes of footage."

"Fuck!" I pick up the eight ball from the pool table and throw it across the room, taking out a lamp before it embeds itself in the drywall.

"I'm not seeing anything on the camera outside either," Heph adds. "But the time didn't jump."

"What does that mean?"

"This driveway is the only way on and off the property with a car, and our security system is on a closed server."

"How do you know that?" Eros asks.

"I went poking around once Athena got those pictures. I didn't think it mattered when she diffused them, but I think that Athena and Paris are—"

"They are what?" I snap.

"They never left the property."

CHAPTER FORTY-FIVE

Athena

My head is killing me as I come to. I try to rub my eyes, but my hands are bound behind me with rough twine that is cutting into my skin. I'm blindfolded as well, and my senses are going crazy.

"Where am I?"

"Don't worry, angel. You are right where I want you. Well, actually, that isn't true. You had to ruin everything. Why?" Paris growls out. "Taking the money that should have been mine wasn't enough? You had to take my brothers, too, and now my mother? What else of mine could you possibly take?"

"I didn't take anything from you." I can feel him step closer to me. His fingers gently lace in my hair like they did when he would kiss me, a comforting loving embrace.

"You took everything," he whispers in my ear as his grip on my hair goes from soothing to painful.

"No," I say. "Your mother is getting the treatment she needs at the best facility in the country. She is waiting for you to come see her. I get daily reports that say she is doing wonderfully. She is now taking all her medications and is completely lucid. We can go see her now if you want."

"Now? It's too late for that now." He lets go of me then rips off my blindfold, taking several strands of hair with it. "You know I was prepared to give you everything. I was going to destroy you, my beautiful angel. I was going to break you, then pick up the pieces and make you my wife."

I blink several times before I can see properly. We are in some kind of small cabin. I can't see much from my chair, just the table next to me with an old oil lantern and another chair and Paris looking all wide-eyed and crazy.

"What? Why would you destroy me if you want to marry me?" I don't really give a fuck what delusions are currently going through his head, but I need to keep him talking and figure out a plan.

"Well, how else was I going to make you dependent on me? I can't have a wife who can leave. I need a wife who relies on me for everything. My plan was simple. I was just going to make you love me, then I would make you let Perseus have the inheritance, and I would continue siphoning from it to support us. Probably get your father to invest with me as well, and I would embezzle from him, too. We would have been happy."

He leans down to place a kiss on the corner of my mouth, and I try to move away from him, but he doesn't notice, or doesn't care about my distress.

"Then you had to go and fuck Eros. I don't blame you, not really. I was pissed, but I should have seen it coming. After all, you are just a woman and a slave to your emotions." Paris moves over to the table. "You know, I even forgave you for that. I did."

"How nice of you." I start trying to twist my arms out of the ties holding my wrists together.

"It hurt me, but you forced me to release those photos. It would just be the scandal I needed to break the conditions of the will. You would go back to your own life, head hung in shame. Eventually, I would find you, broken and alone, unwanted and unloved. I would show you how merciful I can be and take you back. Where you would be grateful for my attention. With your money from your job, and your daddy added to the money I take from Perseus, I was going to refurbish my home and put you there so you could live with Mother. You would have been happy spending your days taking care of Mother and whatever children I gave you, and your nights would have been spent on your knees worshiping me like you were made for."

I press my lips together as I try to keep my mouth shut. But he is making it so damn difficult. The audacity of this man. My god, how did he hide it so well before?

"Then you had to go be a stubborn little bitch and ruin that, too. You had to tell the entire world you are some kind of slut who is empowered to have whatever she wants. Even your mother knew when your father had her beat."

"What are you talking about?" My father? What could Paris possibly know about him?

"Your mother wanted to leave him, but he wouldn't let her embarrass him like that. He agreed to let her live out her days here, put away like the broken toy she was. Out of sight, hidden away in shame. Why do you think she was a recluse?"

"Paris..."

"It wasn't even part of your father's demands, it was all her idea. She knew her place."

"So what is your plan now?" The twine is cutting harder into my skin, but I need to get free so I am rocking it back and forth, trying to loosen the binding. "Are you going to make me tell the world I was wrong, then put me away like a broken doll, too?"

"No, angel." He grabs my chin, pinching it between two fingers. "You are not some broken doll. You are a rabid bitch, and as much as it pains me, the only thing to do with a rabid bitch is to put her down."

"You are going to kill me?" I swallow back any fear I have. "You will never get away with it."

"I already have. Your death will be ruled a suicide. Then Perseus will get the money. I will right all the wrongs that have been done to me and my family. Then I will talk to Perseus and be welcomed back into the group with open arms. It will be like you never existed. By that time Perseus and Heph will be together and happy with each other, fucking finally. And Eros would have already forgotten about you and on to his next conquest. Hell, by the end of the month, he might be four or five conquests beyond you."

"No one will ever believe I killed myself."

"Sure they will. Dumb slut sees what the world really thinks of her and follows the advice of Internet trolls and offs herself. I mean really the things some of these men are saying about you on the Internet are just horrible. Did you know you're famous now? #TripleTeamTramp is trending."

"So you are going to poison me? Or shoot me and hope that no one notices that I am tied to a chair, the marks on my wrists, the signs of struggle in my room."

"Please give me some credit." Paris deadpans before grabbing me by my hair again and kissing me. I try to turn away, but he holds my hair tighter and forces his tongue between my lips, so I bite him. He backhands me across the face hard enough to knock me and the chair over. "Stupid bitch."

The taste of blood is on my tongue, and I'm not sure if it's his from the bite or mine from the hit.

"You're just leaving more evidence. If you kill me, they will find you." My laugh is coming out a little manic. "You are going to spend the rest of your life as someone's prison wife. Assuming the others let you live long enough to see a trial."

"There will be no evidence. I can do whatever the fuck I want to you. When they find your body, it will be nothing but ash."

CHAPTER
FORTY-SIX

Heph

I should have seen this coming. When Athena got those pictures, I checked the security system to see if I could find someone sneaking around taking those photos. I thought that if I found out who was taking the pictures, I could clear Paris's name or know for sure it was him.

There was no one sneaking around on the video, so I thought it was a dead end. It didn't even occur to me then that the pictures came from the video feed of the security cameras. If I had realized that sooner, maybe I could have stopped all of this from happening. Maybe Athena would be safe, Eros wouldn't be on the verge of a murder spree, and Perseus wouldn't look like he is about to pull out all of his hair.

I need to make this right.

Leaving Eros and Perseus to bicker between themselves, I head to the library. It takes a few minutes to politely push a few party goers out of the room, but as soon as I am alone, I open the safe where Freya kept some extra money and the deed. With it, there is a map of the property. This estate is over a hundred acres. It's a lot to search, since we don't use most of it. I start looking at all the buildings on the land. There are many that are never used. This estate used to house tenants in old buildings, and host camping and hunting retreats in the 60s.

Maybe Paris and Athena could be in one of them.

That is assuming he has even taken her out of the house and gone somewhere with a building. He could have just taken her to the middle of the woods.

No, Paris would want somewhere quiet. He would want to minimize risk of something going wrong. Paris has always focused on risk vs reward. He stopped us from doing dumb shit growing up because there was too much risk. Assuming he has Athena captive, he would want somewhere quiet, secluded to hold her.

I just need to figure out where, and maybe what his endgame is. If I know what he is doing with Athena, what his plans are, I will be able to have a better guess but… there is no telling what Paris will do.

I thought I knew him, but Paris has been stealing

from us for years. He might have killed Freya. He has been lying about his mom. Hell, Eros is in love and monogamous, and Perseus wants me as much as I want him. Clearly, I don't know shit. Can my intuition even be trusted anymore?

"What are you doing?" Perseus walks in behind me. "She is missing, and you are just okay with it? You rejoin the party?" He is angry, and I don't blame him. I deserve all the hatred and disappointment in his voice. Part of me wonders if I let this happen. Not intentionally, of course, but maybe subconsciously. I wouldn't think I could do something like this, but if I don't know people I consider my brothers, maybe I don't even know myself as well as I think.

I love Perseus, and yeah, I like Athena. I like hanging with her. I like her fire, and I love the way she rides me, not to mention those sexy little noises she makes when I touch her just right. But it's not love. Not yet. Perseus loves her. I can see it clearly. Maybe I am jealous?

I don't know.

He comes around the front of the desk and sees what I am looking at.

"Where could they be, Heph?" The plea in his voice is enough to break me.

"I didn't see any tracks of an ATV or anything like that around the house, so it has to be somewhere close enough that Paris could walk either fighting Athena or carrying her. I can't see her going quietly if she is conscious."

"She wouldn't. If she was conscious, the staff would have heard or seen something," Perseus agrees.

"Maybe they did." Eros is pacing in front of the desk. I didn't even see him come in. "I am going to go check with them now."

He runs off before I can say anything, but that's fine. Maybe he will get lucky. Paris is smart, so I doubt it, but maybe. At this point, I will take anything we can get.

"Where do you think he would take her?"

With a deep breath, I tell him the answers he won't want to hear.

"Assuming he left the house, and he is on foot, then he has to be at one of these four buildings." I point to the four closest structures.

One is a stable that is used as storage. A garage that used to be a carriage house, a small home that used to be for the caretakers that is currently empty, and a cabin that is a bit deeper into the woods that used to be a hunting cabin. When we were teenagers, we used to sneak out there and party, invite a few girls, drink some beer and make the girls think we were doing something wrong, when really Freya didn't give a shit.

"What does your gut tell you?"

"The cabin is the obvious choice. Paris knows it and would be comfortable there, but it is the furthest and would be the hardest to get Athena to without someone seeing."

"Okay so not the cabin."

"I don't know. I think we should split up. I want you to check the house first. There are a few places on the third floor and the attic we don't ever go to. That would be the easiest option. Then go check the carriage house. I'm going to check the stables and the caretaker's home. Then we will head to the cabin. Call me the second you find anything and take Eros with you."

"Okay." He turns to leave, and I put my hand on his shoulder.

"Perseus, be careful."

"You, too." He grabs my hand and pulls me in for a quick kiss. "Now let's go get our woman back."

CHAPTER
FORTY-SEVEN

Athena

Fear grips my heart as Paris goes into a duffle he has on the ground and pulls out a bottle of lighter fluid and starts pouring it on the wooden walls and floorboards.

"Oh yes, you are going to burn like the bitches of old. You know why they burned women at the stake right? Sure, they said it was witchcraft, but it was always the women who didn't know their place that got torched."

"You are insane," I hiss. I start yanking my arms apart trying to break the binding around my wrists some more, but it's useless.

"No, I am simply doing what needs to be done. Though I suppose there is no reason I have to hurry. I did put a lot of time and effort into you. I suppose I might take something for my troubles." He throws the empty lighter fluid bottle across the room and grabs another. "We have time."

My heartbeat is thundering in my ears again, and I can't breathe. The room seems to spin as I try to break free. The twine doesn't budge, but I can feel blood start to drip down my hands. I rock against the chair trying to break it, trying anything I can think of to get free.

"Oh don't worry, little angel, this won't be any worse than fucking Eros, I'm sure." Paris's cold sneer sends ice through my veins, and I try harder to get away from him.

He grabs the chair I'm on and pulls it back to its legs, I am sitting up again, and my head is spinning. I want to throw up and scream, but I can't manage to open my mouth or take a breath. Tears blur my vision as he unties my feet, then my shoulders. I'm no longer attached to the chair, but my arms are still behind my back.

"Get up, you dirty whore." He grabs me by the hair and flings me to the floor. He grabs the hem of my dress and tries to rip it off of my body, but I strike out with my heel, hit him in the gut, and knock him back.

I am not going down without a fight. He thinks he can rape me? He can kill me? I killed the last fucker who tried to do this. I am the daughter of Freya Godwin and the heir to the entire Godwin empire. I will not be taken out without a fucking fight.

I should thank him for calling me a whore and trying to take what I did not freely give. I have been dealing with men trying to touch me and fuck me since I hit puberty. And I will be damned if this coward who needs to drug and bind me will be the one I let win. I'm not scared in the slightest. I am fucking pissed.

"You are going to regret that." He comes at me again, and I kick out. He grabs my ankle, so I use it to pull him toward me and knock him off balance before I reach out and strike him again, this time managing to hit him square in the balls.

He falls to the ground and knocks into the side of the table. The lantern on the table wobbles for a moment, and both of us stop to watch it. It doesn't fall over and break on the lighter fluid-soaked floor.

Paris wheezes as he struggles to stand back up. I struggle to get to my feet, my legs scrambling to get under me, mostly just slipping on my dress's silk lining. As he comes closer to me, I try kicking out again. He catches my foot and twists it hard enough to flip me over to my front. Then his boot stomps down on my other ankle. Something snaps, and the pain is instant, ripping a strangled scream from my throat.

It hurts more than anything I have ever felt before, but it doesn't matter. I need to get out of here. I need to fight.

The pain from my ankle makes me retch, and I dry heave onto the floor a few times. Paris stands over me, grabs me by the hair, and pulls me to my feet. Another scream rips through me when I try to put weight on the foot he stomped.

"Go ahead and scream. No one can hear you here." He pushes me so I am bent over the table, and while he is trying to rip apart my dress, I nudge the lantern off the table onto the floor and ignite the lighter fluid.

The fire spreads fast. He must have more accelerant in the duffle bag, because when the flames reach that, it explodes with enough force so both of us are thrown back.

When I open my eyes again, the room is engulfed in flames. My entire body is covered in sweat, and I am coughing trying to get air. Paris is lying next to me, unconscious. I need to get fresh air now. It's getting hard to breathe, and I am going to suffocate before I burn. With my arms tied behind my back and my ankle broken, there is no way I can crawl out of here on my own. I look around until I see the damn chair on its side again covered in flames.

This is going to suck.

Ignoring the biting pain in my ankle, I shimmy back toward the chair. The stench of singed hair fills the room, and I try not to consider what that probably means. I hold my wrists to the flames on the chair and pull. The flames are licking my arms, and it hurts. Everything hurts. I use the pain. I use the adrenaline pumping through my body to push me. Finally, the twine breaks, and I can start crawling toward the door.

Even where the floor isn't on fire, the wood is hot and rough, splinters digging into what is left of my silk stockings before embedding into my knees. I am about halfway across the room when something wraps around my ankle and yanks me back. I look behind me to see Paris, with a crazed fury in his eyes. Bracing as hard as I can, I try to pull out of his grasp, but he is so strong. I'm digging into the floor so hard my knees are scraped, and my fingernails are breaking. I let out another scream, and this time I think I hear it answered. It's hard to tell over the cracking of the wood around us, but I think someone shouts. So I scream again.

"Get back here. No one is coming for you. You are going to die broken and alone at my hand, just like your fucking mother did." Paris pulls at me again, and I fight with everything I have.

The door opens, and whoever it is jumps back as the flames by the door intensify.

"Help," I try to call again but I inhale too much smoke, and I start coughing instead. "Help." I try again.

"Athena?" comes the call from outside. I think it's Heph.

"In here," I try to yell.

Paris's hand is now on my throat, and he is holding me down, choking me. The edges of my vision start to go black, and my limbs get heavy. The fight slowly leaves my body, and I can't stop it.

I hear Heph's voice again when the weight pinning me down is lifted, and I am being carried out by Heph.

"Athena, can you hear me? Say something, beautiful, anything."

"Fuck, this day," I croak out, and he laughs.

I am sort of aware of another shout coming from behind me as Heph lays me on the cold damp grass, then Heph is replaced by Eros.

"Baby girl, are you okay?"

"No."

"Paris is still in there," Heph says before running back in.

Perseus is running toward the fire a moment later. Eros holds him back from going into the burning cabin after Heph.

I struggle to sit up, needing to see what is happening, when a loud crack sounds from the cabin followed by the roof caving in and Perseus screaming for Heph.

The screams of sirens fill the air, and before I know it, I am sitting in the back of an ambulance as an EMT is looking over my leg saying something about *shattered* and *hospital*. I'm not really paying attention, but Eros is. He is by my side and is refusing to let us leave until we know Paris and Heph are safely out of that building.

"Sir, I need to take her to the hospital now," the EMT argues.

Eros gives the man a look that is by far the most terrifying I've ever seen. And that's saying something, considering who my father and brothers are.

"We stay until we know the others are fine, then we will take her in. Is that clear?"

The blood drains from the man's face so fast I worry he will pass out as he raises his hands and nods.

"Good. Now give her something for the pain until we can go."

He nods again and starts rifling through the drawers in the ambulance and comes back with a needle. "This might make you sleepy."

When I nod my consent, he gives me the shot, and I lie back in Eros's arms.

"Don't worry, baby girl. I got you." Eros's voice helps soothe me, and the drugs are pulling me under when I hear a shout.

The last thing I see is two stretchers coming out of the building. One of them has two men. One lying prone and another sitting astride him performing CPR as they are being carried to the other ambulance.

My eyelids are heavy, and I can't hold them open anymore. But I know one of my men is dead, and another may follow.

CHAPTER FORTY-EIGHT

Athena

3 days later

It's been quiet at the estate since the cabin burned. Eros spends most of his time in the gym hitting the punching bag over and over or getting on the treadmill and pushing his body to exhaustion. He doesn't talk to me, or anyone. He does come into my room late at night fresh from the shower, and just holds me as he sleeps. If what he does can even be called sleep. He tosses and turns and holds me tighter.

When I wake up, he is gone, and I know I can find him back in the gym punishing his body for what his mind can't cope with. I know he is grieving the brother they lost and worried about the other still lying in the ICU in a coma. The paramedics and doctors have done what they could. Now it was up to him to live or die.

Perseus is handling it far worse. He has locked himself in his bedroom with bottles of whiskey. He drinks as he rages, trying to numb the feelings of loss and hopelessness. He only comes out for fresh bottles, and if he sees me, hobbling around in my cast, he turns and walks away with his head hung low.

I don't blame him. I want to shut down, too. I want to crawl in my bed and never get out, but I can't. Someone needs to make sure Ellen is okay. Someone needs to keep the house running, and someone needs to see to the funeral arrangements.

It's weird planning a funeral for a man I feel like I barely know, but it's not for me. It's not even for him. It's for Perseus and Eros. They deserve to say goodbye. The body was too burned for an open casket, but getting pinned under a burning beam will do that. I don't think any of us could stand to see his face disfigured like that, anyway.

The funeral is being held here. The front room has already been set up. Mrs. Medea is doing a great job, even if she and the rest of the staff are also in mourning.

I just have to get through the next few hours, the funeral, then a meeting with the estate lawyer, and then I can take my pain meds and slip into oblivion.

The funeral is small, really just us, and a few other friends of the guys are there. My brothers come, not really to pay their respects, but to make sure I am okay. The way they keep eyeing Perseus and Eros, I worry they are planning to start something after the funeral. Lucky for everyone, my father is away on business.

Perseus should be the one leading the funeral, but he isn't up for it. Neither is Eros, so I hobble to the small podium to welcome everyone when a shadow passes over the doorway, and I gasp.

Heph is standing there wearing scrubs that are clearly a size too small. He looks horrible, his skin is pale and he has dark circles around his eyes. He could keel over any minute.

Leaving the podium, I shuffle down the aisle as quickly as the cast will let me, tears streaming down my face. Perseus and Eros speak behind me, but I'm not listening to whatever they are saying. I wrap my arms around Heph and hug him tightly, he wraps his arms around me, and he sways a bit. I am pretty sure we are holding each other up at this point, and one stiff breeze and we will both go tumbling over.

"I'm so sorry I didn't get there sooner." He places a kiss on my forehead.

"You saved my life." I hold him tighter. "You're awake! How are you here? Shouldn't you be in the hospital?"

"I had to come. I had to pay my respects. I'm going back right after, I promise."

Eventually, someone pulls me away, guides me to a chair, and Perseus takes my place. He's asking the same question and responding the same way I did. But there is a desperation mixed with relief in Perseus's eyes I've never seen before.

I don't know how, or how long, but somehow we get back to the funeral.

No matter what Paris did in his last few weeks on earth, he was a brother to them and deserves a proper goodbye.

After the funeral, my brothers agree to get a sobbing Ellen back to her room at the care facility but not before giving Eros and Perseus death stares. Heph they just give a nod of respect. It is kind of funny watching my brothers go from dark and scary to giant teddy bear when dealing with Ellen. It's clear to see that they feel awful for the poor woman. I most certainly do and have made a commitment to have her cared for for the rest of her life. I can't imagine what it must be like to lose a son.

The rest of the guests follow them out. All but the lawyer.

"I have the papers you asked for." He drums his fingers on his briefcase. "Did you want to go talk somewhere private or—"

"Here is fine," I say, sitting on one of the couches mostly because the others need to hear this, but also because the idea of getting up and spending more time on this leg is excruciating.

"Did you get what I needed handled?" Perseus

takes a seat next to me. Eros sits on the other side and pulls me into his lap so Heph can sit between all of us.

"I did," The lawyer answers. "I admit I wasn't coming up with a way to do that until Ms. Godwin called me with a proposal. You have both violated the will. As such, you both forfeit sole ownership of this house. Ms. Godwin's expose on polyamory may not have been true tabloid fodder but did cause quite a stir on some of the more... traditional media tracks. And Perseus, you and your friends were tasked with protecting Athena. That clearly went awry as well."

Perseus puts his head in his hands. The guilt must be killing him, but it isn't his fault.

"So neither of you can have sole ownership of the estate and the money. At Ms. Godwin's suggestion, I have placed all of it into a trust. You are both listed as trustees. The terms are simple. You cannot sell the house unless both trustees agree. The money in the trust is to be used to pay for the upkeep of the home and the rest invested or donated. Neither of you can personally gain from the trust, at least not without the other's signature. I have all the paperwork here. I just need you both to sign."

"This isn't what I asked for." Perseus stands up and starts pacing again, always with the pacing.

"No, I couldn't find a legal way to just drop you from the will, and frankly it was against Freya's wishes. Ms. Godwin wanted to give it all up as well, and this was the best compromise I could find."

"You wanted to give it up? Why?" I ask.

Perseus sighs and sits back on the couch. "Because it's yours."

"No." I shake my head. "This house belongs to all of you, not to me."

"Beautiful, you are one of us now. Do you think I would throw my ass into a burning building for someone who wasn't a part of this?" Heph grabs my hand and laces our fingers together.

"You are part of our family," Eros agrees. "Listen to Heph. Listen to everyone."

"Okay." I can't say no to those big brown eyes, not after everything that happened. I lean forward and sign the papers with my right hand, not letting go of Heph with my left.

"No," Perseus says. "This house, everything it isn't ours, it's hers."

"Shut the fuck up and sign the damn papers then drive me back to the hospital before I collapse on the floor."

Eros and I both snicker as Heph bosses Perseus around.

The papers are signed, the lawyer will file them, and in a week it will be official.

No more forced parties. I can leave if I choose to, and I can get back to work.

Or...

I can stay and be part of the family.

A family of four.

CHAPTER FORTY-NINE

Athena

Another week passes before Heph is home and Eros and Perseus start to slowly come to terms with Paris's betrayal and death. There are still many feelings of anger and guilt, but we are healing. I have more energy, and the pain is easier to deal with. Heph starts looking like himself again and is less grouchy. Am I finally seeing the real Heph, and not the asshole who was trying to make me leave? I liked the real Heph... a lot.

Each night, the four of us all climb into my bed. There isn't any sex. It isn't about that. It is about being close to each other, knowing we are all safe. It is sweet and intimate, but if I don't get some soon, I am going to lose my shit.

"So what is your plan?" I sit across the breakfast

table from my father. He has come here to check on me, gain his own measure of the men I am with, and to drag me back to work, kicking and screaming, if he must. His words, not mine.

"I'm staying here," I answer, while taking a sip of my coffee. "I figured I would sell my penthouse, move everything in here, make parts of it feel more like me."

"And Medusa Enterprises?"

"I don't know yet."

He sets down his coffee cup and takes a breath before meeting my eyes. "We need you back in the office. You brought on that fucking hockey team, and all hell is breaking out. The least you can do is clean up the mess."

I smile, liking the fact that my father is now realizing my value. He needs me. He's always needed me, and he now knows it.

"I don't care who you are sleeping with," he continues, "as long as you are happy. But you are a Godwin. That comes with strings. I don't care if you marry one or even all of the assholes living here, and you change your name to some new age, hyphenated bullshit. Hell, they can all take your name for all I care. But this family has a legacy, and it needs you."

"You have two sons who are perfectly capable of—"

He shoots me a look full of daggers and says, "Medusa needs *you*."

"I'm not sure I need Medusa."

"Look, I love your brothers, and they are capable of a great many things. Running this empire fully and alone isn't one of them. It's a massive beast, and you know it. I'm trying to step down myself and enjoy my old age." He takes a sip of his coffee before adding, "I never thought you had it in you, but you came in and made every single man you had to work with your bitch in a matter of days. You have the business sense of a fucking viper and the ruthlessness of a shark. We need you back at work. You can telecommute until you are back on your feet for all I care, but we need you."

I'm surprised to hear my father give praise. I'm even more surprised to hear him say he needs me out loud.

"I'll come back to work," I say, "but things are going to be different. I'm not going to be the same viper you expect. I need to... I need to allow myself to be happy."

"Fine. I want that, too, for you. I know I don't say it. I know I sure as fuck don't show it. But I do care. I do. I built Medusa for my children. For you." He pauses and looks around the house. An awkward silence stretches out between us. I don't know what to say or do with all the free emotions and honesty given. Finally, he says, "Why did you start all of this?" He waves around the room.

"I was searching for something. I thought I was looking for my mother, wanting to know who she was, get some questions answered."

"Did you find her?"

"Yes."

"Was she what you were looking for?"

"No, she wasn't, but I found what I needed."

"And what was that?"

"Me."

I see my father out after more promises to start checking my email and bring the guys over for family dinner at Olympus a week from Sunday, to give him and my brothers a chance to properly intimidate my men.

"So, back to work?" Perseus says from behind me, making me jump.

"Spying on me?" I turn to see him leaning against the wall with his arms crossed over his chest.

"No, okay maybe a little." He pushes himself off the wall and moves to stand in front of me.

"You know eavesdropping is rude."

"You'll get over it. Besides, I don't trust him."

"You'll get over it," I parrot his words back to him. "He's my father. He's not going anywhere."

"So, you aren't going to move back to your fancy city penthouse by yourself?"

"No, I was planning on staying. If that's okay?"

"It's your house," he counters as he slides his fingers into my hair. "But I can see how you might be tempted to go back to the solitude of your own life."

"It's *our* house," I correct. "This is where I belong."

"Good." He kisses me hard, he isn't asking, he

isn't tempting me to follow him. He is demanding my kiss, and I am eager to give it to him.

"Get the others," I tell him. "Meet me in the library."

"You want to be the center of attention, princess?" He runs his hand down my back and grabs my ass as he starts to kiss my neck.

"No, well, yes."

CHAPTER FIFTY

Athena

I stand naked in the library, the candle's flickering the only light. Three men also stand naked before me. Heph. Perseus. Eros.

They were my mother's boys.

But now they are my men.

"Take me," I command, not hiding my desires for all of them any longer.

We've all been through hell, but now it's time to taste heaven.

The three men step forward eagerly, their muscular bodies glistening in the candlelight. I feel their hands all over me, exploring my curves and crevices, and I moan with pleasure.

Heph takes my mouth in a deep, passionate kiss, squeezing my breasts with his rough hands. Eros kneels at my feet, his tongue exploring my folds, sending shivers of ecstasy through my body. Perseus stands behind me, wrapping his strong arms around me from behind as he teases my clit with his fingers.

I feel like I'm floating on a cloud of pure euphoria, lost in the sensations of their touches and kisses. I writhe and moan as they pleasure me, each of them bringing their own unique flavor to the experience. As they continue to please me, I get closer and closer to the edge. I want to come, to let go, and let them take control. And then, all at once, I do. My body convulses with pleasure as waves of ecstasy wash over me.

The three men hold me close, murmuring words of love and adoration. I feel their strong bodies against mine, their hard cocks pressing against my skin.

Suddenly, they all step back, leaving me standing there alone, quivering with desire. I turn to look at them, confused.

"Suck us," Perseus says, grinning wickedly.

Without a word, I drop to my knees and take Perseus into my mouth in turn, feeling his hot flesh, tasting his arousal. I suck Perseus loudly as I stroke Heph and Eros. I taste the musky flavor of his cock, and I like it.

"Relax your throat," Perseus says, his voice dripping with lust. "Relax and take it all."

I draw a deep breath and push my throat out as far as I can, taking as much of him into my mouth as

I can. I gag a little, but I manage to fit him all in. He pushes forward, and I hold still, allowing his cock to move deeper into my throat.

I choke and gag as he pushes deeper, but I relax my throat, and he slides all the way deep inside.

"That's it," he says, stroking my head. "That's it."

I gag again and again as I take him further and further into my throat. I look up at Eros, and he and Heph are smirking in pleasure. Finally, Perseus's cock pops out of my mouth, but only for a moment, and then I'm taking a new dick to fill its place.

Eros pumps his cock down my throat as the other two men stroke their cocks in front of me. I feel like I'm in a dream, like any moment I'm going to wake in my bed and realize this was all just a fantasy. But it's not, it's real, and I want more.

I hear the snapping of a lubrication lid, labored breathing, and my own heartbeat in my ears. Perseus lies down on the ground and pulls me on top of him. Eros comes up behind me, and I have no doubt what is going to happen next.

With Eros positioned at my ass and Perseus at my pussy, they thrust in and out of me, stroking me in unison, their cocks filling me, their hot flesh caressing mine.

I look into Heph's eyes, my breath coming quickly as I realize what I want.

"Fuck my mouth," I command.

Heph stands beside them, pure lust on his face. His cock is rock hard, throbbing with desire.

"I want your cock," I say, looking him in the eye.

Without a word, he steps forward and slams his cock past my lips.

I moan around his shaft as he fucks my mouth, his cock gliding in and out of my throat.

As Heph fucks my face, Perseus and Eros groan, their thrusts growing faster and more forceful. They're all soon fucking me in unison, their cocks sliding in and out of my mouth, pussy, and ass. Their balls slap against my skin as they use and abuse me, and I never want it to stop.

I close my eyes, surrendering myself to their cocks and hands.

I want to be their toy, a plaything for their rapture.

I exist to be used, to be fucked and filled with their hot cum. I want to be that for them, to be used for their filthiest desires. I want to come for them, to give myself to them, to be theirs as much as they are mine.

They're panting and groaning, their thrusts growing faster and more desperate. Heph's cock twitches and throbs deep in my throat. He's close, so close.

I feel the pleasure building inside me, getting closer and closer to the edge. Their skin, my skin, the air in the room, it all pulses with the same electricity, building and growing and exploding with desire.

Eros digs his fingers into my skin as he drives

himself into my ass. "So fucking tight," he says as he drives even deeper.

"Take us, princess," Perseus says as he meets Eros's motion.

I can't hold it in any longer.

"I'm coming!" I moan around Heph's dick, and all at once, the three men release inside me.

I don't ever want to let them go. I never want to be away from them again. They are my men, my lovers, and my friends.

I cry out again, louder this time, and my body shudders as the pleasure explodes from deep within me.

Flashes of lights and stars shoot across my vision. I've never came so hard in my life, and I collapse back against Eros's chest.

As I look up at him, he pulls out and strokes my face, smiling at me.

"Fucking hell, baby girl," he says. "You're the most amazing girl."

I grin back at him, my face flushed and panting, my body covered in sweat.

Suddenly, the other two men are there, wrapping their arms around me. We lie there on the floor, encased in each other's arms, kissing and caressing each other's heated skin. The three of them are all I ever want, all I ever need.

For now, and for always, I belong to them, and them to me.

This is my mother's gift. Whether it was her

ultimate plan, the result is a life-changing inheritance.

It isn't just the men she knew would love and protect me always.

But she left me the gift of finding out who I am. I'm more than Troy Godwin's daughter. I'm not just the ruthless viper I've always been taught I've had to be to gain respect. There's more to me. So much more.

And these men respect me. They love me. I don't have to be a Godwin for that to happen. I don't have to be feared. I simply have to let go and be me.

Happiness doesn't have to be forbidden.

And as I feel three cocks rest against my naked body, the warmth of acceptance surrounds me, I realize that nothing has to be forbidden again.

THE END

Curious about the secrets of HEATHENS HOLLOW? What dark and dirty tales lurk beneath the fog of the island?

Be sure to sign up for my newsletter so you can be the first to hear about my next book...

HEATHENS... Coming Soon!

Alta's Newsletter

ABOUT THE AUTHOR

Alta Hensley is a USA TODAY bestselling author of hot, dark and dirty romance. She is also an Amazon Top 10 bestselling author. Being a multi-published author in the romance genre, Alta is known for her dark, gritty alpha heroes, sometimes sweet love stories, hot eroticism, and engaging tales of the constant struggle between dominance and submission.

She lives in Astoria, Oregon with her husband, two daughters, and an Australian Shepherd. When she isn't walking the coastline, and drinking beer in her favorite breweries, she is writing about villains who always get their love story and happily ever after.

Facebook: https://www.facebook.com/AltaHensleyAuthor/
Amazon: https://www.amazon.com/Alta-Hensley/e/B004G5A6LI
Website: www.altahensley.com
Instagram: https://instagram.com/altahensley
Bookbub: https://www.bookbub.com/authors/alta-hensley

TikTok: https://www.tiktok.com/@altahensley
Join her mailing list: https://landing.mailerlite.com/webforms/landing/c9b6n3

ALSO BY ALTA HENSLEY

Dirty Ledger

Dangerous Notes

Chicago Sin Series:

Den of Sins

Rooted in Sin

Spiked Roses Billionaire's Club:

Bastards & Whiskey

Villains & Vodka

Scoundrels & Scotch

Devils & Rye

Beasts & Bourbon

Sinners & Gin

Evil Lies Series:

The Truth About Cinder

The Truth About Alice

Breaking Belles Series:

Elegant Sins

Beautiful Lies

Opulent Obsession

Inherited Malice

Delicate Revenge

Lavish Corruption

Standalones:

Gold In Locks

Sick Crush

Secret Bride

Captive Vow

Ruin Me

Delicate Scars

Made in the USA
Middletown, DE
14 January 2025

69447425R00241